11 SEP 2018
06 JUL 2019
D0513770
90710 000 362 029

Also by Nick Dybek

When Captain Flint Was Still a Good Man

THE VERDUN AFFAIR

NICK DYBEK

CORSAIR

First published in the US by Scribner in 2018
First published in Great Britain by Corsair in 2018

1 3 5 7 9 10 8 6 4 2

Copyright © 2018 by Nick Dybek

The moral right of the author has been asserted.

Interior design by Jill Putorti

All characters and events in this publication, other than those clearly in the public domain, are fictitious and any resemblance to real persons, living or dead, is purely coincidental.

All rights reserved.
No part of this publication may be reproduced, stored in a retrieval system, or transmitted, in any form or by any means, without the prior permission in writing of the publisher, nor be otherwise circulated in any form of binding or cover other than that in which it is published and without a similar condition including this condition being imposed on the subsequent purchaser.

A CIP catalogue record for this book is available from the British Library.

HB ISBN: 978-1-4721-5386-9
TPB ISBN: 978-1-4721-5385-2

Printed and bound in Great Britain by
Clays Ltd, St Ives plc

Papers used by Corsair are from well-managed forests and other responsible sources.

FSC www.fsc.org MIX Paper from responsible sources FSC® C104740

London Borough of Richmond Upon Thames	
RTHA	
90710 000 362 029	
Askews & Holts	
AF	£16.99
	9781472153869

For Madeline and Veronica

Santa Monica, 1950

The deceased had been a doctor—a surgeon, renowned in his field—but I knew him only as the neighbor who locked himself out once during a storm. I invited him in and we drank coffee in my living room, watching rain pelt the eucalyptus leaves, sharing comfortable conversation and silence. We'd both grown up in Midwestern cities, we discovered—Chicago in my case, St. Louis in his. We both lived alone. As the locksmith rattled up in his truck we shook hands and promised to get together again. We never did.

He was buried in a beige suit, white hands folded on his chest, looking nothing like himself in life, at least as I had known him. The funeral parlor's ceiling was frescoed in a mannerist style: rosy light, lean cherubs, clouds, and fountains. No doubt an expensive place to lie dead.

Though one can never think particularly fondly of a wake, I must admit that I preferred those of my childhood. When my mother died, our neighbors downstairs offered their living room for the viewing so the coffin wouldn't have to be carried up two narrow flights. Mrs. Riley across the hall—who would have taken me in and cared for me as her own if my father hadn't shocked everyone by cabling from France—swept out our apartment and lit the stove with her own precious coal so that our friends would be warm enough to stay as long as they chose.

Though I knew none of Dr. Kepler's friends, I resolved to stay as long as I could. I found his daughter, surrounded by three light-eyed children. She said it was kind of me to come, and thanked me for the dahlias, which I'd guessed were a favorite. I'd often seen him in the early morning, watering his dahlias and pulling weeds from his green jewel of a lawn. Beside the casket, I said a few words to his pallid face, then passed between the clusters of mourners, saying appropriate things—appropriately little—until I found myself listening to a man tell a story with the accent of a British actor playing a German in a film.

At first, I was only half-listening. It felt disrespectful to take an interest in such a story—the story of his life, it seemed—at another man's funeral. But as he continued—blinding headlights, Blackshirts swinging cudgels in an Italian piazza, fires set to the cafés and shops—I realized I knew that in the next sentence he'd be separated from his friends, swallowed by the crowd, beaten badly because the Fascists heard him speaking German, his ribs cracked, his eye nearly gouged out. That is to say, I realized it was not just the story of *his* life he was telling, but mine.

And, of course, though his back was to me, I knew immediately who the man was. Still, I waited what must have been a full minute on the chance the scene would simply fall apart as dreams do. I touched Paul's shoulder—that was his name, Paul Weyerhauser—and when he turned his expression was not so much of surprise as awe, as if the story had somehow conjured me. Perhaps it had—how would I know? What does it feel like, I wondered? What does it feel like to be conjured?

Paul suggested a Viennese bakery. It was late afternoon by the time we left the wake, and the tables were empty. His English had always been perfect, but I could hear the American in it now. He'd had his *gig* at UCLA since '35, he said. He *scribbled* his books in English.

What were the books on? Nineteenth-century American painting, portraiture of the Gold Rush West in particular. When I told him I wrote for the pictures, he asked what he might have seen. I named a few films, and he pretended for a moment before giving up.

"My wife will know your work," he said. "And you? Are you married?"

"Yes," I said, which was true, though my wife and I had not lived together for some time. I wasn't in the habit of covering up that fact, and something in the way I said it—the eagerness, probably—must have betrayed me, because his only response was a sympathetic smile. A bus passed outside. The register rang, and a boy of about nine walked into the evening with a loaf of bread under his arm.

Outside, palms lined Wilshire, thin in the sunlight. Within blocks, the street of bakeries and banks would become a shoulder of brown beach shrugging off a coat of ocean. And Paul, who had bowed to Franz Joseph at masked balls when there still was such a place as imperial Vienna, looked perfectly at home. One can get used to anything, I suppose, from crumbling empires to crumbling sand.

"I have to admit I'm not sure I would have recognized you," I said. He'd aged the way people do in California. His long face was lined and tanned, his hair gone silver instead of gray.

"I spend too much time in the sun," he said. "And perhaps you assumed I had lost the eye?"

He blinked several times, as if to assure us both that, indeed, he hadn't. "You realize that Dr. Kepler was the one who saved it, don't you? It was a close thing. I'd had two surgeries in Austria already before I came to him. I was trying to explain that at the wake—explain his near-genius, but also why I'd needed his help—the riot, the rest of it. Frankly, it's not a story I'm in the habit of telling."

"He lived next door to me—Dr. Kepler. For almost three years now, I think."

Paul smiled, amazed, amused. "I should have preferred to meet him your way." He paused. "I wonder, have you spoken with any *Italian* doctors recently?"

"I believe he died," I said. "In a Nazi camp."

"What, for communists?"

I nodded. We said nothing for a few minutes, eating raisin bread, sipping coffee. Of course, I was wondering how long it would be before one of us mentioned Sarah Hagen. I wanted to prepare myself for what that might feel like.

It would have been a shame, after all that time, to say something about her that I didn't mean. But I had written about love successfully for the pictures precisely because I'd never set out to say anything true. And if I were to have attempted it, I might have said that our sense of romantic love comes from the Middle Ages, along with bloodlettings and the Black Death. I might have left it at that.

But Paul did not mention Sarah, perhaps because he and I were old enough now to be cautious above all else, or perhaps because we quickly became lost in other conversation, in the pleasure of discovering there was much to talk about besides a past we happened to share. And before long, the woman who'd served us coffee turned the sign on the door and it was time to go.

"I walk here sometimes," I said. "To this bakery."

"Do you? I drive from Brentwood once a week. The best raisin bread in California, so far as I know."

"Brentwood? Three miles from here? Four? It's extraordinary."

"Isn't it?" He reached across the table to squeeze my shoulder. His face was so frankly happy that I almost had to avert my eyes. "Isn't it?"

My house was only blocks away, but sometimes the roads seem the least lonely place in Los Angeles, so I kept driving. Past restaurants with men in paper hats carving roast beef in the windows. Past furniture store signs twirling slowly over Lincoln Boulevard. Then out into the farmlands south of Los Angeles, through thickets of trucks heading back to San Pedro. In Torrance, I took a turn into a neighborhood of bungalows and bougainvillea, where two boys wrestled in the street, grudgingly giving way as I approached.

By the time I reached Palos Verdes at the end of the peninsula, it was growing dark, and the road had dipped between hills of chaparral, and I had a long drive back. I didn't mind. The war had shown me the uses of long drives in the dark. Just after I arrived in France, in fact, my father taught me to drive on the empty roads west of the river Meuse. This was in October or November of 1915. He was pleased—we both were—with how fast I took to it, the clutch, the gas, the brake.

But on the way back to Bar-le-Duc we found ourselves on foot. The ambulance had stalled in the cold, then died completely just outside a village. "I don't see us walking the rest of the way," my father said as I followed him over the moonlit grass. "Not in this weather. We'll have to find a floor to sleep on here."

He said the name of the place, but I wasn't sure what he meant. Not because the word was French, but because all I saw were a few stone houses along a low hill, a narrow road of wet ruts. Stars on the sky like a rind of frost. Nothing that needed a name.

It seemed the kind of village left untouched by the war, by the sentiment that outsiders had a place in France. I think my father sensed this, as, almost cheerfully, he said, "Don't worry. They can't turn us away with you here." And he yanked my cap down, playfully. Well, he meant to be playful, I'm sure, but my ears were cold, so it hurt quite a lot.

A woman came to the door in a black shawl, white hair undone on her shoulders. My father spoke to her in French; he gestured to me and then to himself and then down the road in the direction of the ambulance, or maybe that wasn't the direction. I couldn't tell anymore.

There were five other women inside. All pale and thin, though everyone was pale and thin then. The woman with white hair nodded to them, and said something that made my father smile. This is a celebration for her birthday, he translated, but we're invited to stay. The room smelled of onions. The woman began to ladle soup and pointed to a place by the hearth where we could make a bed. The stone floor was warm. Aside from a few candles, the fire was the only light.

She served us the soup, then returned to a round table at the other end of the room. They were stitching needlepoint, the six of them together; a dim blue thread through canvas on a scroll frame, taking turns, the needle looping out and doubling back. I had neither the language nor the strength to ask what they were doing, and soon fell asleep.

I awoke to voices in darkness. From the irregular breathing to my left I could tell my father was awake too. My French was almost useless, and names of places were easiest to catch. *Reims*, *Amiens*, *Ypres*, the women whispered, trying not to wake us.

"What is it?" I asked my father. "What are they saying?"

"They're arguing," he said, and I could hear the laugh in his voice, a sly ironic laugh that was perhaps typical of him, though I never got to learn what was typical.

"About us?"

"They're arguing about where I'm going to die."

They were wrong, though; he didn't die in Reims or Ypres. He died of typhus not far from where we slept that night, just north of Verdun in December of 1915. He was a doctor too—a surgeon with the American Field Service. I sat with him as he lay sweating through three nights of incoherent fever.

I was scared, but not sad, exactly. It was difficult to fully appreciate that the man dying before me was my father. He seemed decent enough, and I was grateful for the time I spent with him, but months later I could remember only that his hair was a metallic gray at the temples, though he wasn't yet forty.

I never lost the image of those women, though. In eastern France in 1915 it was no difficult thing to select a young man for death; it took no special powers. But, for the same reason, perhaps, it seemed like a world in which such powers were possible. In the years after, I thought of trying to find that village, that house. But, that night, I was too turned around in the dark, and the French name was lost to me almost at once, before I knew I needed to remember it.

CHAPTER ONE

Verdun, 1921

On the morning Sarah Hagen was to arrive, I awoke with the feeling of something crawling over me in the dark. A scrape of scale, a scratch of claw. I found Father Perrin in the courtyard, looking as though he hadn't slept either. He waited for me to wash and finish my bread and coffee, smoking cigarettes as if they offended him. He started the car, and we left for the hills north of the city.

It had taken years, but you could almost call Verdun a city again. In late 1919 the famous candied almond factory reopened, and people began to creep back into the streets. A café opened, then a bakery, *then* a school. Well, that's French life for you, Father Perrin said.

By 1921 the roads were clear, the bridges over the river rebuilt, the cathedral stitched with scaffolding. In the evenings the sun reflected red in the new windows. In the hours just after dawn there was a chalky light, as if all the old cordite still hung in the air.

I'd been the *aide de l'évêque de Verdun* for two years by then. My title sounded sophisticated, but my duties weren't especially; I helped the priests of the diocese with whatever they needed, and was offered board and a small salary in exchange. Nonetheless, given Verdun's particular circumstances, it was an important job for which I was hardly qualified. Eventually, I learned to write better in French than I did in English. I often thought in French. I likely would have dreamt in French, but in my dreams no one ever spoke.

On that day we were headed to the Thiaumont Ridge, to the village of Fleury. But there was no Fleury anymore, just as there was no Ornes or Douaumont or Vaux or Cumières—all villages leveled during the battle. The government had declared them officially destroyed. Though it seems that destruction is usually a matter of admission rather than fact, it probably was too dangerous to rebuild. Between February and December of 1916, a thousand explosive shells had fallen on every square meter of ground—ground that had been farmland and forest, then battlefield, then something new, known only as *zone rouge*.

We crossed the snaking Meuse on a new bridge, the water below sleepy and dark—a few ripples, a few branches nodding just under the surface. The road wove up through the hills. The mud remained in some places, but grass had returned in others, a bright, almost hallucinatory green. The earth has never seen anything like this, Father Perrin had said. We've confused it.

I couldn't disagree. Much would be said about the battle's brutality, its exhausting length and strategic peculiarity. But at the time it was waged, it often wasn't referred to as a battle at all. Will the Verdun affair ever end? the newspapers asked, using the preferred euphemism for catastrophe and scandal. Will the French ever recover from the Verdun affair, even if they do save the city? Five years later this still seemed an open question.

As he drove, Father Perrin smoked and smoothed the mustache signed on his lip. He looked like a matinee idol with a bad diet. When he blushed his skin went yellow instead of pink. I'd taught him to play hearts from an American deck that had washed up in the Episcopal palace, the way many strange things wash up at the end of a war. He'd taught me about music. We had no phonograph, but we did have a telephone with a good connection to Paris. Often, Father Perrin would call the last remaining chamber music service and put the receiver on a stack of books as a tin-flecked Saint-Saëns drifted out, costing somebody a fortune.

Other nights, we'd stay up late talking in Father Gaillard's old office or, if the weather was clear, seated on the lip of the koi pond in the courtyard. Just after the armistice a Christian church in Japan had given the Episcopal palace the pond of smooth smoke-blue rocks and five bulge-eyed goldfish. Father Perrin held a special affection for those fish; he told me it amused him to imagine what they thought, drifting in the shallow water. *So this is life. So this is life.*

"Was that you, pacing around in the middle of the night?" he asked now. "How do you feel? Perhaps I should cancel my trip to Bras?"

"I'm perfectly fine," I said. "Unless you're looking for an excuse."

"I am, actually," he said. "It's such an unpleasant story I'd have thought I'd told you already."

We laughed. I was still laughing as he said, "When I was chaplain at the base hospital in Rouen, there was an officer there who'd lost his entire face. Nose, lips, all of it. Can you imagine?"

He was trying to shock me—that was his way—but as Father Perrin well knew, I didn't need to imagine it. I'd seen many such faces when I worked for the American Field Service during the war.

"How much did he realize?"

"Too much. He was still lucid through most of it. He could cough out a few words when he had to. And he lingered. His parents even managed to arrive from Paris before he died."

"That's a mercy."

"Perhaps. It's this boy's father I'm going to see today. He wrote last week, saying that his work would be taking him to Bras and he'd offer a generous donation for the ossuary if I'd be so kind as to meet him there. So, you see, I must go."

"It's so important you go in person?"

"To him, yes. The truly unpleasant part is that when he and his wife arrived at the hospital, they called for me almost immediately. We were standing right beside the boy's bed. His father shook my hand, and said—and I still recall the words exactly—'Father Perrin, I understand what you are doing, and I appreciate it. I'm not like most people. I didn't need to see this boy to feel deeply for him and all the other boys like him. Still, I'm glad I did. I'm not angry at anyone. But please, I think we deserve to see *our* son now.'"

I looked out the window. The car was cresting the hill. I knew Father Perrin would smirk at words of sympathy or—god forbid—understanding. And the horror of the story was only too evident. As was often the case with the stories Father Perrin told, there was simply nothing to say.

I'd opened the car door and was facing the moonscape of old battlefield when he stopped me with a hand on my shoulder.

"In all of this cheerfulness I almost forgot to tell you there's an American woman coming this afternoon. I suppose you'll have to talk to her."

"What should I say?"

He put both hands on the steering wheel and stared out over the destroyed ridge, which always looked to me like a dead crocodile.

"Try to answer her questions. If that fails, perhaps you should say American things. Her letters have been coy about what she wants, why she's coming. To be honest, I'm not sure she's completely sincere. Perhaps you'll know."

His right eye fluttered. I waited for him to say something more, then I got out of the car.

"And will you join me later when I dial Paris?" he called. "Tonight the music will be wonderful. Piano works by Ravel. Perhaps the most beautiful music ever written. I really believe that." I caught a glimpse of the sad, ironic smile he seldom showed anyone but me. "Do you realize," he asked, "how lucky we are to live in such a time?"

The first widow came to Verdun before Father Perrin arrived, before the war was even over. I noticed her mouth right away—I'd forgotten teeth could be so white. It was late summer, and she stood in the palace courtyard wearing an orange dress with white flowers in the pattern, a white hat with an orange flower in the brim. The smile wavered, but she whipped it back, as if it might help to look happy.

"I'm looking for Daniel," she said. "Do you know Daniel Jerot? No, I mean, do you know of him? Nobody seems to."

I was afraid to say anything, afraid even to call for Father Gaillard—the bishop of Verdun, the man who had taken me in when my father died—because I could guess how words, dismissals, promises, had already harmed her. But when I did call, he came at once, black cassock swishing, round glasses smudged. The three of us went into his office, where dim window light fought the dust. I poured her a glass of water.

She told us that she'd met Daniel in a café just off Place Stanislas in Nancy, where they both worked. She explained that after Daniel enlisted in 1914, she'd watched from behind the bar as the mayor walked the square in a white suit yellowing at the collar and sleeves. By custom it fell to the mayor to deliver the news of the missing and dead. She described the tremor in her throat as she watched him pass, the many ways she'd burned her distracted hands.

She described the sunny day in April of 1916 when, instead of turning up Rue Gambetta as usual, the mayor crossed the square, and stood in the door of the café, and took off his hat. The band inside was yellow with sweat too.

She'd imagined she might actually feel some relief at the news—she was ashamed to admit it, but she wanted His Grace to understand everything—but no, all she felt was anger. The little man with the solemn tone and uneven mustache knew just enough to destroy her life and nothing more.

What happened? He didn't know.

Who saw him last? He didn't know.

Would they search for him? He didn't know.

When would there be news?

Other than a curt letter of condolence from Daniel's lieutenant there was no more news. Not for the rest of that year, not in the following year, despite letters to the lieutenant pleading for more information. And all that time she continued to work at the café, continued to watch the man in the white suit with the yellowing hatband ferry the dead across the square.

Had we ever seen Place Stanislas? she asked.

Father Gaillard removed his glasses and rubbed his thumb over the lens. He was a large, even imposing, man, well over six feet tall. But it was his soft face and softer voice that drew everyone to him. He wore, as always, the typical bishop's costume—the cassock, the biretta, the heavy pectoral cross—but he was one of the few people I've ever known who could not be accused of playing a part.

"Yes," he said, "the finest square in France."

"That's true, it is," she said quietly.

They nodded together. She seemed to unclench. Father Gaillard polished his glasses, sweep after sweep with the end of his scarf, as he often did when he was upset, his way of preparing his thoughts.

"Is it the café with the green awning?" he asked eventually. "A zinc bar? Is it just off Rue Girardet?"

Her hair bounced on her shoulders as she leaned forward, alive in a way she wasn't. "You know it?"

"What did Daniel look like?" Father Gaillard asked.

"He looks like everyone else. If you put him in a blue uniform you wouldn't be able to tell him from ten thousand others."

"Come now."

"Like a clown."

"Come now."

"I mean it. Very pale skin, very red lips. English-looking."

"I thought so," Father Gaillard said. He made a final pass with the scarf and replaced the glasses on his nose. "He served me once. It must have been before the war."

She laughed. A sob can't express bitterness half as well. "All this time later? You couldn't possibly remember."

"Perhaps not," he said, "but I do think so."

She opened her purse and rummaged, likely her own way of buying time. I knew a little of how she felt. After all, I had sat in that very chair in the days after my father died, wondering if I could trust the man across from me. Though it was not my place to speak, I wanted to tell her that she should trust him, as I had. But I also felt a sad sympathy for Father Gaillard, knowing the hours of prayer and contemplation this lie would cost him—and it was a lie, wasn't it?

Eventually she looked up with shiny eyes, and said, "Perhaps he put a cigarette on the saucer when he served it? It would have been one of his own. He often did that if someone from the church came. He was shy, he wouldn't have said anything to you."

There was not a trace of falseness in Father Gaillard's smile, but then, there never was. "He did, indeed," he said. "I don't normally permit myself. Perhaps that's why I remember."

After she left, he opened the windows to let out the dust.

"Did you really meet her husband," I asked, "in that café?"

He didn't answer. He was the sort of man who loved reading aloud to children. I used to watch him in the dim rooms of the citadel, his copy of *Grimms' Fairy Tales* held up to the lamp, his voice rising an octave for a princess, scraping low for a dragon.

Father Perrin arrived six months later. The design for the ossuary—the memorial where the thousands of bones left on the battlefields would be interred—had come back from the committee by then. The French government had agreed to pay a portion of the cost, the diocese of Verdun another portion, but much of the money would need to be raised privately, and Father Gaillard announced he'd have to travel to do it, far from Verdun. Someone else would have to face the next Miriam Jerot, and the next. He never admitted it, but he must have realized he was too tender for the job.

Miriam Jerot was the first of many. Almost a million men had died or disappeared on the hills and fields northeast of Verdun, and their parents, siblings, and wives came in a steady line that might have stretched across the entire front. Ladies chauffeured by car from Paris, and illiterate shepherds from Languedoc, and marsh people from Finistère who hardly spoke French at all.

The Father Perrin that appeared in the foyer of the Episcopal palace to greet them was quite different from the man I knew, his expression a mixture of pity and nothing, a void into which they could pour everything they had to say.

And though he said very little, though he let them make introductions and describe their journey, there was something in his manner—in the thin face that looked suddenly honest, the thin smile that looked suddenly kind—that suggested he was *glad* they had come. And that mere fact—that mere illusion, if that's what it was—meant the world to the families standing before him, many of whom had traveled for days in cramped train cars or fuming motorcars or sometimes in carts drawn by horses or sometimes even by foot. Many of them had spent what little money they had to get here. For many of them this was only one notch—perhaps the final notch—in an absurdly long and lonely journey. They had already written letters—to the lost man's lieutenant, to generals, to politicians, to Foch, Poincaré, and Clemenceau. They had waited for replies—from their priest, their magistrate, their mayor—all the while knowing that a letter about their son or husband was just one of tens, hundreds, thousands awaiting its recipient, a letter to be responded to mechanically and in due time.

Father Perrin would usher them through the sliding double doors into the office; he would offer to hang their coats on the square rack with its rectangular mirror. And he would offer them water from a glass pitcher I kept refilled, which rested on a wooden tray, which rested on a Second Empire side table.

Yes, the dust still lingered, no matter how many times I swept out the room or beat the rugs. But if you could ignore it you might not blame a father from Bayeux or a wife from Cassis for feeling that they had been transported back into a time when the death of one man made some impression. That, as they took their seats in the red cushioned chairs with their sloped and polished armrests, as they began to tell Father Perrin their story, they were no longer in a world of empty church towers, the bells melted for ammunition.

When they looked upon Father Perrin and heard him say, "I'm glad you've come. I'll do anything I can to help you," they believed him. For some of these grieving families Father Perrin had to say little else. For some the sight of the churned earth, the rusted wire, the crumbling forts and twisted bunkers was enough. For some the question that had coiled around them for months or years—how could it have happened to my son, my husband, my brother?—began to make horrific sense.

But many others didn't want to understand. They wanted to be understood, and they would lean across the Second Empire desk and clutch Father Perrin's hands. They would weep and talk—for hours sometimes—about the man they'd lost. As if all that talk might help us identify him, as if it might bring him back to life. Bring back to life the man from Poitou who'd walked to Paris as a boy to apprentice as a cabinetmaker, who'd smuggled a young girl in a cabinet he carted back to his village. That young girl, now a woman, came to us in the spring of 1920 to describe every rut in the long road, every bump, the look in his eye when the door finally swung open.

They wanted to bring back to life the boy from Anjou who killed a wolf with a bow and arrow and dragged him home across miles of fields. The boy's mother described his expression as he struggled to maintain the stoicism of his older brothers. She described her delight at seeing pride for the first time on her youngest son's face, even though she could also see it wasn't a wolf he'd shot but a sheepdog.

They wanted to bring back the boy from Lourdes who copied passages of Montaigne out by hand in his letters to his father, to prove that he wasn't forgetting. The boy from Arles who'd lost his right eye when he was eleven—who'd saved money for a glass one to fool the draft board in 1915.

They wanted to bring back the boy who picked apples in Normandy. His father brought a bottle of the family Calvados and insisted that Father Perrin and I drink until we could hardly stand. "He made this," the father kept saying, "he made this."

It was my job to take down these descriptions, to write to the Red Cross and the Ministry of War to ensure that nothing had been overlooked, that no further information was forthcoming. And it was my job to record the family names in a separate set of files to ensure their inclusion on the ossuary's wall of memorial: Abel, Albert, Allard, Barre, Baudin, Belmont, Caron, Chastain, Comtois, even Combs, my own last name. It was my father's family name, bestowed upon me by my mother at birth, though neither she nor I had claim to it, as they never married. Certainly, the fact was not lost on me that, had I died in the war, there would have been no one to come looking.

In some ways, though, the families of the dead were lucky. For so many others, the official telegram printed on light blue paper said *missing, believed dead*. Was it possible, their sad and ashamed eyes asked. Was it possible that in the midst of all they had heard, in the face of all the numbers and statistics, all the warnings from the officers and the mayor and their priest, that *their* son or *her* husband had been one of the ones to survive? Weren't there reports that the Germans had run secret prison camps where the living were kept in order to terrorize the Entente? Weren't there rumors that some soldiers had crossed into Switzerland during the mutinies of 1917, that they waited there now for news of amnesty?

How could Father Perrin, how could anyone, tell these grieving faces that a direct hit from a shell could atomize a man? That the shelling was so incessant during the battle that a man's remains might be buried and unburied and blown a mile into the distance and buried again? That we found hundreds of bones every single day, scattered across the front, mangled and unmatched? How could Father Perrin tell anyone that the fact that such pervasive destruction might lead to hope was the cruelest of ironies?

He could only explain that there were no special lists, no secret camps, no utopian bands of fugitives. He could only say that if a séance or medium helped them feel better, then they should accept that help, but they should believe more in the charlatans who might use their grief against them than in ghosts. He could only say that they had done everything they possibly could already, that they should never for a moment feel they had failed.

But he didn't tell them to abandon hope, and most of them did not. Once a mother from Bordeaux said, "You know, gentlemen, to be honest, I really expected much worse. This couldn't possibly have killed Jean. If you met him, you'd know that."

Once a widow from Lyon told us that she understood our point of view, but that the best medium in France had been searching for her husband in séances for two years without success, that experts in the living world were much more often wrong than those in the spirit world.

Once the wife of a shepherd from Landes handed us a pair of stilts, saying, "If you see him, give him these, please. He'll get home faster."

I left the car on the paved road outside Fleury, carrying the canvas shoulder bag I would fill with bones, and a second, smaller bag stuffed with my canteen, some black bread and cheese, and a half-bottle of Alsatian wine. The door slammed, and the car pulled away, leaving only my shadow in the sun. It was early morning, already hot.

From the new road it was a half-hour climb up the ridge onto the Douaumont Plateau. The ground still looked like a filthy sea. I thought of Chicago, of Oak Street Beach along Lake Michigan, where I had gone with my mother. The lifeguard chairs, the names etched into the wood, the whitewash fading and peeling.

I wondered who this American woman was, what beaches she remembered, what streets. Father Perrin had told me almost nothing about her. A widow, a mother, a sister? A writer looking for a story? A lunatic looking for attention?

I seldom spoke directly to those who came in mourning, but there were others whose welcome fell to me: artists competing for commissions on memorials, metallurgists pondering shrapnel, ornithologists tracking starlings over treeless acres, and, once, a British diabolist wearing an amulet of interlaced snakes.

No matter how rational or irrational their reason, the look these visitors offered me when I introduced myself in careful, but accented, French was usually the same. The mouth tight, the eyes blinking, *Why you?* Not an unreasonable question. Certainly I was the least likely of many people—the parish priests, the sacristans, the other orphans. Of course, I wanted to believe that Father Gaillard had sensed some fundamental intelligence or decency in me when he'd suggested to Father Perrin that I stay on as his first assistant. More likely, though, he realized that his project was expensive, and that Americans had the stable currency. It was a neat trick, I'm sure, to mention casually to a New York heiress or a Pennsylvania industrialist that, in fact, his assistant was American. Weren't we all prey to this horror at Verdun? Weren't we all responsible for its rectification? Look at the young man from Chicago, I could imagine him saying, collecting the bones of the French dead in the fields each day. Will you really not pick up a pen, will you really not sign a check?

After another half-mile I arrived in Fleury. Many of Fleury's orphans had become my friends in the citadel, and I had listened to their stories until they became my own. Fleury had been a village of nearly five hundred people, mostly farmers. There was a church with a gold vestment that supposedly dated back to the time of Saint Denis. A little school taught by a man who'd come from somewhere in the

Alps, whose accent was never fully understood, whose advice was never fully trusted. Two old sheepdogs wobbled through the streets, sleeping by what fires they chose. Livestock snorted into the single-room houses, which were connected to the barns by Dutch doors so that the smell of the animals—the warmth of their bodies and breath—became a part of each home.

In February of 1916 the German attack began in a snowstorm. Just past dawn, the shells blasted open the frozen ground, caving in the roofs of the baker and butcher. My friends described the sparks in the snow. The broken patterns of booms, the shock waves splitting trees and lighting fires, before the next shell struck, extinguishing the fires with a shower of smothering dirt. The school, burned black, scalded with earth. And the tiny Saint Étienne's bell clanging somewhere underneath the explosions. The mayor ran through the streets with snow in his beard and mud covering one side of his face.

They fled with the fires stoked, bread and jam on the tables. They raced into the cold and pulled their livestock from the barns, trying to calm the animals in low voices. Pulling their carts from behind homes. Filing down the ridge west toward Bras-sur-Meuse, toward the range limit of the artillery.

Behind, they left the plows bought once in a lifetime. They left chests containing their most valued possessions, a book no one could read, an embroidered blouse too precious to see the light of day. They left the dinner tables owned for generations, shallow bowls cut into the wood to hold soup.

As they raced away they tried to keep a rough count of who had trudged out through the exploding snow. The schoolteacher was nowhere to be seen. The mayor had disappeared as well. Two men ran back, stupidly shouting, as if the explosions were not warning enough. A shell whistled down and one of the men vanished, leaving neither the mist nor the odor of blood.

Five years later the old tables with the shallow bowls were ash. And over the years I found only a few things that might have been familiar to the mayor or the schoolteacher. A tooth of a plow. Half a spoon. Once I found a green-gold button with a glint of mother-of-pearl. I left it on a burned stump in case anyone ever came back to look.

I returned to the Episcopal palace in the late afternoon to find a woman in a bright blue dress. She was young. Her hair was black, or almost black. As I stood in the archway, she trailed one finger through the koi pond. I could feel the dirt beneath my nails, the sour layer on my neck. I knew, without having to look, that there was a line of sweat across my shirt like a marshal's sash.

"Hello," I said in English.

"My French is fine," she said, looking up, frowning. "You're Mr. Combs?"

"I am. And you must be Mrs. . . ." I knew the name. Hagen. All day I'd imagined asking this woman to sit in the haze of the old office, to lay bare the uncomfortable facts of her life, but I couldn't seem to get the name out of my mouth. Perhaps my tongue already understood something the rest of me had yet to realize.

She scraped a heel, drawing a slash in the gravel—something playfully boyish in the gesture. But her face was too tense to read. "I'm almost sure I've mentioned my name in my letters. Five at least."

She smiled, not especially genuinely, and her eyes went somewhere beyond me, as if she'd passed a test and now Father Perrin would arrive.

"How far have you come?" I asked. "Far?"

"It feels like I did. Up from Udine—I live there, which I've also mentioned in several letters—through Metz. That's France now, apparently. The railway signs are still in German, but they have a Marshal Foch Boulevard. You're American," she said. "You sound like it, but you don't seem like it. Americans are generally punctual."

I didn't wear a watch, and had no idea what time she had expected me. She was right, such questions were seldom asked in Verdun. Father Perrin used to say that our sense of time had been warped by proximity to the afterlife.

"Have I kept you waiting?"

"Long enough, yes."

"Long enough for what?"

"Let me show you," she said. "You'll have to sit beside me, though."

I took a seat at the edge of the pond, the blue-gray flagstone pleasantly warm, as she undid the gold clasp on her purse. Inside, in an inch or two of water, was one of the goldfish.

"I didn't imagine I'd be able to catch one, but it was easy." She laughed, as if she'd truly surprised herself. "How long do you think he'll survive?"

The fish flicked his tail, bulging eyes blank, mouth working on the rim of the water.

"I'd rather not know."

I took the purse from her lap and dipped it into the pond, releasing the fish. I knew how she must be feeling, the long journey on the train. The confusion of the station, the arrival in such a place. And, after all, it was just a fish. All the same, I felt something close to anger. At her disrespect, and at myself for finding her disrespect even a little charming.

"Please don't do that again, all right?"

"I'm not sure I could do it again. That's why I needed to show someone." She caught my eyes, then dropped hers, but her look was more of triumph than disappointment. As if whatever she wanted had already been denied her, just as she had expected.

"I won't tell Father Perrin," I said. "He'd be upset. He's been trying to catch one of those fish for a year now."

She didn't smile. We remained side by side on the lip of the pond, the sun softening as afternoon began to wane.

"You're supposed to ask me questions, aren't you?" she said. "My name is Mrs. Lee Hagen. My husband went missing in the spring of 1918."

In Father Gaillard's office, she kept glancing at the inside of her wrist, as if there were a watch to check.

"You've tried all the other channels already?" It was a question Father Perrin always asked.

She took a breath to prepare. "I've written the Ministry of War, the Red Cross, News of the Soldier, Search for the Missing, and many others. Last month there was a woman from an organization called Help for Families who said she had lists no one else had. Where did she find these lists? How could they know more than the army or the Red Cross? I didn't ask until it was too late. Are you satisfied?"

"It wasn't a test."

"Perhaps everything just feels like a test."

"Those swindlers are the worst on earth."

"We can agree on that," she said. Then she was silent. Usually there was too much to say. Each word we exchanged, though perfectly correct, felt more false than the one before. It was her voice: tired, disinterested, almost bored.

"Do you mind if I ask why you didn't say any of that in your letters to Father Perrin?"

"I suppose I didn't want to have to tell the same story again, over again, over again. It's unavoidable, obviously. I suppose I'm tired of feeling vetted."

"That you deserve help, you mean?"

"That I've suffered enough to deserve it."

More silence, sun on the back of my neck. I rose to open one of the windows. The latch was stuck, and I had to give up.

"Have you been to France before?" I asked.

She looked up from her wrist and smiled weakly. "It's different than I pictured it."

"It's not all like this," I said.

"I should hope not."

"Actually," I said, "other than Paris, I haven't seen much beyond Lorraine. Maybe it is all like this. I don't know."

"Did you see much of the war?"

"Not much, no. I worked in the citadel during the battle. After that I drove an ambulance for a year or so."

Her eyes darted up, and for a moment I saw something in them other than disappointment.

"With who? The American Field Service?"

"For a year, yes."

"Lee was with the AFS."

"Not in the French Army?"

"No, he was attached to the 22nd Division, then he joined with the Americans when they took over the service. His name was Lee Hagen," she said. "He was attached with other Princeton men. Did you—?" She paused. She didn't want to appear foolish, to appear not to understand that most things in the world had absolutely nothing to do with her. All the same, she had to ask. "By any chance, did you know him?"

"Lee Hagen," I said. The name with its hard Germanic syllables felt strange in my mouth. She smiled at the sound of it, and, though she sat only a few feet from me, she looked like something shimmering in the heat at the end of a road. She was a beautiful woman, but to say that I was conscious of attraction or desire would be misleading. It's better to say that I was simply very *aware* of her. Aware of the slashes of her gaze, the impatience of her posture. Aware most of all of her anger, which I assumed—as one often wrongly does—was directed toward me. Was it that simple? That I did not want her to be angry with me?

"Lee Hagen," I said. "Yes. Yes. I did know him. I think I did."

"Well," she said softly.

"Well?"

"Did you know him well?"

"No," I said. "Not well."

There were ripples of light on the desk, beams in the dust. Evening, the sun setting over the rubble along the river. She didn't speak.

"We met," I said, "in Aix-les-Bains. On permission." The words were already out of my mouth before I realized what a good lie it was. For a year nearly every permission had been mandated for Aix-les-Bains, near the Swiss border. It was a fifty-fifty chance that Lee Hagen had gone, and if he hadn't the whole business would have been over. But as I spoke it appeared someone had stolen the bones from her face.

Hardly anyone wrote to their wives about Aix-les-Bains because there were nice American girls there, girls who worked for the YMCA or the Red Cross, who had steamed across the Atlantic, often with their mothers beside them, to do their bit. To share news from home, to dance at the American bar, to smell of familiar soap and speak of familiar things.

It wasn't as if most men reported home about French prostitutes either, but they were easy to write out of the story. While days walking the lake or nights dancing with the American girls at Aix-les-

Bains became the story for many. Better to say nothing to the wife still loved but unimaginably far away.

I got off easier than most, since I had no one to tell, no one from whom to keep a secret. Still, I thought of her afterward from time to time—the girl, not older than seventeen, who'd approached me in the casino. When I arrived at the hotel I had to cut the mud off my feet with a knife. I'd been exhausted beyond words, drinking whiskey-sodas and playing cards. We talked for hours by the lake. She was from Ohio and came over on a ship called the *Esmeralda*. I felt soft from the whiskey. I leaned against her on a stone bench in the dark.

"You look much too young for this," she said.

I tried to kiss her, and felt her lips smile against my lips.

The particular lie came to mind, I think, because Mrs. Hagen reminded me of her. They looked nothing alike. It was a demeanor, a delicacy that seemed to suggest life was not such hard work.

"Yes," Sarah said. "He was in Aix-les-Bains in early 1917, I think."

"He seemed happy there," I said.

"You could tell that?"

"I thought I could."

"He was already losing his mind then," she said.

CHAPTER TWO

"You won't be too lonely, will you?" Father Perrin asked the following morning, as the car wound up the ridge on the way back to Fleury. "I leave again this afternoon." There was thunder in the distance and a thin fog above the river, but no rain.

"Oh yes. For Rodez?"

"You can't have forgotten."

I hadn't forgotten, exactly, but I'd been able to consider little else besides Sarah and Lee Hagen. I had no reason to think I would ever see her again. Even so, several times in the night I'd sat down at my desk to write her a note backing away from the lie. I claimed I'd gone through my old correspondence only to discover I was mistaken: I hadn't visited Aix-les-Bains until early 1918. It likely wasn't her husband I'd met there after all. I was terribly sorry if I'd given her false comfort or hope.

Had I found a way to make the words sound right, I would have sent them, but on three separate attempts the note came out awkward and cold. It was her derision I imagined, not her disappointment.

"I *have* forgotten why you're going," I said.

"It's something of a secret actually. There's a man in the asylum there, repatriated from a German camp. They found him wandering the platform at Gare de Lyon last year, almost catatonic."

"Do you have to go all the way to Rodez to find a man like that?"

I expected him to laugh, but he didn't. After almost two years at his side, I still didn't understand what was permissible to joke about and what wasn't.

"This man doesn't know who he is, and no one else seems to either. He hardly talks, apparently, but claims his name is Anthelme Mangin. Only there is no such person. There's a similar case in Milan or perhaps Sienna, I've heard, but that's the Italians' problem."

"What do they want with you?"

"Oh, these days everyone thinks someone else has the answer. Fenayrou, the doctor there, wants to publish the man's picture in the papers. I probably don't need to go all the way to Rodez to offer my opinion on that, but I said I would. It will rain on the way. The train will break down. I'll sit next to a man who will want to confess all the terrible things he's done. Maybe you'd like to go in my place?"

I had to study his profile carefully to take in his meaning. I knew enough to suspect what he was getting at, though I wasn't certain. "You seemed to do well yesterday," he continued. And then I knew.

"With Mrs. Hagen?"

"Indeed. She sent a note last night. If only she had told me before about her husband. Now I have no time to see her before I go."

"It turns out I knew him vaguely."

"So she said. A surprising coincidence, I thought." His eye twitched, but his eye always twitched. The rain had begun, and through the scrim on the windshield the rolling fields looked even more like waves. Father Perrin pumped the lever to wipe away the mist. "As it is, she's asked to see the provisional ossuary. Since I won't have time to speak with her, I have a mind to say yes."

"I could show her, if you like," I said.

"She's the one that would like. But perhaps you have other responsibilities today."

"Always. But I'll be in Fleury anyway."

"Fine. She must be used to getting her way no matter what she says or how she acts. Probably she comes from some money, which is a curse in a case like this."

"What else do you know about her?"

"Her French is very good." He sighed and brushed his hand across my shoulder. "And I'll see you in five days, my friend." I could tell he wanted to rest his hand there for a moment longer, but the windshield turned opaque, and he had to pull the lever on the wipers again.

"I'm so tired of all the rain," he said. "If only this Mangin could have found himself an asylum by the ocean."

We'd been over Fleury and almost every other inch of battlefield many times already, but it seemed each time I returned, there were more bones. Father Gaillard had said my grandchildren would still find bones in Verdun—we just needed to ensure that they find as few as possible.

It was lonely work, certainly, but I wasn't always alone. Tourists began to arrive before the war was even over, filing through the streets in solemn groups. Soldiers in wheelchairs waited under melted streetlamps, pointing the way to the next site of mourning and triumph. *Here* was Vauban's citadel, where Pétain and Neville strategized the first creeping barrage. *Here* was the Voie Sacrée—the sacred road—from which poured the *matériel* that would save the city, the war, the nation. After the armistice, the tours leapt into the battlefields. To Father Gaillard and Father Perrin, visiting Verdun or Artois or Chemin des Dames was something near to a civic duty. The battlefields would be gone soon enough, overgrown, cleaned up, and then what? Were we to expect people just to remember?

The previous spring, boys from a Catholic school in Tourcoing had spent their vacation on bicycles, helping to collect the bones. The young priest who accompanied them spent much of the time drunk in his tent. In his absence, I helped the boys gather bones in baskets. I walked them to the provisional ossuary like a crossing guard, though they weren't many years younger than I.

Some of these boys worked like the devil, keeping their eyes on the ground, holding the bones as if they were fragile things still in need of protection. These boys knew not to smile or laugh much. To turn away at the jokes of their friends. Some of the others sang songs to pass the time, and talked about schoolwork and the Sainte Roseline girls on the other side of their town.

Once, one of the boys picked up a leg bone from the mud, and stroked it as if it were his penis. It took the others a moment to laugh, and a less determined comedian might have given up. But when he began to moan, to lick his lips, the crowd that had gathered broke into chuckles. They laughed hard when the bone broke apart in his hands and he said, in mock horror, "My god, Father Soucy warned me this might happen."

Some of the boys looked to me as if I might punish him. But punish him how?

Of course, many of them were scared out of their minds. They refused to ride the bicycles unless the asphalt was new. And, though it was safe enough as long as you knew what you were doing, they had reason to be cautious. If you did something foolish like pick up a grenade, then perhaps you deserved what you got.

I headed east past the site of Fleury's old train station, the only remaining section of track curled up at one end like a sneering lip. There were small yellow bones in the dirt. I put them in my bag.

I walked another forty steps before finding much else, all the while feeling Mrs. Hagen's gaze on my face as I said her husband's name. Then, in a shell hole flooded from the rain, I found half a skeleton, mud clinging to the ribs. I knew that I should scoop up the bones and push them into the sack, to dismantle the image of the buried man. It was possible to forget a few pieces of white-yellow carbon. But the skeleton had a face.

I began to wonder—as I often did—if I would have recognized the man's real face. Had this man taken permission in Aix-les-Bains, as I had, as Lee Hagen had? Surely, whoever he was, he had stumbled down the corridors of the citadel at least once. Perhaps he had died with some of the bread I'd baked in his pocket.

Perhaps he was the man who'd kicked me in the hip in the canteen when I didn't understand his French, the man who swore at me in wine-scented shouts as I lay there, too ashamed to move. Or perhaps he was another man, the one who pushed that first fellow away and helped me to my feet.

Let's say he was the second man. Let's say his name was not Lee, but Martin. Let's say he grew up in Jura, became a stonemason. Let's say he had a mother and three sisters but no wife. And let's say that his mother had come down from the mountains in black, begging Father Perrin to explain what had happened to her son.

There really had been such a woman. She'd arrived at the Episcopal palace in October of 1919 without writing first and apologized to Father Perrin, explaining that it was difficult for her to write, that she'd only just learned. She explained that during the war, she'd begged the postman in their village to teach her, because she'd been ashamed that she wasn't able to send mail to Martin. It had taken her months, even though she stayed up half the night practicing. Too long. Because when she finally had a letter to send to her son the only response was a notice from the Ministry of War.

She said to Father Perrin, I understand he's dead, Father. I just want to know. Was I too stupid? Was I too slow? Did he ever receive my letter?

Let's say, for the love of god, that her son, Martin, did receive her letter, that it arrived in the citadel, that he was shocked to hear the postman call his name, pleased beyond words to see his name on the envelope in handwriting he'd never seen but somehow recognized immediately. Let's say he tucked the letter into his breast pocket when he went up to the line the next day.

In July of that year, after pounding the French with artillery, the Germans overran their positions and forced their way into Fleury, driving the French back down the ridge toward Fort Souville. The next morning the French responded, shelling their old positions for hours before the counterattack.

Let's say Martin was among them, feeling—what? An emptiness? A terror? A terrible excitement? A ghost of a wall, a ruin of a barn, perhaps, still stood. The trenches were dug straight, hastily, without time to zig and zag. So, when the French went over the top, when they reached the German lines and half-jumped and half-stumbled into the trenches, those who got up in time with their rifles ready had a clear shot down the line for a hundred meters.

Let's say Martin staggered down a length of trench to where some bodies lay in German uniforms. Perhaps he bayoneted them, one by one. He bayoneted another German through the cheek, the man still alive but buried past his waist by shellfire. And then Martin fell to one knee, thinking only: *my mouth is dry, my mouth is dry, my mouth is dry.*

Later, his lieutenant called roll; a quarter of the names went without answer. The counterattack began before he had reached the letter *T*. It was dark. The sky lit orange, glowing like a hearth. Martin had never thought of the sky so much before coming to the front. But that was his world for three years: mud, rats, the dead, the sky.

The same sky even in 1921, now mopping at acres of cratered dirt. What else was left? Bones in boots, a rusted bucket, a shattered root. Gravel and wheels of motorcars; spokes and strips of rag. A solitary tree, black against the sky, like a finger pressed to the lips calling for silence. I would speak with Mrs. Hagen again in three hours.

Around dawn the French—Martin among them—advance a hundred meters west, and are driven back, leaving the dead as they go. The artillery has inverted the world. The sky falls apart piece by piece, the ground hovers in black sprays of dust. The earth is no longer earth. The water—in flooded shell holes filled with the dead—is no longer water. The air—yellow with smoke—is no longer air. But fire is still fire.

When the order comes that Fleury has been retaken, Martin sits pressed to crumbling walls in a roofless cellar. The counterattack begins just past dawn the following day. Green Cross shells this time. A gas attack. They half-expect it, and have the masks ready. The gas uncoils and sinks. There's always the initial shock, even after many such attacks, but it passes. The masks work. They're just underwater, that's all this is.

There was a lake in Jura so cold you could only swim it in August. The old boulders on the shore were known to aid fertility, and women walked miles to scrape off a bit of dust and drink it with water from the lake. As a boy, Martin would dive down for half a franc (his mother told us all of this!) to the very bottom to catch the most potent water. The lake was ten meters deep. He could have gone five meters down, three, no one would ever have known; he only half-believed in the superstition himself, but he always swam to the very bottom anyway.

At the bottom of a shell hole I found leg bones beneath a few smashed bricks. I put them in my bag. Sometimes I kept count and sometimes I didn't. Sometimes I felt a terrifying sadness, sometimes a strange elation, and sometimes—as was the case that day—I lost touch completely with what I felt and was aware only of what I thought I was *supposed* to feel. I decided I must tell Mrs. Hagen the truth. Not just that I had been mistaken, but that I had misrepresented myself. And if I could find some way to explain why, I would tell her that too.

Nightfall. Fleury smolders. The cellars are gone. A few pieces of brick are all that remain, and Martin, along with the rest of the men in his battalion, trudges back into the darkness. For a moment the shelling stops. No one knows why. There is a buzz of oblivious flies. There is a dead horse in Martin's path. An explosion lifts him into the air. And then?

No. The skeleton I'd found couldn't be this Martin. Anyway, not as I imagined him. Suddenly it was clear that he'd come to in mushy light, to someone speaking German, to hands pulling him to his feet, leading him toward a few mud-caked specters, French prisoners. He stumbles, and the hands stand him up and shove him in the back and stand him up again but gently this time, and then he hears a voice in broken French. If you keep walking, it says, it's all right, you're going to live.

By the time I arrived at the provisional ossuary, I had only a few minutes to wash in the drum behind the building. The groundwater still wasn't trusted. I splashed my face to the rumble of a car engine and practiced the apology a final time. *I meant only to help, but I realize my words have likely had the opposite effect. I was unprepared. I was foolish.*

The sky had emptied, but thunder still reported from a long ways off. I found Mrs. Hagen waiting in the road with her hand out to me. I offered her my arm. Even in midsummer the mud never really dried. Perhaps it was our slow pace along the duckboards that made me see the provisional ossuary through her eyes. A house with glassless windows on either side of a pine door, looking less like a monument than a dry goods store.

Nevertheless, we'd done our best to make the inside feel like a sanctuary. There were candles on the windowsills, garlands and wreaths on every beam. Along the back wall stretched a banner with a wild-haired woman holding a torch aloft, reading "Et à la Sainte-Alliance." Everywhere was the sweet, yeasty odor of the bones, like the smell of a sneeze.

I waited for her eyes to adjust, for the names of the villages engraved on the boxes to emerge from the murk. Father Gaillard had commissioned a plaque for each stack, corresponding to its sector of the battlefield. Order is a sign of respect, he said. But the bones seldom fit, and, despite how we tried, the piles jutted in ghastly fractures.

She dropped my arm and waded away, her hair falling to one side as she turned her head to read the inscriptions. The light was confusing. The flickering candles, the glaring panes of sun. *I was unprepared. I was foolish.*

"You collected all of these?" she asked.

"No, no. There used to be a lot of us."

"What happened to everyone else?"

"They moved on."

In the beginning, twenty of us left the Episcopal palace six mornings a week in the bed of a Renault truck. Twenty of us walked into the hills, through the destroyed villages—mostly the orphans of those places. Verdun was still disputed territory then, filled with an almost Pentecostal spirit of nationalism. The cathedral pews were full on Sunday. The hallways were full of the strained voices of generals, politicians, and cardinals, all trying not to mix the pure water of national pride with the oil of self-interest. And yet it all seemed only a collage of disagreements about whose official letterhead certain notices went on, or how to respond to claims of war benefits, or where and how to bury the dead.

Everyone did seem to agree, though, that such pettiness couldn't continue. Verdun was a sacred space—at once the symbol of victory and loss, glory and horror—and, like all such spaces, it demanded austerity, even self-abnegation, from those entrusted to watch over it. That, I think, was why the military finally allowed Father Gaillard and the diocese to take the lead in the construction of the ossuary, in the administration of the cemeteries, in the counseling of the families. They simply didn't trust themselves.

Certainly, both Father Gaillard and Father Perrin—in speeches to the sacristans, the orphans, the kitchen staff, the gravediggers—had always been clear about the discipline our jobs demanded. There are many places in France, in Europe, they would say, where grief had been used to selfish advantage. Verdun would not be one of them. Did we understand?

"Would you like to light a candle, Mrs. Hagen?" I asked.

"No, thank you," she said. "But may I touch one of these?"

She smiled, as if daring me to stop her. She reached into one of the boxes, marked *Ornes*, and lifted out a pelvic bone and held it up in the candlelight.

"Would I know?" she asked.

For a moment, I pretended not to understand her question. It was said that the ground was so infused with bacteria that wounds would fester in the *zone rouge* faster than anywhere else on earth. Sometimes I imagined that something else—some essence of the dead—might have remained in the ground as well. I imagined that, digging through the soil, I might suddenly know how to refit track in the Paris Métro, or navigate the streets of Hamburg by heart. That I might take a woman's arm and immediately match her stride to my own.

"You'd be the best judge," I said. "But no, honestly, I don't think you'd know."

I returned the pelvic bone to the box and when I turned to face her again she was crying.

"That wasn't him," she said, once we were outside.

"I'm sure it wasn't," I said.

"I know it wasn't him because he went missing in Italy, not here."

I didn't say anything.

"Well, you can guess why I didn't tell you. Who would I have been handed off to if I'd said that?"

She apologized immediately, but only with her eyes. Indeed, her eyes and mouth rarely seemed to agree. The effect was a vague and lonely face. The face of one who has given up on ever being understood. And, I thought, when was the last time someone tried?

"Was he transferred after Caporetto?" I asked.

"In late '17, yes. And in the spring of 1918 he wandered off during a barrage. Near Gorizia."

"He *wandered* off?"

"His CO's word. He was kind at least, the CO. He reported Lee as *missing, believed dead*, not as a deserter. When I visited him after the war, I had to practically force him to tell me what really happened."

"That's the hardest thing in the world," I said.

"No. If we'd had children, then it would be worse."

"Why come here, then? What did you want to see?"

"I suppose I just need to try everything before . . ."

She trailed off, and I didn't ask what was to come after—I had no right to her future—but I did find myself bringing up my own past.

"There were rumors our group would go to Italy too," I said. "Most everyone wanted to."

"Didn't you?"

"That's partly why I left the service after the U.S. Army took it over."

"You wanted to stay here?"

Usually I said that I stayed out of a sense of loyalty to Father Gaillard. Because I'd been in the Verdun sector for almost three years by then and felt I had a duty to see it through the war in whatever small way I could. Both statements were true, but there was another reason as well.

"I was scared to go," I said. "It sounds strange, I know, but I could tell you a hundred stranger things."

"No," she said. "It sounds like you were the smart one. The car should be back soon. Will you wait with me? And will you do something else for me too?"

"If I can."

"I plan to stay a few more days."

"I'd be happy to show you whatever else you'd like to see."

"Even in Bar-le-Duc? There's something I very much want to see there. Would you go with me?"

Santa Monica, 1950

In the early thirties, when I was working at Paramount, Ernest Hemingway came onto the lot for a screening of *A Farewell to Arms*. He didn't think much of the picture, and said so unequivocally—though, to be fair, not many did. Not even those like myself who had worked on it. The script had only come past my desk because Frank Borzage, the director, had heard I'd driven an ambulance like the protagonist, Frederic Henry—like Hemingway himself. Normally, any personal experience with a picture's subject matter was enough to get you removed from a project, but Borzage admired Hemingway and thought he might be impressed by the touch of authenticity.

But he wasn't impressed. He could scarcely have been less interested in trading war stories with me. And by the time of the screening, I couldn't have said what I'd contributed to the film and what I hadn't, which was the case just as often as not.

I do remember, however, that I tried and failed to save the novel's famous lines about the meaninglessness—even perniciousness—of military rhetoric. *Abstract words such as glory, honor, courage, or hallow were obscene beside the concrete names of villages, the numbers of roads, the names of rivers*, he'd written. *Finally, only the names of places had dignity*, he'd written. The language was beautiful, the sentiment true enough, but I did wonder if Hemingway ever considered what it was like to live in a place with the *dignity* of Verdun. What it was like to walk along a river with the *dignity* of the Meuse.

Part of what first seduced me about California was that the names of its streets and sites had almost no meaning, and certainly no dignity—not in the way Hemingway meant, anyway. Sea View Avenue. Briarcrest Road. Or Rockingham Drive, where Paul lived, and where I drove for lunch the Saturday following Dr. Kepler's funeral.

It was a tony address—north of Sunset, just down the street from Cole Porter. Visiting homes on this sort of street was a part of life in the pictures, even if I hadn't been doing much of it lately. I'd reached a rather interesting moment in my career, where I no longer needed to attend tennis parties and Sunday drinking sessions in order to work. The arrangement suited me, I found, and I discovered a shyness in myself that I'd never had the chance to cultivate.

Nevertheless, I was pleased to receive Paul's invitation. The house was smaller than the others on the street, and, though it was built in the same Spanish style, a slight shabbiness set it apart.

The man who answered the door looked marvelously healthy, however—all the more so now that he wasn't dressed for a funeral. He wore a white linen shirt, open at the collar, and asked if I'd like to take my drink in the backyard, where three golden retrievers waited patiently on the lawn.

"Do you know what this is?" he asked as he handed me a boomerang.

"I believe so."

"The dogs love it. Care to throw?"

I said I'd prefer to watch. He gave an order in German, and the dogs lined up at his heel. We stood like that for quite a while, chatting in the late afternoon sun, Paul throwing the boomerang, the dogs tearing out into the lawn and leaping in turn. There was something pleasant about watching them hurl themselves into the air with such abandon, then wait at our feet with such apparent calm. And their game made our conversation easier. Sometimes I regretted that I'd never had many of those talks that take place in backyards, two boys throwing a baseball. Paul and I were a bit old for that, however.

"I didn't train them," he said. "If I had I would have used English, not German."

"Have you been back to Austria since the war?"

"My wife discourages me—I'm sorry you won't meet her today, by the way."

"Won't I?"

"She's visiting family in the east before the weather changes. Her mother's been ill for quite a long time, actually."

"My sympathies. And what about your family?"

He said nothing, but he didn't release the boomerang, his rhythm of throwing and retrieval briefly syncopated. "My father's newspaper was quite outspoken on *Anschluss*. Once the Nazis came to power, I suppose it was only a matter of time. Quite funny—somehow, I assumed you already knew that, but of course there's no way you could have."

We took a second round of drinks at a small table on the back patio, the dogs panting at our feet.

"I've been meaning to say, I saw one of your pictures this week." Paul said the name.

It wasn't one of mine, and I told him so.

He rubbed a hand over his face and laughed. "Dear god. I only went because I thought I recognized the name in the paper, I thought you mentioned it last week."

"It doesn't matter," I said. "Did you like it?"

"Yes. Well, are they all like that? So melodramatic?"

"Some are much worse. Most of the ones I've worked on, in fact."

"Oh, I'm sure that's not true." He paused, took a drink, and made a face. "I saw *Robin Hood* just this last year. A friend screened it. I didn't know what it was until it was too late."

"With Douglas Fairbanks," I said, slowly. "What did you think?"

"He was very graceful, forceful. I couldn't think of a worse sobriquet for that poor creature in Bologna. Could you?"

I'd driven there knowing that we'd be obliged to talk about Bologna and the man there we'd referred to as Douglas Fairbanks, about Drummond Green and Dr. Bianchi, about Sarah and Lee Hagen. I knew, also, that it would do me no harm to discuss those things—but that didn't mean the prospect was pleasant. The fact was, I didn't know how revisiting that time—those places, those people—would feel. I did know that I felt very well at the moment, more content probably than was typical for me. The fizz of the gin and soda, the perfect weather, and especially the old friend before me. I didn't answer. And when it was clear that I wasn't going to, Paul nodded in a genial way that could have meant anything, though I took it to mean that he understood perfectly, and said, "Well, you probably met Douglas Fairbanks, the real one."

"No. I never did," I said. "But I met Douglas Jr. Now there's a poor creature."

CHAPTER THREE

Mrs. Lee Hagen greeted me in the lobby of the Hotel de Guise wearing another blue dress. The de Guise had been spared most of the shelling and was the nicest of the three hotels that had reopened. I'd hauled the bags of generals and politicians up the looping staircase, wishing each time that the room I moved toward was my own. I always looked forward to listening in on the conversations in the lobby, each person far from home, starting from scratch. Like so many French words, I thought of it by its English homonym. *Disguise.*

Her hair was held back in two mother-of-pearl combs, and she wore a necklace of silver flowers. She was reading an English newspaper.

"I didn't know you could get those," I said.

"You can't. I brought an entire stack with me from Boston."

"I see," I said.

"I'm sorry. I'm only joking. I'm not *that* hysterical. It's yesterday's paper, from Metz. In Metz you can get the paper. I ordered coffee. I hope you don't mind. Will you sit down and tell me?"

I sat. "What should I tell you, Mrs. Hagen?"

"It's all right to use my first name, isn't it?"

"If you permit me."

"I do permit you. I was hoping you'd tell me what you're doing here."

"There are a hundred stranger things."

"Yes, you said that yesterday too."

She folded the newspaper and laid it flat on the table. The second half of a headline read, "DOUBTS WILSON." A man stepped in from the sunlight and said a few words to the concierge, his head bowed. He left as if rushing from a bad dream.

"There isn't much to explain. When I left the AFS, Father Gaillard asked me to help him. I couldn't refuse."

"To help him retrieve bones?"

"Among other things, yes. But when you say it like that it sounds—"

"How do you say it?"

"I never do."

"I really meant, how did you come here originally."

A waiter in a black jacket pushed the kitchen doors open with a brushed steel tray, then deposited saucers and cups on the tables, delicate spoons and dishes of brown sugar cubes. He bent, with the same formality, over our table. I have to admit that I felt a certain pride, sitting with a woman for whom such pleasures were routine, a woman who could speak to anyone she wanted but wanted to know about me.

"My father was American but he was born in France. He was a doctor with the AFS. He brought me here," I said.

"Irresponsible."

"No one ever accused him of being responsible."

"A strange thing to say about a doctor."

"He was an adventurer first."

"That's a kind light."

"Perhaps. He claimed to know Shackleton and Percy Fawcett."

This made her laugh. "He was interesting."

"He probably was. When my mother died, the Rileys—the neighbors who took me in—cabled him purely as a formality. Anyway, I hardly saw him, even once I got to France. I was boarding with a family around Bras. But when he died, there was no more money to pay them, and I moved into the Episcopal palace with Father Gaillard, and later into the citadel."

"Wouldn't it have been sensible to return to the States?"

"Yes. But, as you probably know, it wasn't a very sensible time."

"No grandparents wondering where you'd gone?"

"I've been told my father's parents are still alive in California, but I don't know them. My mother was another adventure."

She blushed, stirring her empty cup with a slender spoon. But anything I'd once felt about my parents' arrangement had washed off me years before. And it was a pleasant feeling to sit at that table and find that things that had once made me feel ashamed no longer made any impression.

"Father Perrin was afraid you were a journalist," I said. "I begin to wonder."

She laughed again. "I'm just used to asking questions. There's no reason you have to answer them. At least not truthfully."

"I don't mind. And don't worry. It's not entirely true."

The truth was that before my father died, I met Father Gaillard at a Casualty Clearing Station in a rye field outside of Souilly. My father had insisted I come, but then he worked for twelve hours straight, and even when he stopped to eat, I could see my questions glancing off his glazed eyes.

Father Gaillard had come on a pastoral visit. He sat down beside me, a giant man with tiny glasses. Much to my surprise, he knew my name. "Tom," he said, "if you wanted, you could be a great help to me. Would you mind very much?"

No, I didn't mind. I'd sat like a statue for hours watching the surgeons, bearers, drivers, nurses, and orderlies rush and stagger through the tents. I'd watched them dressing wounds; shaving for surgery;

administering morphine, saline solution, and brandy. I wanted nothing more than to be of some use myself.

I followed Father Gaillard into a tent set off from the rest of the CCS by a path worn in the unthreshed rye. There was little light, little movement, and almost no sound from the rows of cots inside. A single nurse sat on a pallet of sandbags and wrote in an enormous notebook. The tent flaps were open at both ends, but the space smelled powerfully of lavender and festering wounds.

Father Gaillard relieved the nurse and opened the notebook to a page near the back.

"Mark a cross next to each name at my nod, would you, Tom?"

The task was mercifully easy. I followed him from bed to bed as he inquired after the needs of the few soldiers who were conscious, said prayers for those who weren't, and, just before passing on to the next bed, gently touched the tip of each soldier's nose with his palm. If he nodded, I drew a careful cross in the margin next to the name.

Only later did I understand that we had arrived at the moribund ward, that these men were not expected to survive and could not be afforded the doctors' precious time. Only later did I understand that it was the chaplain's responsibility to write to these men's families in order to prepare them, but that the inevitable dying could go on for weeks, sometimes months. If the nose was cold, if the cross was marked, it was time to begin the letter.

Even to my fifteen-year-old mind such a method did not seem especially scientific or sound, yet, when I asked my father, he said Father Gaillard was seldom wrong. In fact, three months later, I watched Father Gaillard touch my father's nose in just that way. Soon after, he began to administer extreme unction, and, soon after that, he pulled the blanket over my father's face. Later that afternoon, Father Gaillard drove me back to Verdun himself, offering anecdotes about the parishes we passed on the way. More than once I thought he might cry.

"How do you feel, Tom?" he asked. Mostly, I felt angry that Father Gaillard seemed more affected by my father's death than I was.

"Tom," he said. His English was good, but with his accent my name sounded like "Tome." He kept repeating it, "Tome, Tome, Tome. I've gotten to know your father well. You might not be aware, but he was a decent man in many ways. And he would want me to help you. You think that you don't have a choice about what happens now, but you do. Have you thought about what you want?"

I'd already thought plenty about what I didn't want: the steamer ride home, the train ride across the northeast, coasting past Chicago's squealing stockyards. I'd thought of the kind but thinly stretched Rileys, waiting at Union Station. Then the familiar hall, smelling of cabbage; the familiar stairs and the apartment where I'd lived all my life with my mother, no doubt filled with someone else now, peering out, wondering who the new boy was.

I could also imagine the train as it picked up speed, heading west. Yellow fields and mountains and, somewhere beyond that, California, where my grandparents supposedly lived. Then: nothing. I couldn't picture them at all; even worse, I knew they couldn't picture me.

"What would it mean to stay here?" I asked.

It meant the orphanage in the Episcopal palace and shifts in the kitchen. After the battle began, it meant ten months traversing the passageways of the citadel, baking bread, and working in the canteen. But it also meant a promise from Father Gaillard that he would get me into the AFS once I turned eighteen, and, in those days, the AFS was reserved for men of a better class than the one from which I'd come. And it meant the illusion of choice for the first time in my life, the feeling that my choice was brave and possibly even noble.

That day at the CCS, after we had finished in the moribund tent,

I'd listened as Father Gaillard assembled the surgeons, orderlies, and nurses for prayer. *God has given us all a purpose here,* he'd said. *Our lives are difficult, certainly, but they are no longer futile.* Those words had meant a great deal to me. Though at the time, my French was still miserable, and it's possible I misunderstood what he was saying completely.

Several times on the way to Bar-le-Duc, I'd considered asking the driver to turn around, to take me back. I'd considered pleading my obligations for the day, of which there were indeed many: the letters to be typed and signed with Father Perrin's stamp, the stretch along the river near Forges to be walked for the sixth or seventh time.

It would be romantic to say that I didn't protest because such responsibilities seemed distant in comparison to the woman sitting beside me in the car. Truthfully, I allowed myself to continue because Sarah herself hardly seemed real, because it seemed that if I were to touch her, my hand would pass right through.

Her car dropped us on the outskirts of Bar-le-Duc, where the Voie Sacrée met Rue St. Michel. We fell into step with a crowd arriving in their second-best clothes, crossing the field toward twin tents the grimy yellow of kitchen aprons. The grass was damp, the hem of Sarah's dress shaggy with it by the time we reached the gate and I paid the twenty-centime admission to a man in a shapeless hat. Beside him two other men who could have been his brothers—the same raisin-like eyes—smoked hand-rolled cigarettes. The swarthier of the two held the flap up just high enough for us to duck inside.

The tent smelled of lamp smoke. We took seats on a long bench in the front row and watched the crowd file in, eating nuts from greasy paper bags. On the far wall a curtain with the faint outlines of waves or mountains hung on a wire between two knotty posts.

"The show might not be very good," I said to Sarah, as if it had been my idea to come, as if I should impress her, as if impressing her were possible. The crowd smelled of livestock and loam. Their backs were stooped, their faces dirty. I realized just how out of place we—or at least Sarah, in her blue crepe dress with its pleated skirt—must have appeared. And yet some of the tension had already left her face.

The oil lamps came up, and the man who had taken our tickets, now wearing a fur vest, stepped out from behind the curtain. Everything about him suggested exhaustion. He leaned on a cane and began to speak.

"What did he say, what did he say?" the man to my right asked. His neck was thick and glossy with sweat. He'd somehow made it to the tent without losing the shine on his shoes. I shrugged and we shared a smile.

The trainer's Pyrenean accent was so thick, his dialect so heavy, that I could barely understand a word. As he spoke, his gaze swept the tent, appraising the audience. Then he waved his cane as if to dismiss us, and withdrew behind the curtain. Just as he did, two bears emerged from the wings.

They were led by chains attached to iron rings looped through the backs of their mouths. They were an identical deep brown, except one bear had a smudge of white above his right eye, like an old man's wild brow. They plodded, snouts to the ground, to the front of the stage, then reared up and roared. Sarah gasped, and—pressed next to me by the crowd as she was—I could feel her body quake. She laughed at herself, and I could feel that too.

One of the bears fell back to his paws, but the other—the bear with the white eye—remained with two black pads exposed, admonishing the audience until he was tugged down by the chain.

The bears circled like boxers. They rose to their hind feet again and touched noses. They took three steps back, then toddled forward like jousters, each with a paw outstretched, narrowly missing the other. They roared in frustration, but Sarah and the rest of the audience were prepared this time, and applauded to show they were not afraid.

The man with the thick neck didn't applaud. His hands were busy holding a blue handkerchief to his brow, trying to shield his eyes so that he could look at Sarah instead of the performance.

The trainer stuck two chest-high posts into the stage. Slanting his eyes up toward the audience, he removed the chains. Freed, the bears reared again and placed their paws on the posts to steady themselves. From behind the curtain came a thin music, played on a brass instrument, a trumpet or cornet. The bears bowed.

They began to dance.

First two steps to the right, then two steps to the left, a semi-pirouette around the posts, another two shuffling steps back. The music was major-keyed, a galloping staccato. Someone behind us whistled, and I stole a glance at Sarah, who was smiling with her hands clasped. Though the man's leering was repugnant, I couldn't blame him for wanting to look at her face, alight with thrill.

The bears spun like ballerinas, paws flared around their heads. I could picture the white curled wigs, the sunlit parlors. A few dainty turns, another press of paws, and the song ended. More applause. The pure brown bear bowed to the audience, but the white-eyed bear sat down and began to scratch his ear, until the trainer came from around the curtain and, with a hooked pole, yanked the ring in his mouth.

"He's the bad bear," Sarah whispered to me.

The trainer appeared again with his cap held out. Sarah whistled.

"Is it like you thought?" I asked.

"It's horrifying," she said. "It's fantastic. Which one do you prefer? White-eye or Pure-brown?"

Before I could answer, the bears reemerged from behind the curtain wearing togas, laurels of waxy leaves shadowing their wet eyes.

Pure-brown reared up on two legs, placed one paw on the post, and raised the other. Performing again: a string of growls that seemed in their cadence almost like human speech. In fact, he seemed to be giving a speech, perhaps in the Roman forum, perhaps about Gallic barbarians on the northern frontier.

The audience chuckled as the slobber collected in the corners of his mouth. White-eye crouched at his side, but, as Pure-brown grunted and purred, White-eye stood on four legs, stalked a few steps, and began to urinate, the laurel coming loose and slipping down his brow, the toga flapping around him. The audience erupted.

Pure-brown dropped to all fours, blasting a black-hearted roar, showing his yellow teeth. White-eye cowered, and Pure-brown resumed his speech, pawing the air in exclamation, his growls almost plaintive.

White-eye sat motionless until one of the men stole out from the side of the stage and strapped a short knife with a triangular blade to his paw. As Pure-brown crescendoed—*empire, empire, empire*, he seemed to growl—White-eye waded toward him on his hind legs. Then White-eye raised the knife and the curtain fell.

The man with the thick neck leaned forward in his chair, and, reaching across me, offered Sarah his handkerchief. "For your eyes," he said. The eyes she raised to meet his were glittering cold.

When the bears emerged next, White-eye wore a blindfold and clinking chains. Pure-brown followed in a red officer's kepi, the kind that had cost so many lieutenants their heads in 1914.

One of the trainers shook loose a cigarette, put it in the corner of White-eye's mouth, and lit a match. More applause from the audience. Then Pure-brown reared up, paws on the post, and the trainers put a rifle on his shoulder, strapping it there and fastening it with snaps until the barrel ran along his arm and pointed at the blindfolded bear.

"Italians, obviously," the thick-necked man shouted through cupped hands. He laughed, but no one else did. He elbowed me in the side and said quietly, "Let me apologize. I should have realized you were together."

"Indeed. I ought to feed you to these bears," I said, my voice far sterner than I intended.

"I misapprehended, my friend. That's all."

"It's quite all right," I whispered.

The two other Pyreneans passed through the curtain and saluted the shooter. Ready, they yelled, as if the moment finally demanded their carefully guarded energy. A smattering of applause from the crowd, a rustle of whispers, the popping of peanut shells. Outside the sun swung up, and the tent burst with yolk-colored light. White-eye was panting. Aim, the men yelled, a few voices from the crowd joining in. The cigarette fell from White-eye's mouth. Fire! A bang that sounded like the report of a real gun, and the bear collapsed. No pirouette or death roar. He just went down and lay in a pile.

Pure-brown allowed the rifle to be taken from him, the men to lead him away. I half-expected the mournful sound of the cornet, but the tent was silent. Only the executed prisoner lay in the middle of the stage.

"They didn't really . . ." Sarah whispered. No, even as she said it, the prisoner was flicking his ears. He put up his head and yawned, pink tongue lolling. The audience applauded, but immediately one of the trainers ran onto the stage and began to shout something in dialect. It seemed the bear had risen from the dead too soon, throwing off the show. This was the bear who had misbehaved all along, and the little man who had seemed too ground-down to care about much of anything minutes before was waving his arms now, roaring as if in imitation.

The other two trainers came out from behind the curtain, exchanging a look I couldn't help but find worrisome. The little man's expression changed too, his voice softened, and he ran his hand gently down the bear's brown back. There was something in the man's face that had been absent until now, a tightening of the lips and eyes, a flinch that flickered past and was immediately masked, but I knew it well enough as fear.

He backed away. There was mud in the bear's claws, spittle on his teeth. The trainer stumbled, making a pulling motion at his fellows. Where was the hook? Where? They didn't have it. And everyone in the crowd could see that by the time they got the hook it would be too late.

The man with the blue handkerchief had already jumped from his seat and fallen on his backside; he was trying to pedal backward through the mud. The bear blurred toward the front of the stage. And somehow I knew, and it wasn't just the narcissism of fear, that the bear was coming straight for *us*. Not the crowd, but Sarah and me. I put my arm across her chest, but couldn't find the strength in my legs, and then the bear was before us, directly before us, and I could feel Sarah against my arm, stiff as the dead but blaring heat. The bear reared on its hind legs. We were close enough to smell its breath of earth and meat.

Then the bear smiled. He smiled. The corners of his mouth turned up like a man's. He smiled. And galloped back to the three trainers and the other bear, the men standing with straight backs, then the five of them bowing to the crowd.

In the years since, I've told the story many times. But I tell it without Sarah in it; I don't mention the pleats in her dress that I found myself clutching as the rest of the audience applauded, or the slow descent of her breaths, or the soft hand with which she untangled my fingers.

I told the story recently at a dinner with some young actors. I'd had a little too much to drink and was feeling the strange euphoria that comes at the end of a huge meal, a feeling of invulnerability but also acute mortality. One of the actors and I had teamed up on the rest of the table. I'd been charming and had grown a little too confident.

After I finished the story there were chuckles, much draining of already empty glasses, much stamping of already crushed cigarettes, but I could read their faces well enough: this old man is crazier than we thought. Finally, my actor friend, a comedian famous for starring in a picture about a talking motorcycle, said, "You know, that reminds me of a story my great uncle used to tell. He was a jockey in Buenos Aires many years ago—the twenties, I think, or before even. Apparently there was a horse that was supposed to be sent to the glue factory, but then my uncle gave him a try, and they started winning races. He wasn't a champion by any means, but a winner. Anyway, my uncle swears that the night before he left for America, he paid the horse a visit in his stall, and the horse knew immediately that he was leaving. Not only that, he swears the horse started to cry! Real human tears, real human sobs, and my uncle just had to hold this horse's snout until morning."

No one said anything. The actor looked at me in the sour way the young look at the old. If not for that look, I might have thought he was trying to help.

But how can I blame him for not knowing what the world had once been? The Pyrenean trainer would no sooner have believed in the concrete freeways that all of us would take home that night. The hot showers we'd run and the lights we'd flip on and forget. The comedian couldn't have known. He couldn't have known that a lifetime is a sad thing, that, in the end, it is a bridge between two worlds that don't believe in one another.

CHAPTER FOUR

I stole a scarf from Father Perrin. I hadn't wanted to. I had some money saved that I'd planned to spend on new clothes at a shop called Pingouin's. The original building had been demolished during the battle and the owner had recently reopened in a new storefront along the river with only a fraction of the former space. The racks were stuffed with a fairy tale's worth of gowns. Half-buttoned shirts piled in wooden boxes, mannequins wearing cocktail dresses and bowler hats.

The proprietor—a rather penguin-like man, as it happened—only glanced up from a desk covered in dinner crumbs. He seemed to think his store needed no explanation. I thumbed through trousers and misshapen jackets, giving him time to come over. I considered a few shirts, and played with the buckles on a pair of shoes, but still he didn't come. I walked out without closing the door behind me. Why hadn't he asked me how he could help, what I was looking for? Why hadn't he given me the chance to say, Perhaps something a bit special. Tonight I need to dress for dinner.

Mrs. Lee Hagen seemed to have no shortage of clothes. She was waiting in the lobby in a green dress with bows at the shoulder and waist.

"We have time for a walk first," she said, and we stepped out into the evening. It was a warm Saturday, and the tables along the river were full of the men who had come in droves to rebuild the city.

We passed a table of Italians, sipping little glasses of something strong. Beside them, a table of Poles sat sweating in the damp dusk. All were smoking. The river didn't smell right, and cigarettes almost masked the odor.

I felt their eyes follow us as we passed, felt them wondering who I was and why I was walking with her. One of the Italians interlaced his fingers, then pulled them apart like an exploding bomb.

"Did you understand what he said?" I asked.

"Yes." She didn't say any more.

"Verdun will probably never be so cosmopolitan again," I said.

"At least until another war comes," she said. "Who are those women?"

At another table, six or seven women sat in long, loose dresses. They had dark eyes and hair, though the eldest of the group wore hers up in a twist that had gone white.

"Mediums," I said. "Verdun is lousy with them now."

"Perhaps someone should put a lighter to the street."

"They tried that already."

We cut inside the arc of the river on Rue Levalle, where much of the wreckage was still untouched. The skeletons of broken buildings played on the imagination. The remains of a mossy window looked like an animal gone bad in the teeth, or a stroke victim dragging a frozen eye up to meet your gaze. But there also could be a certain beauty to a smattering of plaster left on stone, to a slash of rose wallpaper on a gutted interior.

As I walked with Sarah, I thought mostly of her—the length of her step, the fall of the green silk over her narrow shoulders. I hadn't noticed her shoulders before, I realized. I hadn't noticed anything about her body. I wasn't allowing myself to, but then suddenly I was.

It was growing dark as we crested the bluff and began to descend past crumbling garden walls and the zigzag of crippled shadows. Our steps didn't sound as they should have on the empty street, the echo coming back only half-pronounced.

"What was Verdun like before?" Sarah asked. "Do you remember?"

"Not like Paris, not like Chicago. Small, I guess. Dreary, a lot of people say."

"Do you think it will ever be the same again?"

"If they work very hard they might manage to make it small and dreary again someday," I said, but she didn't laugh, and the joke no longer seemed funny. "The restaurant is just up here," I said.

We passed the old primary school. Inside its half-leveled walls nine or ten boys were kicking a football, some shirtless, their voices rising. They were losing the light and their game would be over any moment. One boy, who clearly didn't understand the sport, yelled above the rest, "Pass it here. It's my turn. It's my turn."

The restaurant was completely empty. Even so, Sarah was forced to insist that her concierge had made a reservation before the dark-eyed host finally offered to take her wrap. I would have been just as happy to leave. There were low electric lights on the moldings, and candles on the six or seven tables—far too few to fill the room. The host removed the silver plates. Sarah spread a scalloped napkin on her lap. I felt shabby.

"I've been looking forward to this aperitif for hours," Sarah said. Her perfume smelled of violets. I felt my pulse like an insect at my neck.

"I think I need to know why you asked me to dinner," I said.

"And why is that?"

"Because then I might know how to act."

"Would you?" she asked, eyes amused.

"Probably not, but I'd still like to know."

The host—also the waiter, it seemed—bent to present the menus, a thick wooden cross falling from his shirt. In his unbuttoned black vest and open collar he looked more like a village tailor than a sommelier. It occurred to me that he hadn't been planning to work that night.

"Campari? Campari, two please," Sarah said in French. "We're going to have a grand meal."

"That pleases me," the waiter said, "but, I'm sorry, we don't have Campari. I think you'll prefer Suze anyway." Then he withdrew to the kitchen as if he'd been whipped.

"One thing I *can* tell you," Sarah said to me, "I asked for the most expensive restaurant so it would be impossible for you to pay." She glanced around the empty room, the green walls flickering in the candlelight. "Apparently it's impossible for everyone else too."

Marshal Pétain had dined here—I'd driven him, in fact. He'd complimented the pork knuckle and decided the future of Europe with three tables of attendants. But now the room was so quiet I thought I heard someone calling for a *coup de rouge* at one of the cafés by the river.

"I understand why you're asking," she said. "You're thinking that I've invited you here because I want to know about Lee. That I'm going to drink enough wine to have the courage to ask you about him. Well, I probably am going to drink enough wine. So perhaps I should just ask now."

That's her way of answering my question, I thought. And it was the best and kindest way she could. Any other ideas I'd invented I'd have to tap from my mind. That was all right. That was for the best.

"I wish there was more that I could say."

"But everything there is, please say it now."

In the previous five years, I'd rarely had to make anything up. I didn't quite know how to go about it.

There was a man in Aix-les-Bains, I told her, with hair longer than was customary. He looked like he was inviting lice, I told her, yet there was a glow about him that suggested he couldn't be touched by such things. All this was true. There really was such a man.

I was lying on the hotel terrace above Lake Bourget, I told her. My mind had decided that it was safe for my body to feel again, and I found that I was constructed of materials that didn't work together. My legs were rubber. My neck wood, my arms tin, and so on.

The man strolled out into the sunlight and sat down beside me, smiling as if we knew each other. After a moment, he began to sing.

I fled to the sea, the sea was too small
But I still had a ball, I still had a ball

I drove into town, the girls cried in the hall
But I still had a ball, I still had a ball

I arrived in the summer, it was already fall
But I still had a ball, yes, I still had a ball

The melody was vaguely familiar, better suited to a smoke-dim room. His cadence changed and the notes slid minor.

I kissed my girl out in the park
There's better light, now that it's dark

I stumbled home at the end of the night
There's better dark, now that it's light

I left in the summer, and arrived in the fall
But I still had a ball, yes, I still had a ball

The snow covered the window and spread to the mirror
The perfect end to a perfect year

What are you supposed to do when a stranger sings for you? I was too tired to clap or whistle. "What's that song?" I asked him.

He turned to me and smiled, shy and proud. This, too, was true.

"I wrote it. With a friend. We used to sing in the ambulance, you know." He had the grating cheerfulness of an Englishman, but his accent was American.

"Time passes that way, doesn't it?"

"Any interest in learning it?" he asked.

"Sing it again if you want," I said, and he did. The second time through I could join him on the refrain. I liked the song, melancholy and hopeful. The lyrics seemed ironic, but something about the man suggested irony wasn't his traffic.

"Any interest in cribbage?" I asked when he finished.

"Why not?" he said, and we began to play.

I described the entire scene to Sarah just as I recalled it, as we sat at the table, as the waiter brought the Suze in little stemmed glasses, quickly drained. But what else did the man say? There was something that had brought him to mind.

"I wrote it for my girl," he said, returning to the song midway through our game. "She understands music better than I ever have. I'd like to surprise her with it when I see her again. Have you a girl?"

I shook my head. And then, in the dreamlike way that time passes on permission, we drifted to a meal and apart, and I don't think I saw him again.

I imagined Lee to have the man's easy style and purchase on the world. I thought that if I had met Lee, he would have said something like that about her. It didn't feel completely like a lie.

She took the white linen from her lap and dabbed the corners of her eyes. I'd meant the words to comfort her. They clearly hadn't.

"Thank you for telling me. Really. No one else mentioned that."

"You've talked to many others?"

"Everyone I could find. His fellows. His lieutenant. His major. A woman he slept with in Padua. He seemed all right to you otherwise?"

"As all right as anyone."

"He was already getting sick."

"As I said."

"And then I found out he went mad. They don't write to tell you that. You have to go looking for it, if you want to know."

"You don't have to talk about that," I said.

"And what if I want to?"

The waiter brought a salad of bitter greens, lardons, and soft cheese. He presented a bottle of Riesling from before the war. We hadn't ordered either. He placed the cork next to me on the table and splashed the first pale drops into my glass.

"Can you picture Boston, at all?" she asked. "Try."

I had remnants from grammar school: the three-point hats of the minutemen, musket blasts at the massacre.

"I can picture John Adams," I said.

"In that case, picture my family's house."

They lived outside of Boston, she explained, in a garrison-style colonial. Fireplaces in the bedrooms, claw-foot tubs in the baths, flowers on the wallpaper. There was a full-length mirror on the door to her mother's bedroom and she remembered standing in the hall as a small child—perhaps two years old, perhaps three—looking at her reflection, listening to her mother coughing on the other side.

Sarah was six by the time her mother returned from the sanitarium. She remembered waiting in the foyer, jerking the chain on the electric lamp, off, on, off, on. But there was nothing of the moment of return and little of the months and even years that followed. Only her mother smiling weakly from across the living room, the fire snickering between them. Smiling from across the lawn, shaded by poplars. Smiling from across the dinner table, serving herself green beans and bacon from her private platter.

The doctors claimed she'd been cured of the tuberculosis, but she remained so afraid she was still contagious that she refused to touch Sarah, refused even to linger in the same room with her. Eventually, Sarah stopped believing the doctors too.

"What about your father?"

"He never argued."

It was acknowledged by everyone, including him, that he'd married up. He had more or less cheerfully put aside any pleasures, including his own opinions, to practice law and earn the living that was expected of him. His only extravagance was an unshakable confidence in his memory of maps, in his unwavering sense of direction. Sometimes he would take Sarah to the Boston Common, where they would stroll with ice cream cones while he waited to present his services to tourists looking for Paul Revere's house or Faneuil Hall.

"He was afraid to contradict my mother. Afraid that perhaps she was right. We were all afraid," Sarah said.

"Why not send you away?" I asked.

"Because she loved me, all the more since she felt she couldn't be near me. That seems strange, I know, but she came from the kind of family—a rich one—where there was no expectation of acting like other people. That was my aunt's assessment, anyway."

She said her aunt's name as if I should know it.

"Well, when I was little I thought she was famous."

The aunt lived in Paris, where she wrote music criticism for

The Daily Telegraph. She was a fierce Wagnerian, an early champion of avant-garde Russians: Stravinsky, Prokofiev, and especially Scriabin.

"Do you know Scriabin?" Sarah asked. "His dream was to write a piece of music so powerful it would bring about the end of the world."

"Finally I know who to blame."

"He never finished that particular piece," she said, smiling. "Or so my aunt told me. It was the kind of thing she'd go on about in her letters."

When Sarah was a child she and her aunt exchanged many such letters. And, from the spring she turned fifteen, every letter came with an invitation to visit—on the condition of her mother's permission, of course.

But Sarah never asked for her mother's permission. Instead she wrote to Maud that her mother had refused to let her come. She described how angry she was, how disappointed. She would simply have to spend the summer in Paris in her mind, she wrote. Imagining the blooms in the Tuileries was the only thing that would get her through to fall, she wrote.

"You didn't want to go?"

"It's not that I didn't want to. I was afraid."

"Of what?"

She shrugged. "That the boat might sink. That a war might start, trapping me in Europe for years."

"That actually sounds more like clairvoyance," I said.

"Hardly. But I was right. Wasn't I?"

The waiter returned with a platter of asparagus in cream sauce, sweat beaded on his brow. He replaced our half-full glasses, and poured a richer white.

"Listen," I said. "Could we perhaps have some say in this?" The waiter made a perplexed face and thumbed his cross, as if it might answer my question.

"The lady asked for a grand meal," he said, finally.

"The lady would still like a grand meal," Sarah said. "Bring us everything."

"I'll certainly bring you everything we have," he said.

"Tell me," she said once he had returned to the kitchen. "Were you afraid when you first came to France?"

I thought for a moment, feeling I owed her an honest answer. "No. The fear came later. I didn't know enough at the time. My father's telegram completely changed my thinking. Did something change yours?"

"Not exactly. Around the time I was to graduate from high school my aunt, without telling me first, wrote directly to my mother, begging her to let me visit. As it turned out, my mother was actually quite excited about the idea."

The waiter appeared to relight the candle, to refill our glasses and take our plates. He returned with a platter of *rouget* baked in breadcrumbs and parsley.

"You're supposed to laugh at that," Sarah said. "You realize, it's supposed to be funny."

"You told me that you hadn't been to France," I said.

"I lived in France for five years."

"You implied it then, certainly."

"I don't recall that, but why should I have told you anything true?" she asked.

"Why should you now?"

In May of 1914 she left for Europe in wet weather. As the ship lurched into the Atlantic, Sarah was relieved to see her mother—

blowing kisses with both hands from the safe distance of the pier—fade into the crowd. But she was too afraid of the liner's listing to enjoy walks on deck. She was afraid of the card games and of the magician who pulled scarves from the mouths of debutantes and dowagers. She was afraid of the small crowd gathered at Le Havre, afraid of the single man playing trombone along the quai.

She was afraid of Maud's apartment in Montmartre. The smells of pork fat and pipe smoke flooded her new bedroom; the thunder of footsteps on the stairs jolted her awake. Maud kept the windows open in the rain.

Sarah was afraid: a blue tinge to the streetlight gleaming on the greasy faces of maids and dishwashers coming home from shifts in the bowels of hotels. Stone staircases grouted with moss, dead-ending up Montmartre. The carts of rag pickers, piled with sheets and shirts washed gray. Waiters staring out from empty cafés, faces mangled by warped glass.

"What about your aunt?"

"I wasn't afraid of her. But I didn't like her nearly as much in person."

Maud was thin, with hair that had gone white early, kept long and braided over one shoulder. She was prone to talk for hours, prone to touch you on the arm if she didn't feel you were paying absolute attention.

"Now that you're here it's time to find yourself," she said. "Obviously, it's a cliché, this idea of finding oneself, isn't it? That is, it's cliché for a man. And tragically not so for a woman. I need only mention your mother."

"What would you advise?" Sarah asked.

"Simply that you *listen*."

Sarah tried. Sometimes they'd go to Chat Noir to watch the cabaret and sing along to the piano played by a friend of Maud's. But more often, her aunt would usher her to a particular flat lined with Persian tapestries where a host in purple satin robes greeted them. Sarah would sit, propped on a cylindrical pillow, conscious of little more than her effort not to betray her own confusion, as someone—often her aunt—lectured on the secrets of the Rose Cross, or Schopenhauer's influence on Wagner's late work. Once, her aunt gestured at the full moon, glowing above the sooty rooftops. "That will is our will. It's the same will," she said.

And Sarah tried to listen, seated in a velvet box at the Opéra, as the third act of *Parsifal* began. She could feel her aunt turning her gaze toward her in the dark, willing Sarah to gasp, to shudder, to fall in love. Sarah felt nothing, but she didn't want to disappoint Maud. As the holy knight held up the lance that had pierced Christ's side, Sarah pressed her thumbnail into her palm and thought of her father, alone on the Boston Common, offering directions to strangers. Finally, just before the house lights came up, she was able to cry.

Father Perrin often said that a face looks different when you know its story. I'd pictured Sarah's face at five and fifteen, transposing the green of her dress to the ocean she'd crossed. I could see traces of pink on her nose from when she'd cried as the curtain fell. Surely, Lee was in that face too. But I couldn't see him. Perhaps that should have come as no surprise. Stories, after all, are told to conceal the truth just as often as they are told to reveal it. Father Perrin often said that too.

The waiter cleared the table, plucking the wineglass from my hand, changing out the dishes and flatware. "You'd like the Pommard with the duck, I think," he said. "But we have other Burgundy."

"Don't dare ask my opinion now," Sarah said.

He poured the wine into our glasses. It was like nothing I'd ever had.

"It's leather," I said.

"Yes." The color of the wine was on her cheeks too. "Very good leather. We haven't toasted."

"To what, then? What should we drink to?"

"In my family, we don't actually touch glasses. If my father is in a jovial mood he raises his to the founder of the feast, like the Cratchits in *A Christmas Carol*."

"To begin with, Marley was dead," I said. I only realized then that I was drunk.

"Deader than a doornail," she said.

"My mother read it to me every December. I used to love ghost stories."

"Do you?"

"I used to."

The waiter presented the duck breast, sliced in dark sauce, ringed with juniper berries and sprigs of rosemary. Already my body felt like a thing only vaguely under my control, and I realized how alike pleasure and fear can feel in their extremes.

"Just a moment," the waiter said. "Perhaps I could tell you about this duck?"

"Please," we said, roughly at the same time.

"Because you are speaking English, I will try in English." He held his palm in front of his face as if he might find the words there. "So, you know—maybe, perhaps!—it is difficult but special to grow ducks in Lorraine. The bad water, because of the bad dirt, you understand." We nodded. There were few things I understood better than the bad dirt and water of Lorraine. "These ducks my wife and I raised. When we left in 1915 we brought them with us to Bordeaux. Bordeaux is a very different region for ducks, much easier, even before the war. These ducks taste, I don't know how to say, they taste very particular, very good."

"It's the best I've ever had," Sarah said. The waiter flushed pink.

"Perhaps no duck will taste like this one ever again," he said. "I hope you like it. His name is Michaud."

"That's a bit unappetizing," Sarah said, and the waiter began to laugh, embarrassed.

"No. So sorry. It is my poor English. The duck has no name. *My* name is Michaud."

He had the kind of thick, round face you couldn't help but call honest.

"There are days," she said, "when I have to remind myself how I got here. So then I have to step back to the thing before that and the thing before that. I suppose that's why the story's taking so long. Is this all terrible for you?"

Her face had relaxed. Her soft expression suited her soft features. It seemed to me this was how she was supposed to look.

"If anything you're going too fast," I said.

Sarah began listening to Cleo Muller in May of that year. At least the plaque on the buzzer read Muller. Her husband called her Cleo, or when he was pleading with her, as was the case most nights, Clo, Sarah could hear them through her thin bedroom wall when they shouted. What was he pleading for? Sarah took an interest at first because she assumed it was sex.

Cleo had auburn hair, feline eyes, and two children, a girl and a boy. Sarah guessed Cleo to be about forty years old, though it was difficult to say because she glimpsed her in person only a handful of times. She could set her watch to the sound of the children's steps echoing in the stairwell everyday at 13:00, to the view from the window as they filed toward Sacré-Cœur, the girl first, then the boy, then their governess. But never Cleo.

Why? Because most days, it seemed, Cleo would wake up completely paralyzed, unable to get out of bed, unable even to sit up. When René—that was her husband's name—came home in the evenings he would explode in rage, then grief and shame. He promised to take Cleo to Cannes and buy her the best view of the ocean. He promised to take her to Cannes and drown her. He promised to kiss her feet if she would only walk across the room, if she would only agree to resume psychoanalysis.

"It was hysteria?" I asked.

Sarah's smile was wry and amused. "You really think there is such a thing?"

Not in Cleo's case, certainly. Often Sarah could hear her pacing her bedroom at night—like Sarah's father, René seemed to have his own room. She could hear the strike of a match, perhaps the crumple of a newspaper. She could hear René's heavy steps in the hallway, but never a knock at the door.

"You were planning to help her?" I asked.

"No. I was planning to *find myself* paralyzed. To wake up like that one morning."

In the restaurant, Sarah pressed a bare forearm to her brow as she laughed. This time, I laughed too. But then, I couldn't resist.

"What about Cleo's little girl?" I asked. Sarah looked at me, annoyed.

"You *do* want me to skip to the end, I see. It is late, I suppose. You're right, once I pictured her standing outside her mother's closed door it wasn't fun anymore. And, yes, I felt an unbearable disgust with myself. That summarizes it pretty well. I found an address in my suitcase, wrote a quick note, and went down the stairs to send it before I could lose my nerve."

"To whom?" I asked, though I didn't need to.

We finished the duck, leaving the rosemary sprigs on the plate like a trampled wreath. I tried the bottle, but there was only sediment. The candles on the empty tables had all gone out and a velvet darkness filled the room. Not a single customer had come in.

"Was there really a Cleo Muller?" I asked.

"Why do you ask that?"

"It's not uncommon—there are so many reasons why the people who come here make up stories, or pieces of stories. You learn to tell when things fit together a little too well."

"And do you usually try to embarrass them?" she asked.

The answer, of course, was no. But I wasn't trying to embarrass her. I was trying to impress her.

"Don't worry about the bottle," she said. "He'll bring Sauternes with dessert, I'd bet my life on it. No, it didn't really all happen quite that way. There was a Cleo, though. There still is. And there was a René, but he died at the Marne. I suppose I should also say that my childhood wasn't quite so gothic either. I just wanted to give you a sense of it all."

"A sense of what?"

"Well," she paused, as if embarrassed. "Of why I fell in love so fast, and so deep."

"You enjoyed Michaud?" the waiter asked, still laughing as he cleared the final set of plates. We clamored to compliment him.

"Excellent, excellent. The crème brûlée is named Maurice." He laughed and presented a bottle of Sauternes

Sarah clapped, and said, "Sauterne, you see? I live."

I felt myself drifting, less than aware of what I was saying, feeling somehow that I had already said the wrong thing, but unsure of when or how. The right thing to say in the moment seemed clear enough.

"Lee was in Paris?" I asked.

"Yes. He'd gone over around the same time I did—just before, actually. He was working at the Paris branch of a bank. His father's bank. He was the only person I knew in Paris aside from my aunt. Fate or not-fate, you decide."

"I'm not sure that's my place."

"It's just something Lee and I used to say. That was the sort of thing we began to joke about almost immediately. Fate or not-fate that we came together as we did."

"You knew him well before?"

"Not well, though I'd known him all of my life."

He'd grown up one town over and in those days there were many Lees, many boys with mild, northern European faces, who sat politely at church, or spoke politely to her at picnics. Many boys she avoided.

In high school he played the Pauper to her Lady Jane Grey. He looked the part, all right. He was tall with silver-blond hair and the kind of round chin that looked like it could take a punch. He was almost supernaturally untalented, though, with a tendency to falsify even the most inconsequential moment with oddly placed pauses and cramped expressions.

Later, in Paris, he would claim he'd only auditioned because he wanted a chance to talk to her. It was true that at their chaperoned wrap party he brought over a plate of Linzer hearts and asked if she would like to sit outside. Of course the answer was no. She was sixteen by then and there were still many Lees.

"I can imagine," I said, my tongue too loose from the wine. She rolled her eyes.

"What I think a man really wants from a woman above all else," she told me, "is fear. So I was very desirable. Not because of the way I looked especially. They could sense my fear."

"You don't seem afraid now."

"No. That's changed."

Maurice had arrived. Michaud poured more Sauternes.

"Would you like to do the honors?" she asked, pointing to the crème brûlée and offering me one of the spoons.

"No, you, please," I said.

"Good. It's my favorite part of the whole meal." She crashed the spoon through the burnt sugar like a boy falling through ice on a lake.

Lee had plans, a trip to Chartres with the son of his boss, but he begged off when he received her note. And, as they walked through the blooms of the Tuileries, Lee told Sarah that her mother had written and asked him to look in on her, but that he'd known enough not to.

"Known what?" she asked.

"That if I did you'd never speak to me again."

"It's likely I never would have spoken to you anyway."

"I know," he said. "But you have."

He touched her arm to signal that they might stop and sit on a bench. When he held the door to the café on Rue Custine he touched the small of her back as she stepped through. And yet there was no expectation in his touch, only warmth. And this difference surprised her—just the feel of his hand on her back, at her elbow.

When he invited her to dinner the following Friday, she asked that her aunt come as a chaperone. Maud agreed to meet them at the brasserie, but never showed up.

"I'd be happy to call someone," Lee said. "I'm just trying to think who." They were already seated at the pewter-topped table.

"No one else seems to mind," Sarah said. "Perhaps I shouldn't either."

"It's one of the nice things. No one seems to mind anything here. One night, I slept under an embankment."

"Why would you do that?" Sarah asked.

"Adventure, I suppose. I guess adventure always seems more appealing when you're lonely."

Sarah had always felt the opposite to be true. Even so, she said yes when he asked her to marry him. In the month they'd been together she'd done everything wrong—did I understand? Everything. She'd had the intoxicated feeling that nothing could harm her. She had invited him in everywhere. And still he asked.

In June they glided across a grassy patch in the Tuileries, holding hands, pretending they were on Lake Waban in Wellesley. Just weeks before, she would have found such behavior maudlin and embarrassing. Now they ignored the Parisians who jeered because they assumed Lee and Sarah understood no French. Just as they ignored the cables from her parents asking that they at least wait to marry in the States. Just as they ignored the note from Lee's mother wondering if he understood what an eccentric family he was marrying into.

"It was very interesting," Sarah said. "Suddenly it was so, so easy to shut everything else out. I didn't expect that."

I nodded, thinking of my room in the Episcopal palace, the creak of the bed slats, the steam on the windows, the clink of the lamp chain—often the loudest sound in the hour before I tried to sleep.

"I must confess something. We do have Campari," Michaud said. "But I don't like it. Fernet-Branca, though, is better than anything in France. I don't often admit that." He set the bottle on the table beside two small glasses. We asked him to join us, and he set out a third glass and pulled up a chair. He asked after Father Gaillard in a sleepy voice. I only realized then that he'd recognized me when we'd come in, that he must have been wondering who Sarah was and why we were together.

As he refilled the small glasses we spoke of his childhood in a village outside Strasbourg—his family had moved west after Alsace was annexed by the Germans in 1871. He'd always planned to return, but now it felt like a duty to stay and help rebuild Verdun, even if he was going bankrupt in the process.

"You must excuse me for interrupting you so much," he said. "I'm supposed to be invisible, but I'm not used to cooking for such happy people."

By the time we left the restaurant I half-expected daylight. I could smell the roasting almonds and hear the din from the cafés on the river. It was still before midnight.

"Verdun was famous for its almonds before the war," I said.

"Mmhmmm," she said, as we turned back toward the hotel.

"What are you thinking about?" I asked.

"How happy we looked," she said.

Without the detour it was only a few minutes back to the de Guise. She stumbled on uneven stone. I steadied her with my arm and she shrunk away. As we turned the corner on Rue Margot, the hotel awning, ringed with electric bulbs, blistered the darkness. As I opened the door for her she said she could do with another drink.

A barman in a red jacket was polishing glasses with a white cloth. I ordered. He poured two red wines and shook out his aching fingers.

She'd put powder on her face unevenly, and I could see the perspiration just above her lip.

"Do you want to go on?" I asked.

"I don't know. The fight may have left me."

It was the time of night when glasses are left half-full. I didn't want her to ask me to leave.

"You stayed on in Paris after you married," I said.

"Indeed, yes. In July. In the Luxembourg. The same day Jean Jaurès was killed. Do you remember that day?"

"Vaguely," I said. "Maybe not at all."

"Well, you were somewhere in Chicago, weren't you? It probably couldn't have mattered to you less. They say he was the only man who could have kept France out of the war, so it was quite a scene. What do you think you were doing on that day? Late July. How old were you?"

"I was fifteen. In late July, I was probably at the Indiana Dunes with my mother."

"Perfect. I have no idea what you mean."

"They're sand dunes around Lake Michigan. That was where we vacationed if we had enough saved. As it happened, that year we did."

"And what would you do on these vacations?"

"Swim in the lake. Climb the dunes. Eat ice cream."

She smiled, and finished her glass. She stood up.

"Now," she said. "Have another drink at the bar. You know the stairs, don't you? When the clerk isn't looking come up. Number seven."

I felt my chest begin to dissolve. I wanted to say the absolute right thing before it did. "What if he sees me?" I asked.

"Kill him," she said.

The first woman I slept with claimed her name was Destin. I'd been the last in a line of three or four of my friends from the Field Service. When my turn came I promised myself I wouldn't close my eyes.

There had been other women after that. Sometimes we'd take the ambulances to farmhouses: strange, sad places lit by candles set on staircases and drooping sideboards. No one cared if these places burned down. Red wax was the cheapest, so there was often an occult feeling to the rooms, like something out of "The Masque of the Red Death."

Once, in the garret bedroom of one of these places, I looked out the window to find the ravaged field beyond the house—a black barn, a husk of tree, brittle wheat—covered with heavy green gas.

We were well past the German artillery range, but I jumped from the bed and grabbed the woman by the wrist and swam blindly through the house. I had masks in the back of the ambulance and my only thought was that I might reach them before we both inhaled too much. Outside, the frozen grass crumbled under my bare feet. I smelled nothing, could breathe normally. I thought I was hallucinating—you heard about that from time to time—but she pointed at the moon glowing green and looked to me as if I might explain. We were both naked and I was still holding her by the wrist. It was just green fog. I never saw anything else like it again.

Fortunately for him, the clerk wasn't at the desk when I finished my second drink.

Sarah answered the door as if she had just whispered a secret. Her eyes looked glassy in the electric lights. Her lipstick was fresh; she'd caught her teeth. I didn't know how much time had passed since she'd left the bar, but one needs only a moment to doubt.

"I wonder if we've drunk too much," I said.

"Have you?" she asked.

"Not like that. Too much to decide."

She shrugged, the way I could picture her shrugging onstage, so the balcony could see it. “How else are these things decided? Just know that I want to. Do you?”

I wanted to. I wanted to. So often, desire and reality are so far apart that, on the rare occasions they intersect, it can feel as if desire itself has pounded reality into shape. That's why I allowed myself to do it. I believed that neither of us would be hurt later, because I didn't want us to be hurt. That neither of us would be angry later, because I didn't want us to be angry. That I wasn't betraying Father Perrin, or Sarah, or, for that matter, myself, because I didn't want betrayal to be defined in such terms. Such is the power, for a moment, anyway, of getting exactly what one wants.

The walls were done up in whites and icy blues. There was an electric fan on the ceiling and a balcony hidden by white drapes. The window was open, but there was no wind. I kissed her neck. She grabbed my hair, and pulled my lips to her collarbone. Her eyes were open. Her eyes were closed. As I touched her I expected her to ask me to stop and I tried to stay near enough to the surface that I could. And then when I knew that she wouldn't ask me to stop I expected her to disappear. The dress slid from her shoulders. She'd taken everything off underneath.

“How long will you stay?” I asked.

“In Verdun? How long do you want me to stay?”

“It can't be up to me,” I said.

“No, it isn't.” She'd risen from the bed and opened the curtains, but there was nothing to see, only an unlit city on a dirty river. “But it just so happens that at the moment I'm at a loss.” She returned to the bed and lay down on her stomach.

“Won't you go back to Udine?”

"I might. I don't know what else to do. I used to think I knew, but then it leads me here."

"Is that so bad?" I tried to ask the question with a lilt in my voice, to joke, but I really did wonder. I got up and went to the sink. The carpet felt exquisite under my bare feet.

"I didn't know he was a singer," she said to my back. "I didn't know he wrote a song."

I splashed my face over the basin, once, twice, trying to decide what to say. I felt no guilt whatsoever—how was that possible? I suppose because what I'd told her about Lee, what I'd told her about the man who sang to me in Aix-les-Bains, had led me to this room, to her, and *that* felt like the truth.

"Is that so surprising?"

"No. It's just that it's reminded me of something, something I've been trying not to think about. But then I remember that I came here to learn things like that, and to be reminded, and to think. The thing is, when he came back to Paris on permission around Christmas in 1916, he'd lost so much weight. And he had a terrible stammer. I told him that he needed to have himself declared, to at least be examined. He claimed that he had been examined.

"There was a cartoon in the *Telegraph*. It was a picture of the grim reaper and the devil, or maybe Mars, looking at an endless field of crosses. And that was what the caption said. *An end of a perfect year*. Or *the end to a perfect year*. Something like that."

"Like the last line of the song," I said.

"Yes," she said. "He kept bringing it up, he kept saying that they shouldn't print things like that. I asked him why. He tried to explain, but the stammer. He kept trying, but he couldn't get past the *P*, and then he walked into the other room, and by then I'd learned not to follow him."

"It's awful," I said. In the darkness she kissed me again.

"Yes. But, in the end . . . That's the kind of thing one wants to know."

"I shouldn't be here when the light comes," I said.

"I shouldn't have said anything."

"It's not that," I said. "You can't want a scandal."

"Perhaps you've noticed I've stopped caring. I understand if *you* don't want one."

I probably did want a scandal. I already could have said, honestly, that I loved her, but the choice to act on my feelings likely had as much to do with hatred. Hatred for the solemnity of my work, for its stifling honor. Hatred for a fate—no, not a fate, I chose it, after all—that had turned the simple arrival of a woman from my own country, near my own age, into an extraordinary occasion.

"I was wondering," I said. "If you were in Paris, why did he go to Aix the next year? Why didn't he come home to you? That's what I would have done." She made a sound, not quite a laugh.

"You do actually listen."

"Shouldn't I?"

"I'm just not used to it. Had I known, I wouldn't have said so much. I only found out later he had lied. He was afraid to see me by then. Or afraid for me to see him. He told me that his leave had been canceled. Which did happen all the time, you know."

"That's true." It was a disappointment I remembered well.

Santa Monica, 1950

Paul insisted I stay for dinner—it would be a favor to him, he said, since his wife was away. So we sat on his veranda and ate spaghetti prepared by his housekeeper, an exceptionally tall woman from Puglia who joined us for a Fernet-Branca after the meal. She told a wickedly funny story about the Fascist syndicate in her village exiling the priest in the weeks after the March on Rome, forcing him to wipe the dust of the town from his feet before walking off into the hills. There was plenty in the story that might have brought us around to our shared past, but Paul didn't press. Instead, he talked of Charles Russell's work in bronze, ethnographic portraiture, the malleability of light in oils. I was happy to listen. These weren't subjects I often thought about, and he made a good teacher. And—just like any good teacher—he knew when he had said too much.

"Tell me something about what it's like to work in the pictures," he asked. "What would I not expect?"

"I'm not sure there is much. It's the kind of world that tries very hard to give people what they expect."

"I doubt those writers expected to go to prison," he said.

"No. They didn't."

"Anyone you knew?"

"Yes."

"You weren't involved, I take it."

"I'm not political."

"That's absurd," he said. "How could that be?"

It was absurd, but at least I'd found something Paul didn't expect. If you worked in the pictures, you knew that twilit verandas were no place to talk about politics. And it didn't take the Congressman Dies of the world, dragging screenwriters to Washington to testify, to remind you.

In the early thirties, for example, when I was just starting out and still cared very much about my career, I'd had the good fortune to get some interest in one of my scenarios from Columbia. I was even promised five minutes in Harry Cohn's office. I'd worked on my pitch for a week, but when the day came, I rambled and stammered. Cohn was surprisingly genial, but I could scarcely do more than stare at the autographed picture of Mussolini on the wall behind his desk.

Paul didn't insist I say more, though he did insist that I accompany him to a birthday party for an old friend from Vienna. It was too early to go home, he said, and the party wasn't far. In addition to the gin in the afternoon and the amaro after dinner, I'd drunk a bottle of wine on my own by then, which I wasn't used to. Good wine, which I certainly wasn't used to. Even though I'd made enough money to afford good wine, I never had gotten the taste; drinking it always felt like a dull performance.

Paul drove us to the party. As it turned out, we could have walked. And, as it turned out, the friend he referred to was one of the most famous living composers in the world. We arrived late. The chocolate cake had already been cut, and a crowd had gathered around the piano in the living room to sing *lieder*. The party had reached the stage when the arrival of new faces arouses unaccountable enthusiasm. I may have been the only guest whose first language wasn't German; all the same, I found many faces I recognized. Some I knew quite well and others I'd admired from afar for some time.

I realized now how polite Paul had been to take an interest in my work, to ask what I made of the pictures. He knew as many people in Hollywood as I did, and better people too.

"You were a little modest," I said.

"How do you mean?" And this was what was easy to forget about Paul—he wasn't being modest, exactly. He had grown up in these circles. It should have come as no surprise that his life in the new world was like his life in the old, in social terms, at least.

The German émigré community in Hollywood wasn't quite what it had been during the Second World War. Many of the most famous expatriates had gone back to Berlin or Hamburg or Vienna now that the Nazis were gone. But their parties—where the Mann brothers argued, and guests traded stories of daring escapes across the Pyrenees—were still legendary.

No one seemed to be discussing anything of great philosophical import that night, however, and in many ways the gathering seemed like an ordinary Hollywood party—the same gossip, the same cliquishness, the same suspicious peering through partitions of cigarette smoke. But there were obvious differences too. The parties I knew usually began this way: young women talking to older men, curious as to what the men could do for them, the men curious in turn. But more often than not their answer to one another was: nothing. And, as the night continued, people tended to forget they were at work, and the kids found each other to dance. The old men found each other to chaperone and regret. Certainly I regretted it the first time I found myself in that group of old men.

But, here, I could make out at least three generations cradled around the piano, singing together. The ceiling was crowded with balloons, the patio crowded with tiny girls with giant bows on their dresses. Exhausted little boys asleep in chairs. Teenagers playing cards. Which is all to say that people of every age seemed to be having fun, and it seemed like I might have some luck with it too if I tried.

Yes, the host was already in bed—it was his eightieth birthday, after all—but Paul promised to bring me back to meet him another time. We took pieces of chocolate cake and some kind of sweet wine onto the back patio. There, he introduced me to a stream of friends, most of whom broke back into English once they realized I knew no German. Someone pulled Paul away. I caught up with a writer I knew from RKO, drifted to a producer I'd worked with a decade before, until I found myself standing beside a composer who had literally slammed a door in my face earlier that week.

His name was Max Steiner. If the stories can be believed, his first opera—which he himself conducted in Vienna at the age of fifteen—had brought Strauss to tears. Perhaps or perhaps not, but it was unquestionably true that after he left Vienna for Hollywood he invented film music as we know it. Many composers of his pedigree—the evening's host, for example—would have been deeply ambivalent about such a distinction, but not Steiner.

He wore rimless glasses and stiff collars in the heat, and was said to do his best work before six in the morning. He was the kind of man you didn't expect to see drunk, though he certainly was that now. No doubt he'd made an exception for the host's birthday, which Steiner must have considered a very great occasion.

"You know Paul?" he asked when I said hello. "How do you know him?"

"It's been so long I can hardly say."

"Ah, but that is an untruth. I can never seem to remember how I meet my new friends, not the old. How do *we* know each other again?"

I reminded him. He slapped his forehead, slapped my back.

"Now I am embarrassed," he said. "How is your progress?" He meant my progress on the project we were working on, a picture in the vein of *The 39 Steps*. The plot went like this: An American spy posing as a Viennese psychoanalyst comes into possession of critical Soviet intelligence. As he feels the Soviet agents closing in—with mere minutes to spare—he subliminally implants the intelligence into the memory of one of his patients, an American innocent named Arthur Bradley, who has come to Vienna for treatment.

Soon after, the spy-psychoanalyst is murdered, and Bradley must elude the Soviets, who are desperate for information the American does not realize he possesses. The rub is that the intelligence—Soviet radio codes—can only be accessed from Bradley's unconscious at the sound of a particular trigger, a poem his mother used to recite to him as a child.

Somehow, the studio convinced Robert Frost to write the poem, but problems arose halfway through filming when the actor playing Bradley insisted the poem be turned into a song—it would make much more sense emotionally, he said. The director agreed, but Frost refused to have his work set to music. Steiner, who was contracted for the score, was pleased at the chance to write the song, but the producer doubted his command of English, which was indeed suspect. Predictably, the studio's solution to a dispute between three geniuses was to bring in a fourth party to write a compromise so mediocre no one could bother to be angry. I was their man.

I couldn't blame Steiner for his irritation with me earlier that week. And, at the party, I found him to be gracious and warm.

"Why don't we work on it a bit now?" he asked.

"On the song?" I looked over at the piano, where someone was plinking Kurt Weill.

"You don't think they'd mind?"

"I don't mean here." He looked at me sternly. "Obviously this is a house of many pianos."

We ended up in a back room that fit an upright, two chairs, and little else. A practice room. There was a bust—Brahms maybe—wearing a Bruins baseball hat. And on the wall a framed poster advertising a performance of Mahler's Fifth Symphony with a red X slashed across it.

"Old scores," Steiner said, seeing me look. "You see?"

He laughed at his own joke and produced a bottle of Slivovitz.

"Tell me now. What have you? What do you have?"

I had nothing, frankly. I would have liked to explain that I was no songwriter, but years of living in the wrong place had given me the wrong reflex.

"You'd agree the song must be right for the character," I said.

"He was in the army, was he not?" Steiner began to play a bouncy march, his hands far more steady than his head.

"That's good," I said, "but isn't the idea that the song came from his past?"

The bottle bobbed between us while Steiner considered.

"How do you remember all these points?" he asked. "Why do you bother? So he was a baseballer, was he not?"

"That's right. He was a pitcher who gave up a promising career to go to Europe to fight the Nazis. He hurt his elbow and was never able to go back. That's part of the trauma."

"Yes! Yes. Now how does it go? Is it something like this?" He began to play a rather mournful riff on "Take Me Out to the Ball Game."

"But I think it should go back even further. He went to college at the University of Missouri. Do you happen to know their fight song?"

"I certainly do not!" Steiner shouted. And we both laughed, and drank more. I had just made up the part about the University of Missouri. I was enjoying myself. We moved back through Bradley's past, recounting details—some alluded to in the script, some made up on the spot—and Steiner turned each detail into a line of melody. He could play anything without seeming to think at all—Tin Pan Alley, jazz, Second Viennese school dissonance—but none of the melodies were quite right for the picture, in his opinion. I had no opinion. I'd stopped thinking about the picture. The drink had worked its way behind my eyes, had made everything soft and unthreatening. I felt in that wonderful state when life seems wholly inconsequential. Pity that there are such dire consequences if one lives like that too often.

"It goes all the way back to his mother," I said.

"Ah yes, his mother sang it. Yes?"

"Yes."

"So a lullaby, then?" He played something soft, soothing but minor, and it was close enough. I began to sing.

I fled to the sea, the sea was too small
But I still had a ball, I still had a ball

I drove into town, the girls cried in the hall
But I still had a ball, yes, I still had a ball

I kissed my girl out in the park
There's better light, now that it's dark

And stumbled home at the end of the night
There's better dark, now that it's light

Steiner followed me the whole way on the piano, knowing just where the changes would go. I can't say quite what I felt, or what I thought I was doing. I suppose a sense of loss often accompanies a sense of relief.

"Well," he said, once we'd finished. "I don't know. It is interesting, but it sounds very lonely to me. And if there is one thing a lullaby would not emphasize, it is loneliness. Do you not think? But let us play it again."

CHAPTER FIVE

In 1918—more than two years after I'd come to France, and almost a year after I'd joined the Field Service—the United Sates Army arrived, marching past the base at Souilly in clean uniforms, laughing gleefully at their own bad French, boasting about the *Boche* heads that would roll.

"Hallo?" I heard a voice call one morning from the top of the stairs of my *abri*, the French-style underground bunker. I'd been sleeping the sleep of the dead. The man must have called and called. "Any English spoken down there?"

I'd driven all night and, as I took the stairs to the entrance, I could still feel the running board vibrating in the soles of my feet, could still hear the grind of the clutch, like the sound of a man retching. The Americans, three of them, stood in their comical helmets, dressed up as soldiers. "Sorry to bother you, friend," one of them said.

He looked like a baby. I don't mean that he looked merely young. I mean that he appeared to be an adult-size, rattle-and-pacifier baby. "It's just that we haven't glimpsed the front. We're not sure where it is exactly," the baby said, his English quite intelligible despite the fact his teeth hadn't come in yet. His companions, who seemed older, but whom I couldn't quite get to come into focus, grunted their assent.

"It seems quiet today," I said, which was true. "I'll take you up to Tunnel Kronprinz, if you like."

We single-filed through communication trenches. The whole while, the baby went on about breasts, which he contended were like snowflakes, like fingerprints. Could the eyes tell the difference? Sometimes, obviously. But the mouth always could tell. Then he switched to nipples. Just in color there were endless variations: brown nipples, rose-pink, sunburn red. An 808 whistled overhead and exploded half a mile off. The two men and the baby dove onto their stomachs.

I felt disconnected from the earth and the air, from my own body—it wasn't an unpleasant state, actually—and I didn't understand why I'd volunteered to take these men, whether these men were even real at all. The Kronprinz was real enough, though. The Germans had dug the network of timbered tunnels and galleries when they'd held Mort Homme—an ancient and presciently named ridge east of the city—in the spring of 1916; it was a bunker so elaborate that whispers of German ingenuity even reached us in the citadel.

Perhaps they'd built it too well. When the inevitable French counterattack came, the Germans refused to give up the Kronprinz, even after they were surrounded and presented with terms. The French responded by gassing every last man inside. Later, they blasted the doors to find a labyrinth complete with lamps and fans on electric generators, gleaming surgical wards, officers' quarters with wing-backed chairs and Persian rugs looted from fine *maisons* in Laon, all buried a hundred feet under the earth. A neat and useful spoil of war, but for the fact that the tunnels were also crowded with hundreds of German corpses.

Americans loved the Kronprinz, loved the idea that they were fighting on the side that would beat these ingenious engineers, that they, in fact, would be the ones to tip the balance. Even the baby drooled happily as I led him and his friends to the doors of the auxiliary tunnel.

"Should it smell like that?" he asked.

"No. But everything does." I shrugged. "Try to get used to it. The electric lights still work. There's a switch at the end of the chamber."

I waited by a hunk of burned chassis as the two men and the baby dissolved into the tunnel's mouth, leaving me to imagine their slow, stupid walk, a hundred meters through the dark, the smell thickening with each step. Leaving me to imagine them feeling along the walls for balance, suspecting that they were being had but too afraid of looking weak to turn around. The light switch really was a hundred meters or so back. I saw it flicker on. What must they have seen in that instant? Empty eye sockets. Flesh deserting bones. The image gave me no pleasure, at least I can say that. One of them screamed, then I saw them moving toward me—I say *moving* because I couldn't describe exactly how—they seemed to have been spit more than anything else. And when they came out they breathed in fast and long. The baby looked at me with angry, natal betrayal, but I knew he would say nothing, lest he begin to cry.

It's hard to keep a sense of right and wrong when you've lost your sense of what is real and what isn't. But that's no excuse. My madness was small. Small enough that I usually recognized it, and it was obvious to me even then that those boys from Kansas City and Cleveland were guilty of nothing but arriving in France a bit too late for my taste.

The morning I left the Hotel de Guise I could scarcely imagine why I had done such a cruel thing. And, as I washed, I wondered if, in the years to follow, I'd feel the same shame, the same sense of a very different type of temporary madness, for having spent the night with Sarah.

It all came to mind because I was scheduled to drive up to Mort Homme that very morning. But I'd found no bones there in months. I didn't want to be reminded of any of it, not when I could still smell the sheets of her hotel room, her violet perfume on my skin. I realized that what I wanted most was to spend the day at a café. There was nobody to tell me not to.

I passed the old opera, where two men were hoisting a new door. I walked through the old town gates, across the drawbridge, then north along Rue Mazel, turning when I saw a pair of bright red shutters on an aching brown hinge, a cat licking its tail on the splintered sill.

On Rue Saint-Pierre the windows were polished, the woodwork stained dark. Signs had been painted on the glass in looping gold letters: a tailor, a fromagerie, a hardware store with a movie projector in the window.

As I approached, Sarah stepped out of a shop, carrying a parcel wrapped in butcher paper. She passed me without saying anything with either her mouth or her eyes. I felt hot blood in my face. I kept walking.

"Tom," she called. And I spun to see her standing, half-turned up the street. I waited as she hurried toward me.

"I was just surprised," she said. "And I didn't want you to see."

"To see your candle?" I asked, gesturing to the parcel.

"I suppose you know what it's for. My aunt's a firm believer. I imagine you aren't."

"Well, no. Because they're all frauds," I said.

"I know," she said. "Actually, I don't *know*. What makes you so sure? Have you ever been?"

I knew only the names—the Madame Misteriosos, the Madame

Houdinis—the mere mention of which would send Father Perrin into a rage. It was funny how skeptical he could be, except when it came to the subject of God's word made flesh on earth.

"You must be going somewhere," she said.

"I suppose I am," I said.

"I want to come with you, wherever it is. Can I take your arm?"

Reality felt loose. She slid her arm into mine and we continued up Rue Lemper. The citadel was only two streets away, so there wasn't time to say much before we turned a corner and stood before its gray stone walls.

"Did Lee ever come here? To the Vauban Citadel?"

"There was a lot he never mentioned, but I don't think so."

I was glad. I wanted to show her something that was mine. The citadel had been the headquarters for the general staff, and the center of life in the city during the battle. I'd spent my seventeenth birthday in its galleries, a dungeon of twisting alleys and vague green walls. The light so dim that I always felt like my eyes were just on the edge of adjusting.

The rumors in such a place were lethal. I often woke in the night to whispers running through the barracks: The Germans had taken Fort Souville. They were one ridge away, the city was lost. The roof was finally ready to collapse.

But for three years the roof held, and Fort Souville held, and, after September of 1916, the Germans never came particularly close to the city. The shelling tapered off. It must be admitted: the citadel felt safe. Something that could not be said of many places in eastern France.

The place bustled with a kind of begrudging, melancholy life. A narrow-gauge railroad clattered through the galleries, delivering flour and bullets. In the canteens, scratchy music skipped on overworked gramophones. The men had no one to dance with, but sometimes would stagger to their feet and sway as if holding some invisible love.

It was part of my job to serve these men in whose desolate eyes, in whose scraps of conversation, I found dim and horrifying hints of life outside the walls. Once, I brought glasses of water to a table of three men—fresh water was at a far higher premium than the thin wine they called *pinard*. Their uniforms were splattered, their lips scabbed. One of them waved me over. "Smell this cup for me, would you?" He held it out with a blistered, trembling hand, though his voice was steady. I did as he said. The water was fetid, smelling of the particular kind of decay that was all too common in Verdun, probably from a barrel contaminated by groundwater seeping in.

"I'll get you another," I said, "from a different barrel."

There was a mark just below his right eye, as if from the press of a scalding thumb. He took back the cup, and sipped, and licked his lips.

"You should try this," he said to the other two. Their blue caps were pulled low over their eyes. "I said you should try this." He pushed the cup across the table with his knuckles. "Go ahead. It tastes just like Jean. Go ahead, tell me I'm wrong."

The other two men exchanged a glance. One adjusted his cap, pulling it lower, as if the best answer was just to go to sleep.

"Go ahead, go ahead, it's Jean, it tastes just like him."

Eventually, the second of the two men took out a pack of cigarettes.

"Have one," he said to me. "And leave us alone."

"Should I take the water away?" I asked.

"For god's sake, yes!" he shouted.

Those were difficult months for me, and I thought often of Chicago, of the games of ring-a-levio I'd played with neighborhood boys whose names I'd already begun to forget. I thought often of my mother. She couldn't afford a salon, but on Sundays her friend Helene always dolled her hair. We'd ride miles down to Oak Street Beach on the trolley even though we could have walked to the beach off Sheridan Road.

Her typical answer to my complaints about the ride was that she wanted me to meet nicer children. Though, one afternoon not long before she died, she raised her round sunglasses and said, "The truth is that I met your father here." After that I didn't complain. I thought she meant that Oak Street was a place of special significance, that returning to the beach in the summers was a way to feel closer to my father.

But one night, when I was trying to sleep with a hundred orphans snoring around me, I realized she hadn't meant that at all. She'd been looking for a new husband. Even though they were both dead by then, I felt as if something had been taken from me, just an impression of affection, I suppose.

Even so, compared to life in the citadel, the past felt like safe harbor, at least at first. The soldiers glowered in passageways and spat at my feet when I helped to serve the meals of crusty bread and weak wine. My French improved month by month but I never got the accent right. I worked as hard as anyone, and, eventually, the glances and jabs began to be replaced by offers to sit and talk at the end of mess. But then those soldiers would go up to the line, many never to return, and new soldiers would come cycling in, mocking my accent, pushing past me in the dim halls.

The rest of the orphans distrusted me too, but they had nowhere to go. In March, a boy named Alain whose parents had died in Fleury arrived with a shoulder wound. He refused to talk to anyone, even Father Gaillard. For days he lay in his bunk in our dormitory. The surgery on his arm was clean and he'd avoided infection, yet his eyes remained a sickly, scornful yellow.

"I have a fever," he kept saying. "I have a fever."

He said this for five straight days and thrashed on the bed in a strange sort of rage. He put up such a fight that Father Gaillard himself came to kneel next to him and read from *The Count of Monte Cristo*.

"Alain," he said gently, "you can see what is happening here. I know you can. You can see how important it is that you live?"

"I don't have to do anything. I can't do anything. I'm on fire."

"You are fine," Father Gaillard said. "Many others aren't, but you are."

"I'm on fire."

I sat with him one night, picking up the book and beginning to read—as much to prove to myself that I could as for any other reason. "How's your fever?" I asked when I finished the chapter.

"Very bad. I don't care if you say it's not."

"You might want a cold towel," I said. "It might help you."

He glared up at me with the yellow eyes, as if I were trying to trick him. But eventually he nodded, and I dipped a piece of a field coat we'd shredded for rags in water, and pressed it to his cool brow.

"Thank you. Why doesn't anyone else believe me?" he asked.

The better question is why did he insist on the fever? I thought I understood. His village had been destroyed, his parents had been killed. He couldn't possibly be fine. That would make no sense at all.

I kept the rag to his forehead until he fell asleep. And a few days later I taught him how to knead dough for the bread. How to gauge the big ovens, and set the crust, and pull the wooden peel back from the heat at just the right moment.

"Can you tell me about Chicago?" he asked one night.

I could hear the other boys shifting in the dark on their bunks, could hear the murmured conversations die. I described the elevated trains. The downtown streets. The cold lake. They asked me about American girls, American food. Were most American men really two meters tall? Had I ever killed an Indian? Would the Americans ever come into the war?

Somehow a ritual was born. There was no one watching over us. If we wanted to talk in the electric light of our dormitory, there was no reason we couldn't. Yet many nights we'd turn the lights off and wait until the rumble and din of the corridors and galleries had died. We would slip into our coats—old field coats, far too big for most of us—and light the kerosene lanterns stolen from the kitchen where most of us worked. We would put the lanterns against our chests and button up the coats so that only a glimpse of light bled onto our chins and mouths. We would talk.

Why go to all the trouble? Perhaps there was a reason in the beginning, but it was quickly forgotten. It was a means of granting permission, really, of confirming that we weren't *just* talking. Alain described the evacuation of Fleury, Serge the fall of Ornes. Franck described his village on the edge of Lorraine, the prehistoric rock there, once a site of pagan worship. He told us how the parish priest had stuck an iron cross into the rock and how, despite the devout nature of his village, the cross was ripped down in a matter of days. Why? Because the rock was and always had been a place for bodies, not spirits. Franck himself had been pushed behind the rock with a girl from the village, and in the darkness they had found their mouths pressed together.

"And who did you tell them about?" Sarah asked me as we turned back toward the river.

In a different time and place, the medium might have been famous just for her eyes, large and shallow-water blue. She met us in the street below her flat. I'd seen her before, I realized, at a table by the river, drinking alone. I never learned her real name, but she went by Madame Goyas.

"The address is hard to find," she said in perfect English, "so I always come down."

She led us up a narrow staircase to a door with a glazed bowl hanging upon it, painted like an eye. Inside was the room of a pauper: a sagging table and three unmatched chairs, a cloudy oil lamp on a windowsill. The walls were bare except for a row of telegrams of condolence in French, German, Italian, and Russian. One was addressed to Mr. and Mrs. John Fields of St. Louis, Missouri.

"I can speak many languages," Madame Goyas said. "It's all the same to me. Which do you prefer?"

"What language do the spirits speak?" I asked.

"It's all the same on the other side too." Even as she narrowed her eyes they seemed huge. "I know who you are. You've come to discredit me, no?"

She may have been a fraud, but she certainly wasn't a fool. She looked from me to Sarah, those eyes asking what kind of friend I was supposed to be.

It was a fair question. Sarah and I had eaten lunch, poking fun at acquaintances who'd buried fingernails in flowerpots and slept with photographs under their pillows. She asked me to accompany her to the séance, and only after I agreed did I realize she was serious. No matter. I'd already decided to give myself over to her wishes, whatever they might be. But now I didn't know what I was supposed to do or say, let alone what I was supposed to feel. Madame Goyas needn't have worried. I was a fool but not a fraud.

"It's right to be cautious," Madame Goyas continued. "There *are* many charlatans. The dead don't want to talk to the living. It isn't easy to make them."

She gestured to the table. Window light slashed toward a basin filled with an inch or two of water. Madame Goyas stepped toward the mantel of a collapsed fireplace and lit white candles with a long match. Sarah unwrapped her candle—the duplicate of the half-burned others—and placed it in the center of the table.

"Why don't they like to talk to the living?" Sarah asked—skeptically? Sincerely? I couldn't tell.

Madame Goyas smiled and dropped the match into the basin.

"They're happy," she said, "and we upset them."

"Heaven, you mean?"

"There's no heaven," she said. "Only the other side."

It was obviously a show, but a good show. The show was in the poverty of the room, in its disdain for the luxuries of this side. The show was in the absence of heavy drapes, or silver bells, or crystal balls, or iconography of any kind.

The show was in Madame Goyas's parochial dress, modestly covering her from ankles to neck, but too small and cut for a girl, so one's eyes adjusted to the rounds of her shoulders and hips, the swell of her breasts, as if to the dark. The show was in her body, hidden in plain sight, emanating aliveness more than sexuality. And the show was in her face, in that expression some people—powerful people—can summon. The expression that says, *Yes, I understand.* Father Perrin's expression. I began to grow nervous because I feared that she *did* understand; I feared she understood what was happening between Sarah and me far better than I did.

"Where are you from?" I asked.

"France, of course. Aas," she said. "In the Pyrenees. And you?"

"Shouldn't you know?"

"Should I? Are you dead?"

"He's also American," Sarah said.

"American? I had no idea, you see?" She smiled.

The slash of light fell from the table. Madame Goyas peered into the basin and nodded her approval.

"The match is pointing toward Mrs. Hagen," she said. "We should begin."

The match *was* pointing toward Sarah, directly at her, in fact. It floated, unwavering, its head splintering bits of black sulfur.

"I ask you to close your eyes, and to put your foreheads to the table. Don't think that I have left you. That is the one thing that will not happen."

"All right," Sarah said, her voice snagging on something. This was no lark. She was nervous, perhaps even afraid.

"But first light the candle you brought, Mrs. Hagen."

Sarah's face flared yellow above the match. She put her damp hand in mine and I reached to take Madame Goyas's hand, wide rings on every finger.

I closed my eyes. It was too late to get away. The tabletop was surprisingly cold.

Silence. Then Madame Goyas began to whistle. Or not quite. She began to speak. But the words, vaguely French, would phase in and out like wind whipping through branches, like the breathing of a man shot through the throat.

"There," she said in English. "There. Now don't move."

"What was that?" Sarah asked.

"The dialect from my village. No one speaks it now."

"But the dead do?" I asked.

"I asked if you had a preference. This is my preference," she said. "But now I must explain, Mrs. Hagen. Ask questions. Ask what you want to know of Lee. Do not speak of anything other than the questions you want him to answer. That is important. Do you understand?"

"When?" Sarah asked.

"I hope you'll know."

For a time there was nothing to do but listen to Sarah's breath. Then I heard footsteps. I thought someone had come into the room from behind the curtain opposite the window, but the picture of the room in my mind had broken into shards. Madame Goyas whistled again, and the sound now seemed to carry a chill. I felt drops of sweat on my neck.

"Lee?" Sarah said.

Madame Goyas's fingers were stiff as the bands of her rings. Though I knew I was still holding Sarah's hand, I couldn't feel it. The footsteps circled the table. More drops on my neck, on the backs of my ears, in my hair.

"Lee?" Sarah said again. "Lee. Lee. Lee."

Silence.

"Lee," she said.

"What is that?" I whispered.

"Rain," Madame Goyas whispered. "Don't talk."

Rain? Yes. The entire room seemed to rustle with the sound of falling water. It smelled like rain too, warm and light. My eyes were still closed, but I could see it all around us. Cloudless, wolf's-wedding rain, with the sun shining through. The steps squeaked and slid across the floor, nimble, insouciant, a child's. *Lee. Lee. Lee.* The darting tongue of the name lashed like brambles along naked legs. *Lee. Lee. Lee.*

The steps were running now, not over floorboards but through wheat; there was the crush and swish of a field giving way. Birds startled in the underbrush and fluttered past my face. I could smell the ashes of an old fire, could hear the tolling of a church bell, faint and far. The footsteps skidded through a brook. The ringing fell away. But where was the question? *Lee. Lee. Lee.* Madame Goyas's hand had started to shake.

I tried to rise, and felt Madame Goyas's grip tighten, her arm going rigid to hold me in place. I didn't move again. The specter, the actor, the illusion—whatever it actually was—had reached a road.

"Say something, Mrs. Hagen," Madame Goyas said.

"Lee," Sarah said. "Lee, what was it that tasted like berries?" The words came out all at once. My stomach clenched. The rain shut off. Someone was coughing. Madame Goyas's hand jerked away and I opened my eyes. The sun had faded entirely and the room was lit only by candlelight. She was the one coughing, and pink-tinged slime poured out of her mouth and down the front of her dress.

She coughed as if she had been pulled from the bottom of the river; the slime came out in spurts on the table. I pushed my chair back. Finally, she released me from her grip and put up the hand to cover her mouth as fresh slime slid through her fingers.

Madame Goyas shook her head as if to say there was nothing to worry about. She ducked behind the curtain and returned with a glass of water and a rag.

"I'm sorry," Sarah said, as Madame Goyas wiped her mouth. "I couldn't think."

"No. I'm sorry, Mrs. Hagen," she said. "You must have known. That wasn't him."

We walked back to the hotel. We undressed. We made love. Well, no, I wouldn't have put it that way even then, but I don't know what else to call it. The married couples I write about sleep in separate beds, after all. I take that as a good bit of fortune actually, as sex is difficult to aestheticize. It becomes funny so quickly, and there was nothing funny—or even pleasurable, in the typical way—between us that afternoon. Perhaps it's enough to say that there was confusion in it, not the confusion of pain and pleasure you see in dirty books, but the confusion of comfort and fear.

Afterward, I searched for something to say beyond the obvious, but in my mind there was only blankness, and outside was her bed and her body.

"What did the question about the berries mean?" I asked.

"It was in one of the last letters he wrote me," she said. "*They said it would taste like berries. It doesn't taste like berries.* It doesn't make a difference. I know it's absurd."

Madame Goyas had returned half of Sarah's money. She'd apologized. She'd said all the signs were right, but signs were only approximations, trickles of light from a buried fire. We hadn't talked about the rain, the footsteps, the slime in her mouth. Once we left, it didn't seem to matter whether any of that had really happened.

"I wonder if you would have asked something else if I hadn't been there."

"I don't believe in any of it, Tom. That's why I invited you."

"To prove that you don't believe in it?"

"Yes. But I shouldn't have."

"You think I kept him away?"

"No, but I'll tell you what I do believe, if you really want to know."

"That he's still alive?" I hadn't realized I knew until the words were out of my mouth. I couldn't even wish to take them back. She would have told me as much in the next instant.

She sat up in bed. "I suppose you've seen this a hundred times?"

"Actually," I said, "if you want to know the truth, I've never seen anything like you."

She rubbed her face with the heels of her hands, looked at me from the corner of her eye, smiled with the corner of her mouth. I started to laugh. At her expression, or at what I'd said. Or perhaps at neither. I always laugh hardest when I'm not quite sure what's funny.

And she laughed too, though not as much. She understood the joke better than I did.

"This—with you—it isn't common for me. Suddenly I was afraid you might not realize that."

I touched her arm to no effect. "I couldn't think that, not unless I was completely blind."

She nodded. "I suppose that's why I bring it up."

The room still felt like the inside of a jewelry box. The city outside was the same dusty black. Her back curved against my palm as it had before. And yet.

"You don't have to go on searching," I said. "I'm not saying you shouldn't. But you don't have to."

"You're right, of course. But my train leaves tomorrow morning."

I saw Madame Goyas once more before I left Verdun. She wore the same black dress, but I almost didn't recognize her. Her mouth was different, her eyes different, and her bearing suggested someone younger, someone who had seen far less of the world. Her voice was different too, shy and a little wild, as she invited me to share her café table along the river.

"You usually sit alone," I said.

"Since you already doubt me, what's the harm? And I have a question that I'd like to ask you."

I nodded.

"You lied to her about something. What was it?"

"I thought you were out of character," I said.

"Can't *you* tell a liar?"

"Yes, I suppose."

"Will she forgive you?"

"I may never see her again, anyway," I said.

"Really?" She showed a face unlike any I'd seen her make. It must require enormous discipline to never appear surprised. "You'd disgrace yourself for a woman you don't hope to see again?"

"I didn't say I didn't hope."

She poured me a glass from a carafe of red wine. I put my hand up to block the sun so I could look her in the eyes.

"How much longer will you stay in Verdun, do you think?" I asked.

"Until there is a better place for my work. Forever? I take great pleasure in not having to decide."

"I don't understand that," I said.

"No. I don't think someone like you could understand, but if I had stayed in Aas, I'd have married years ago, and then my future would be quite certain. At least for the women there every day has been identical for hundreds of years. Certainly, I wouldn't be able to sit out at a café and share a drink with you." She finished her glass and poured another, as if to prove the point. "Shouldn't I make the most of the few advantages my life has offered me?"

The river glittered in the late afternoon. A waiter whistled past. I think I wanted to hurt her feelings, to see if I could.

"Perhaps if you'd married, your husband would have died in the war. Wouldn't that change things?"

She looked at me, laughter sparkling in her light eyes. "Who's to say that's not exactly what *did* happen? And who's to say that my husband and I don't get along better now than we ever did when he was alive?"

"That's right. What did you say? The dead are truly happy?"

"No, that was a lie." Her expression darkened, and she lowered her voice. "It used to be true, but now the dead are desperate to talk."

"Why is that?"

"They don't recognize the world they left and they come to ask us why."

She was a fine actress. Had she met the right person on an ocean liner she might have been famous for a little while. Once I arrived in California I looked for her sometimes in nightclubs and on soundstages. Somehow, it seemed wholly possible that I would see her.

And a few years ago I thought I heard her on the radio in a Paris hotel. My wife was angry with me, and rightfully so. We'd taken a trip. The first time I'd been to Paris in twenty-five years, the first time she'd ever been, and I found myself desperate not to leave the hotel room.

Faye gave up and went out to meet the *Mona Lisa*, leaving me alone to listen to a program about the smuggling of Jews and dissidents into Spain during the Nazi occupation. The host described the language that locals used to help the smugglers, a whistling dialect that could carry from mountaintop to mountaintop. *Imagine, listener,* he said in a grave and gravelly voice, *that you are one such refugee, that you have been traveling for weeks. You are tired and terrified. Imagine what you see across the mountains: a peaceful valley, a huddle of buildings, and a slender church tower amid the shadows of peaks. This is Spain, this is freedom, and this is the sound that guides you to it . . .*

"What do you intend to do now?" Madame Goyas asked from her seat at the café by the river. It was the last day I ever sat in one of those cafés, I think, my last evening on the Meuse. I never went back to Verdun. I saw the completed ossuary only in pictures. An ugly thing, rising from the ridge just past Fleury near Fort Douaumont. A cold cement box with a bell tower like the hilt of a sword. According to *Life* magazine, the bones we'd collected had been interred finally in a basement vault, visible only through knee-level windows.

The end is in the beginning. Comedians have always said so, and, more recently, physicists. When Father Perrin arrived in Verdun in the spring of 1919, he called me into the office and paced in front of the big windows above the courtyard.

"I must admit, Tom, I find it strange that you'd want to stay on here," he said. "Brave, perhaps, but it's a nasty effect of war that bravery—so-called bravery—is valued so highly. So let me admit to you that I'm terrified that I'll fail at what I set out to accomplish here. You're not French. You're hardly Catholic, I think. Are you telling me you're not afraid you might not be able to help?"

He took a packet of cigarettes from his pocket and tapped at the foil with one finger, frowning.

"Father Gaillard has asked me not to smoke in his office," he said. "You see, I'm learning my limitations. Just when I think I've met them all, a knock on the door."

"Sometimes a friend knocks," I said.

He nodded skeptically, as if to say that a turn of phrase was worth nothing. He sat down on the edge of the desk and arranged his face, practicing, I think, for the job ahead. "My mother died when I was eleven, Tom. And this was seen as a great stroke of fortune for my family. My father saw hellfire in her eyes. Don't misunderstand. That isn't an expression. He *saw* hellfire, and dumped the water from every pot and pan in the house so she'd have no way to put it out. And also don't misunderstand, my father was an exhaustingly ordinary man." His expression softened, as it always did eventually. "I understand your mother is also dead. Can you tell me how?"

I told him what I remembered. The public ward. Her yellow lips, her yellow tongue. How she had died with open eyes, how the nurse who closed them had been her high school classmate, as it happened. She smoothed my mother's dry hair on the yellow pillow. "You know what a looker she was when I knew her?" She smiled at me. "Now she will be again." My dead mother, the looker.

Father Perrin touched my shoulder. "You see? You see?"

I never fully understood what I was supposed to see, but he agreed to let me stay. And, two days after Sarah boarded the train for Udine, a day after he returned from Rodez, he invited me in and waited patiently while I poured myself a glass of water from the tray on the Second Empire desk. He poured himself a glass of wine.

He already knew about Sarah—our affair—obviously. Still, he let me tell him in my own words. A truck pulled into the courtyard, the engine idling. A door slamming, the driver—his name was Clarence—calling to the cook with whom he often played cards to come out and take delivery of the week's vegetables.

Father Perrin closed the window. His right eye was fitful. He was worn out, and not just from the trip. In the two years I'd known him he'd aged ten.

"Perhaps you think I'm partially to blame," he said.

"I don't," I said.

"Perhaps you think you shouldn't feel ashamed." He swallowed some wine. "You may be right. But you should be careful. Suffering speaks a language all its own. And that language is seldom literal. Do you understand me? *Do* you feel ashamed?"

The cook walked out into the courtyard, shading his eyes. He accepted a cigarette, as the truck continued to idle. If I could have met Sarah in a hotel in Aix-les-Bains or in a train station in Chicago, I would have. But I would not have changed anything else.

"You're saying she may not love me," I said. "But I didn't say she did."

"Am I still managing to overestimate you? Didn't you at least do this because you thought you were in love?"

He lit a cigarette and smoked it in three draws. The cook, Michel, laughed over the grind of the truck and said, "Too true, too true." The room reeked of smoke and exhaust. Father Perrin's eyes were red and didn't seem to see me. My eyes burned.

"I have pity for her, for Mrs. Hagen, for all of them—all those that come here, you know that. But I have to admit to you: pity is difficult to maintain all of the time. Especially when I can see in each face the same wish: if only it could be someone else. What I mean is that the grieving are just as selfish as the rest of us, perhaps more."

"You're saying that . . ."

"That, in my experience, suffering does not bring sanctity. What I mean to say is that you don't believe in God, I suspect, though I know you wouldn't tell me. So, if the world is all atoms and void, who could begrudge you a few unclaimed atoms that might lend some comfort? Who could begrudge her? Only I don't believe this will bring any comfort to you, Tom. Not in the end. Perhaps that is why I'm so upset."

"Too true, too true," Michel shouted again; this time, Father Perrin tapped the window. The two men threw down their cigarettes and set to work.

"No, that's not entirely true, Tom. I'm upset because you were wrong. Very wrong. And it was a mistake from the beginning to put you in such a position. It was my mistake. Just explain to me what you were thinking. How you justified this—what can I call it?—a romance, a dirty weekend? Just tell me that?"

I don't think he expected an answer, though he certainly deserved one. He'd shared wine grown in vineyards around his village in Languedoc, and admitted to me he was once so poor that he stole those same grapes for food. He told me he hadn't heard piano music until he was seventeen and had just arrived at the seminary in Toulouse. At first he mistook the sound for rain.

"I've never understood why he doesn't turn off the engine," Father Perrin said. "I hate to have to talk to him about it, but I suppose I will." He waved his hand through the cigarette smoke, as if to say that was all.

"At least she wasn't French," he said, and smiled sadly. "No. I shouldn't joke. I won't tell Father Gaillard. Rather, I'll tell His Grace you decided it was finally time. I'll say we decided. And, once you are gone, no one will remember what you've done. I will. But only because you're my friend."

He rose from the desk. I looked up to see Michel carrying a box of mirabelles past the windows. One fell, and Clarence picked it up and pretended to throw it at the back of Michel's head, laughing to himself.

"Do you know," I said, "do you know that I found Mrs. Hagen sitting on the edge of the pond? Somehow she'd caught one of the fish in her purse. It was the strangest thing."

Father Perrin opened the door to the hall.

"Why do you tell me that now?"

"I don't know," I said. "Because I promised her I wouldn't."

CHAPTER SIX

In Paris, I took a room on Rue du Temple, next to a building being gutted at double-time. The work began each morning at seven, hydraulic drills and hammers smashing away at the bricks and beams. On weekend mornings when the work ceased, I'd wake to the sound of a tambourine. From my window I could see a dark-haired child, perhaps a year old, standing up in her crib, dancing to the jangle.

The room itself smelled like cat spray but got good light; if the windows were open, there was nothing to complain about. Of course there were bugs in the wallpaper that came out at night. As my neighbor pounded on his wall, they would migrate in ripples down mine. Or perhaps I only dreamed that. In Paris, I mostly slept well.

There was hammering—typewriters all morning, the press in the back room all evening—in the small office I shared with seven other men at the weekly newspaper, *La Voix du Soldat*. Father Perrin had made one call, and the job was mine. In certain circles, it seemed, he was almost a celebrity. Marcel, *La Voix*'s publisher, asked me timid questions about him, and from the first day treated me with a deference I certainly hadn't earned.

It was a relief to find that the job for which I'd been hired—assistant classified editor—required little more than cleaning out a mailbox, writing up a bill of sale, and typing up a notice. Anyone could have done it, but I appreciated the continuity with my old work; at least I never began to feel that the world was a decent place where people weren't suffering.

> Looking for any news about Pierre Barcolle. Disappeared in the Champagne sector, in February 1917. Last seen on patrol on the night of the 17th during a gas attack. Please write with any information.
>
> Or:
>
> Please! Does anyone know the whereabouts of Michel de Parne? Taken prisoner in the Konstanz camp in 1916. Caught typhus but was later said to have recovered. Loved Arsène Lupin. Loved still by wife and young son.

We charged little for the ads, but—since so few had money to spare, or had already spared what they could on less desperate methods—their writers tried to work in every possible detail with every centime. "Lved B. brds," one said. But what was *B*? Blue? Baby?

The irony was that we charged by the word, not the letter, so the abbreviations saved no money at all. Sometimes, I tried to change abbreviations to words, though I was always afraid of getting something wrong. It was difficult to think of the men and women who had written these notices deciding on the detail that would best represent an entire person. All the more so because, by late 1921, those details were almost certainly useless. The mass graves were all exhumed, the last prisoners repatriated, the names already chiseled on memorials. And the memories of the living—compromised from the start—were fading by the day.

Otherwise, our weekly covered whatever news might be of interest to veterans. And Marcel was smart enough to know that there were many voices of the soldier—some hopeful, some bitter. We published updates on the innumerable memorial projects in Toulouse, Nantes, and every other corner of the country. We published stories about masons rebuilding Amiens; hoisting stone blocks, too heavy for shaking hands. We published stories about the splinters in the hands of boatmen returning to work in Brittany, their palms actually softened by the war. We wrote of women in the Rhône valley, returning to the home after years in munitions factories—the yellow of the nitric acid having faded from their skin and hair, but not their taste for independence. We wrote of men who'd never be able to work again—missing hands, missing half their minds—who scraped by on disability pensions that were hardly enough to support a family.

But no matter what else we published in the fall of 1921, we always made space for the story of Anthelme Mangin, the amnesiac of Rodez. The same man Father Perrin had gone to visit the day after Sarah arrived in Verdun. The amnesiac, as he was known, had become a sensation in France that fall. The doctors at Rodez, against Father Perrin's advice, had asked that his picture be published in the major newspapers. The story had stunned the nation and delighted editorialists. Was this the luckiest man in Europe? they asked. The only man free of the chains of history? Or was he the inevitable omega of Europe's most shameful moment?

More importantly, who *was* he, really? The doctors at the asylum in Rodez were flooded with letters—from wives and parents who hoped against hope, and against reason too. By the fall of 1921, three women had put in legal claims on Mangin, and the claims of countless others had already been discredited. There were many times I wanted to write to Father Perrin, to ask his opinion on Mangin, to ask his opinion on many questions.

Instead, I worked. I typed up the advertisements, set them, calculated the price, and moved on to the next until evening came and I left for the Chevalier Vert, a café with Sir Gawain painted on the window glass.

Marcel had introduced me to everyone at the Chevalier Vert and welcomed me to his tab. I shouldn't have taken advantage as much as I did, but I got the impression he'd been waiting for a friend to drink with for years. And, like many people just starting out, I felt the world owed me more than I'd received.

Marcel must have been in his mid-forties, but he had that child-like quality of men who never marry. He could talk articulately about a great many subjects in both English and French. But around women he became deathly shy and drank too much.

"I've done many things to make myself a better match," he said. "Before, I had a terrible flat. I had a terrible tobacco habit. I had terrible manners. I changed all that. But still, no luck. And then, miraculously, my odds improved. It was as if all Europe got together and said, Isn't it time that we got Marcel Sirac married? But what can we do to improve his chances? Aha, I've got it, the kaiser said. But still here I am with you. Not that you're bad company."

I tried to help, but when I invited women to sit down at our table, when I began to boast about Marcel and the important work he was doing for France, he went almost catatonic. Once, he even pretended he'd fallen asleep.

Other nights, Marcel took me to the cinema. Though I'd been to the nickelodeons in Chicago before the war, with their sticky chairs and signs saying "Stay All Day," I never much wanted to stay. But, in Paris, for the cost of a drink, you could take a seat in the Gaumont-Palace near Place Clichy, with its blazing marquee and velvet seats, and listen to the orchestra tuning up. And then the lights would go down and you would be somewhere else entirely, in Spanish California with Zorro, in the lair of Dr. Mabuse. And nothing that happened on the screen mattered unless you wanted it to.

After I'd known Marcel for a few months, after I'd shown him that his small secrets would be safe with me, he said, "I'll show you what cinema truly is."

I followed him to the café in the Latin Quarter that had been his Chevalier Vert before the war. He bought me a *coup de rouge* and ushered me to a back room smelling of bicycle grease and scattered with kitchen chairs. They'd fancied the place up with old cognac ads in which a cat in a suit and tie holds up a snifter. On the far wall a bedsheet hung from a clothesline, and, on the other end, a man with the shoulders and beard of a Viking smoked a pipe and prepared the film on a hand-crank Cinématographe from the early years of the century.

"That's Loti," Marcel said, pointing to the man, pointing me to a seat. "Watch him. I want you to watch how fast he cranks the film. Pay very close attention."

The back room filled with a small and run-down crowd. A man sat down to a half-tuned piano and began to plink. The film started. A series of reels starring Max Linder. I'd seen one or two before in the citadel, the screen glimpsed through kepis, the soldiers mostly too tired or frightened to laugh.

Now the prints were scratched and faded, bearing the scars of a thousand performances. And the frames flew by: Linder lying down by the fire to find his shoes smoking, attempting to clean his bedroom window and finding himself hanging from the ledge. All in a herky-jerk, out of step with the ragtime piano. When the lights went up and we walked out, Marcel asked me what I thought.

"Too fast," I said.

He nodded. "I thought so too. But I never know if it's my imagination. It means that Loti is back together with Marie. It means he's eager to get home. She is the most beautiful woman in the world."

"She used to be yours?" I asked.

"Almost. Very nearly. Not quite. Now you tell me. Who is it *you* dream about?"

On the morning Sarah was to leave Verdun, I'd slipped from her room while she was still asleep. I'd had coffee on a silver tray in the lobby; the waiter charged it to her account without asking. I'd returned to the Episcopal palace to work, sorting correspondence for Father Perrin's return. Her train left at noon. Verdun to Metz, Metz to Zurich, Zurich to Milan, Milan to Udine. I'd never watched a woman other than my mother pack a bag.

At 9:30 I washed my face, wishing for colder water. I went to the kitchen looking for someone to talk to. I ate a chunk of stale bread. I watched the fish in the pond. *So this is life. So this is life.* The sky looked like a sponge poised to wipe out the earth. The flat stones laid along the walk whorled, fossil-like. I'd never noticed.

I started back toward the hotel, hoping it wasn't too late. It started to rain, then stopped. There were Italians along the river, but they didn't look up. My nerve had dissolved. Once I arrived I was too embarrassed to ask the clerk to let me up to her room.

I had another coffee and paid for it myself. Her luggage came downstairs at eleven. She followed five minutes later. When she saw me, leaning in the doorway, she didn't quite smile.

"Will you come to the station?" she asked.

The same car that had taken us to Bar-le-Duc, the same driver. The light outside was hard, and the car's shadow reached halfway across the street. Doors slammed. She touched my hand while watching the ruins through her window.

"Would you come with me to Udine?" she said. "I'd buy your ticket right now."

"Would you like me to?"

We crossed the river and turned on Rue des Capucins. A man in the middle of the street was bandaging his sheepdog's paw. The driver honked, and the man looked up from the greasy fur, startled.

"We don't have long to decide," Sarah said. "If this were a few years ago I'd have asked if you loved me."

I would have told her I did love her if she'd asked. It had only been two days, but I knew something had changed because I'd never felt so desperately alone and I didn't know what else to call that. But she meant that love was beside the point. Maybe it was the point once, the way that salvation was once, but not anymore.

"I'll write to you," she said.

The train station was new, rebuilt from scratch and painted a dull brown. The lobby was empty, the ticket window shuttered for lunch. And under the low ceiling already bearing smoke swirls, I was reminded how little Verdun actually mattered. They build beautiful monuments for concepts, but beautiful stations for places. And here there were no trains running west, not even to Paris, and the trains to the east terminated in the new French city of Metz.

At first, I hoped Marcel might hand me a perfume-scented letter. I imagined I might find an envelope addressed in her hand among all the other envelopes in the morning's post. I imagined that she might arrive at the office purely by chance, having come to post an ad in person. Or that she might arrive having given up on Lee, having returned to Paris to find me. I imagined her eyes snapping open in the middle of the night, certain of her mistake.

If she'd written to me care of Father Perrin—and perhaps she had—he'd forwarded nothing. I couldn't bring myself to write him to ask. The shame had time to gather. I dreaded his letter almost as much as I desired hers. At the same time, I thought of him often; I thought especially of what he'd said that final day in the office. *The language of suffering is seldom literal.* Certainly I wasn't the first person caught between desire and shame, but that knowledge was of no help.

I could only imagine how Sarah and I might meet again: at a bookstall by the river as we both reached for a copy of *Le Matin*. As the only two people crossing an empty square at midday or midnight. The Eiffel Tower was involved, as were the Luxembourg Gardens and Les Halles, and many times I thought, *Imagining the blooms in the Tuileries is the only thing that will get me through the fall.*

One should probably not trust feelings in need of landmarks. Or perhaps the problem was that, in Paris, dreams that might have felt particular seemed only reiterations of someone else's. Verdun—now there was a place to fall in love in the twentieth century.

And then she did write. The letter did arrive with the mail at *La Voix*, in a light blue envelope that was somehow exactly as I'd pictured it. I ripped it open, which was wise because, as it turned out, there was little to savor.

After turning the piece of hotel stationery—the Unita in Trieste—over in my hands several times, I did my best to forget everything I'd read. Within a day I knew it almost word for word. The letter opened with pleasantries—she was human after all—and then:

> *I'm glad, very glad, that you didn't come with me. To have allowed that would have meant to lose all hope. That's no way to begin with someone. And, frankly, I fear it was only hopelessness that made my feelings for you possible. Quite honestly, there have been times when I*

have felt ill used by you. But I know that's only my own guilt, and that you did nothing I didn't invite. I don't claim to know the future, and, sometimes, I imagine one in which you take part. I do indeed care for you. I would indeed like to see you again. The truth is, though, that I would need to be another person entirely to ever fully be with you. And, given how we met, I believe you might need to be a different person in order to fully be with me. Nevertheless, know that I'm not sorry about anything. Stay my friend. I owe you a great deal, I really do.

Also, I would not have had the happy news I've just received, which I owe at least in part to you. And to Father Perrin, especially. He wrote to me soon after I returned to Udine to put me in contact with a priest here in Trieste who has put me in contact with a new group—that is, a new organization looking for the missing. There are Austrian archives on prisoners of war that have only just been discovered. This is a very real thing, Tom! And there is a Hagen who showed up in one of the camps near Graz in the summer of 1918, just months before the armistice! That's all I know for now. But the world is completely different. You can tell, probably, how hopeful and stupid I am, but I'd rather be humiliated than hopeless. I know how it sounds: facile, clichéd, foolish. But I wonder if it's fair that we associate those words with the things we say when we are happy. I wonder if I care.

With affection,
Mrs. Lee Hagen

I couldn't be angry with her. Instead, I was left with a far more particular and improbable feeling, that of having my worst fears and regrets so clearly—to say nothing of so elegantly—expressed in another's words. I told myself then that only those truly in love ever have that feeling. And because love literalizes everything, because it closes distances—ironic distance in particular—I began to consider how I might become another person entirely.

* * *

In November, Dr. Fenayrou, the director of the asylum at Rodez, and his already exhausted staff received more than two hundred queries about the amnesiac, many of which—heartbreakingly—described a man that couldn't possibly have been Mangin. Some wrote of blue eyes when Mangin's were brown—but wasn't mustard gas known to affect eye color? Some set the man's height at six feet when Mangin was only five feet, three inches—but certainly such strain could shrink a man? Some wrote of augers and visitations in dreams, as if these might strengthen their case.

Meanwhile, Mangin's resolve to remain unidentified only seemed to deepen. When the doctors asked him for a sample of his handwriting, he scribbled muddy waves. When they asked what he remembered of his profession, he looked back with the gentle, stupid eyes of a deer. When they presented him with trowels, threshing scythes, and levels, he let them clatter to the floor.

Ironically, Marcel wrote on our editorial page, *this man's lost memory is a reminder for the rest of us. But can't we also see him as a man who rejects the crude tools of the very industry that led to the machine gun and the green cross shell? A man who rejects any semblance of identity, only because he has learned that, in the age of industrial war, an identity can be stolen on the whims of strangers and at a moment's notice? These are only the most rational of responses, and yet he finds himself watching the night stars through barred windows. He might be the greatest artist of our time, yet he wears a straitjacket.*

"What do you think?" he asked me. "Too sanctimonious? Too romantic?"

"Do they keep him in a straitjacket, really?"

"No. No. By all accounts he's quite docile, even sweet."

* * *

As is well known, the artists left Montmartre for Montparnasse during the war. By the time I arrived in Paris, the quarter Sarah had described in her stories had become *passé*—one of many new words I'd never needed before. I asked Marcel about where we lived in the 3rd—there must have been part of me that saw my life in Paris as something I would talk about, perhaps even brag about, later—but he said no one should brag about life in our neighborhood. I decided I'd have to take pride in being out of fashion. I'd take pride in the Chevalier Vert, for example—that haunt of shy editors of minor papers, with its chipped glasses and yellow windows. Why the name? Marcel said there had once been a flower factory on the block; the flower girls had come drinking in the evenings, their hands still green from the arsenic dye. Indeed, you could still see their poison fingerprints smeared on the bar.

The Vert was the kind of café that filled with immigrants, not expatriates. Yet I met Shelly Harris there one evening in December. I have no idea how he found the place, but he asked in surprising Dixie vowels if he might sit at our table.

Almost immediately, and for reasons I couldn't quite follow, he began a story about a party he'd recently attended in the 6th. There, he'd chatted and drunk as always, until a bell rang and the guests assembled in the living room, each holding a length of rope. Promptly, everyone but Shelly fell into a trance and began to channel the dead with fluttering eyes.

The host, Shelly later learned, had begun this ritual some weeks before; the ropes were meant to tether his guests to the world of the living. But, on that evening, Shelly looked on, first with bemusement, then horror, as they began to fashion the cords into nooses, as they began to hang the nooses around their own necks. What a time! What a world! Thank god I was there, Shelly said, to shake them all awake.

It was a gripping story, I suppose, though there was something immediately off-putting in the sheer performance of it. The next time I saw Shelly, he told the story again, almost word for word. And the next time too.

"Does he always do this?" I asked Rose Pemberton, who'd arrived at the Vert with Shelly and a group of his American friends a few nights later.

"That's just Shelly," she said. "Never wants to say the wrong thing."

Like Shelly, Rose became a fixture at the Chevalier Vert. Rose wore men's pants and her hair undone to her waist. She was married to an English lawyer she told everyone she'd never liked very much.

Rose introduced me to a dozen other Americans. Wilson Rohn, for example, who had the manners of George V and even looked a bit like him. There was something alluring, I had to admit—after a childhood of cabbage dinners with the family across the hall—in eating with friends who ordered oysters and lean meats. There was something alluring, too, in the realization that, had I met any of them in Chicago, they likely wouldn't have given me the time of day.

Perhaps Marcel sensed my excitement. Anyway, as these Americans began to haunt the Chevalier Vert, he found excuses to leave early, saying that he had fallen too behind in his work to sleep, let alone to drink and socialize.

I probably didn't try as hard to convince him otherwise as I should have. Though there was truth to his excuses. Interest in the Mangin case had nearly doubled the circulation of *La Voix du Soldat*, and, as Marcel devoted more and more time to the story, he let me pick up some of the slack.

My first article covered a new marble monument in Le Mans, a subject now relegated to the last page. Next, I wrote a series of articles on *La Voix*'s most stalwart topic: the inconsistent and often unfair payment of benefits by the Ministry of War. Next, I wrote a feature on a soldier who was mistakenly reported dead in the Nivelle Offensive; when he rang his mother's bell in Pigalle, she died of *joy*.

Marcel was appropriately hard on my copy. Nevertheless, he continued to publish what I wrote and to offer more assignments. Eventually, he abandoned the Chevalier Vert altogether. I felt guilty going without him, but, by February, when the snow fell through the chimney smoke, there was little choice but to watch it through the Chevalier Vert's steamy windows. A glass of wine was cheaper than the coal it would take to heat my flat, and I often stayed until closing.

By then—though I had written her several times care of the address in Trieste—I hadn't heard from Sarah in six months. Some days I still woke with the sting of her on my mind. And some mornings I woke to the pinch of Rose's nails because, in the night, I'd pinned her long hair to the mattress. She made clear that our relationship would never be serious. Despite that, my life began to feel slightly more than provisional, as it often does when one outgrows his first friends in a new city and makes a second set.

"Why here, of all places?" I asked Wilson Rohn one night, after he'd ordered a second bottle of Bordeaux, after everyone else who had to work the following morning had left the Chevalier Vert. Wilson had a slim and witty face, and as I'd gotten to know him I'd realized that his politeness shielded a good-humored maliciousness.

"Haven't you heard?" he asked. "There's an American who drinks here, who used to pick up the bones from Verdun. This is quite the chic place."

Santa Monica, 1950

My house nearly has an ocean view. That's what the agent said when I bought it several years ago. Nearly. If the house were three stories instead of two: ocean view. Three blocks further west: ocean view. She said the phrase as if to imply that I was close, so close, to a standard of attainment that I obviously didn't quite grasp. She was right. I didn't care about an ocean view. Partially, that was due to my education. The French don't like to look at the water, except in August.

Still, I bought the house—an Eclectic Revival cottage with a catslide roof and eucalyptus trees in the front yard—when several others would have been just as suitable. And when I signed the papers, the agent said that I had been both wise and lucky, which led me to believe she'd had a hard time interesting anyone else. Indeed, the house would have been small for a family. "So many people don't realize there's no reason to buy space you don't need. Yet," she was quick to add. I suppose it's possible she just didn't realize that I was on the other side of *yet*, that I was at the end of something—a marriage, in this case—rather than the beginning.

At least I can say that I've never had cause to regret the house. Though I don't have an ocean view, every day I do see people walking to the beach. There's something salubrious in just that. The zinc-tipped noses, the sandals and oxfords without socks. The easy conversations tossed over shoulders, the striped sun umbrellas and towels.

In fact, I was watching a young man walk two spotted dogs in bandanas past my window when the phone rang the morning after the composer's birthday party. It was Max Steiner.

"How do you feel this morning?" Steiner asked. His tone suggested he'd already written two scores and a sonata.

"I don't remember giving you my telephone number," I said. "Does that answer your question?"

"But obviously I have your phone number," he said. "I did not think you would mind speaking at home."

"It's an honor, actually. Did I tell you that last night?"

"Like you, I am somewhat unsure what we spoke of last night. Nevertheless, upon reflection, I believe it to be perfect."

"You believe what to be perfect?"

"Your song, of course."

The song. The ridiculous song. I tried to massage back my headache, to find a little lucid space to think. "By the piano?" I said, dismissively, as if my tone of voice might sway him away. But then—all the more ridiculously, since it wasn't even my song—I couldn't help myself. "You said you didn't like it, though, didn't you?"

"I believe that I said it was too lonely. The reason I do not often drink is that my mind becomes too literal. Loneliness, of course, is the perfect subtext for a lullaby."

"That may be," I said. "The problem is I don't remember any of it."

"None?"

"I'm afraid not."

"You made it up on the spot? Impressive." Though a click in his voice suggested he wasn't feeling very impressed.

"I must have channeled something in the house," I said.

"I would not say that," Steiner said. "But it's quite all right. I remember everything perfectly. Isn't it . . ." And he began to sing. His voice was bad by any standard, but the words were exactly right. The moment should have been funny—the unexpected call, the deeply accented performance in which "the snow covered the *vindow.*" Only I was too afraid to laugh. Truly, I was afraid. Who would care, really, if that song ended up, improbably, in a picture? Who would even know? Yet my chest clenched.

"*That's* impressive," I said when he'd finished.

"Naturally, I don't forget music."

"Naturally." There was a pause on the line, and I realized just how ill I suddenly felt.

"But I have forgotten," Steiner said. "Why were you at the party?"

"I came with Paul Weyerhauser."

"Yes, yes. That was it. How do you know Paul again?"

"We met in Italy," I said, feeling too dizzy to lie or deflect. "Almost thirty years ago now."

"Is that right?" he said. "Fertile soil, I suppose."

"It didn't seem so at the time."

"I mean only that he met his wife there too, after all."

CHAPTER SEVEN

"I received an interesting letter from Bologna today," Marcel said one morning in the spring of 1922—late spring, late May, the butter on the dish at our café table soft enough to have caught one of the season's first flies. He'd asked me to lunch, as he did at least once a week. I knew I'd disappointed him by drifting over to the Americans at the Chevalier Vert, but he was the type who went out of his way to be more attentive when he was hurt. I was trying to learn from his example. I took my *croque madames* the way he did—the barely touched egg running yellow off the bread—thinking that sometimes it's the smallest things that make a person feel less alone in the world.

Spring was splitting into summer, and what a spring it had been for Marcel. His work on the Mangin story had earned him a small award, and circulation of *La Voix du Soldat* continued to rise, even as ads for missing men were replaced by advertisements for shirt collars and quack cures.

Marcel, with an acumen I think he had only just discovered in himself, announced in the March 1 issue that our publication would henceforth be known simply as *La Voix*. It would continue to tell the story of the men and women who sacrificed for France, of course, but shouldn't it be acknowledged that all the French had sacrificed, that we were all *soldats* in one way or another? It was *La Voix*'s job to speak to, and for, us all.

"Bologna," he said, "is the new home of the Italian amnesiac."

We'd been following the story of the Italian amnesiac only vaguely. Like Mangin, he'd been a prisoner of war, but the Austrians, in the death throes of empire, had nowhere near the Prussian proficiency for record-keeping. They completely lost track of the man in the camp. He had no identification, and didn't look particularly Italian, so they sent him to Serbia after the armistice.

It soon became clear to the doctors in Belgrade that the man was no Serb. For one thing, he spoke no Serbian. Not that he spoke much of any language, but he could follow basic commands—sit, stand, undress—in French, Italian, and English. Since Italy was closest, they sent him there. First to a military hospital in Udine. Then to another in Sienna, then finally to an asylum in Bologna at the request of a famous doctor who'd taken an interest in his case.

According to the report Marcel had just read, the man had spoken his first word in three years. The word was *ball*. According to the report, the man's picture had been released to the Red Cross and all the usual groups. But the Italian papers still hadn't shown much interest.

"Part of their excuse," Marcel explained, "is that nobody knows if he's Italian. But if he *is* Italian, they don't want to pollute the glorious image of Roman masculinity by putting the focus on a catatonic coward."

"That's your opinion?"

Marcel sliced the fly off the butter and flicked it into the street. "I don't much care for Italians. At least their newspapermen."

On another day the conversation might have ended there. There was much work to discuss, and an Italian amnesiac was just a curiosity, as relevant to *La Voix* as the price of pearls. But the mention of Udine—even in passing—had caught my attention. And, as the waiter emerged from the door of the café with our lunch, only to pause to greet a guest at another table, I knew we had an extra moment.

"If no one cares, where did the report come from?"

"A letter from the man's doctor. A Dr. Bianchi, I think. He believes 'the international press,' as he terms it, might have more interest in this amnesiac than the Italians."

"What on earth is 'the international press'?"

"I suppose he means the papers Americans read. He believes the patient to be an American, in fact."

The waiter arrived. Sometimes people claim their words come out before they're aware of what they're going to say, but, in that moment, if I had trouble finding the words, it was because the picture in my mind was *too* comprehensive and vivid. An American woman in Udine coming across the notice, dreaming a familiar face upon the smudged photo, booking a ticket to Bologna in perfect Italian. *I'd rather be humiliated than hopeless*, she'd written.

"I'd like to be the one to go," I said.

"What one? To go where?"

"To Bologna."

Marcel laughed. "We have plenty to say about France, my friend."

"I'll pay my own way," I said.

"Can you even pay your way home tonight?"

"Just."

"It makes me feel good, really, that you would ask. That you would think I could say yes, just because you asked. People must have been very kind to you in the past to make you think that. I suppose you've always wanted to go to Italy, is that it?"

"Since you ask, I once went through considerable trouble *not* to go to Italy. But I'm going now. And you are going to Rodez."

He laughed, harder this time. The laugh was so good-natured that I started too. "I am?" he said. "I seem to have forgotten."

"You'll need to in order to profile the families coming to inquire about Mangin. Meanwhile, I'll file from Bologna. What if we published them side by side? The experience of the missing in two different countries. Has anyone done that?"

He bit into his egg, breaking the yoke, drizzling his napkin in yellow. And he chewed slowly, sneaking glances, not wanting me to see that he was considering my proposal.

It must be said: I had no idea if she was still in Udine, if she was still in Italy at all. I may have hoped, though I certainly didn't expect, to find her in Bologna. But as I imagined her reacting to the news of this poor amnesiac, I felt a sense of attachment to her I had not known in months.

As Marcel chewed, I tried to look something other than desperate. Only when I was older and had some concept of money did I realize how generous he had been. Only when I had responsibilities and deadlines of my own did I realize how recklessly he'd assigned me work. There were many friends I was unable to track down after the second war ended, but I did manage to get back in touch with Marcel. He'd run a press for the Resistance during the occupation; he'd done some time in one of the camps but had come out all right. They no longer made the cheap scotch we used to drink in the Chevalier Vert, but I sent him a case of Cutty Sark, and he sent me a picture of two healthy-looking children, standing in front of his home in Grenoble, though there was no mention of their mother.

"No one else is doing such work, I have to admit," he said eventually. And then he smiled in a way he never smiled. It was a cynical smile, even a little mean. Seeing that expression on Marcel's face reminded me that I knew nothing of what Father Perrin had told him about me, about why I had left Verdun, about Sarah. "And perhaps it will be good for me to go to Rodez," he said. "Perhaps I'll meet a beautiful widow."

At Dijon, my train compartment emptied. I moved to the window. A white-haired man slid open the glass door as we left the station.

"May we?" he asked, in a thick English accent. "No. No. *Peut . . . nous*?"

"Oh, yes," I said. "I speak English."

He saluted this happy coincidence with a lift of his white brows, then led his wife into the compartment. He was a small man, and she was nearly twice his size. He lifted their suitcases onto the rack with shaky arms and smoothed a wool blanket over his wife's knees.

"Ah, now that's done," he said, turning to me. "For a few hours, anyway. Not enough hours, but a few."

The train shook across flat fields and gentle hills. The man's wife pulled what appeared to be a wedge of cotton from one ear and fished a brass horn from her bag.

"My name is Edna," she said. "And you are?"

"Tom," I said.

"That's it, young man," her husband said. "I'm Derrick. She won't say very much more, young man. But it's not personal. You see, her hearing is going. She can hear some with the horn, but you can't walk the streets of Dijon, let's say, Tom, with a horn in your ear now, can you?"

His face told me I should laugh, so I did.

"That's it, Tom. It's not all gloomy, is it? Even in France. You must be hungry, young man. When I was your age I was always hungry."

I hadn't brought a thing to eat and admitted I was hungry. He set to work emptying a basket of food, cans of *pâté de canard*, brown bread, soft cheese.

I told him I was on my way to write a newspaper story in Bologna, and he insisted that Edna put in her ear horn so I could explain to her as well.

"We're traveling for the pure pleasure of it," he said. "Geneva next. Might as well, shouldn't we?"

"Oh yes."

"We live in Essex, have you been to Essex? Beautiful country. The ocean is always gray, but that's the real ocean, isn't it, young man?"

"Yes, I suppose so."

As we finished the *canard*, as Edna's eyes closed, as her mouth dropped open, Derrick described the famous trees and bloodlines of Essex. I could have almost predicted what he would say next.

"Yes, well, that's always been our home. And if home becomes a gloomy place, let's even say a sad place, you can't just change it, can you, young man? And you wouldn't want to, not really. But you might want to get away if you could, wouldn't you?"

"Yes, I think I would."

"Oh, but put that aside. When you're my age, you'll want to take the waters like we do. Geneva is for that. Have you ever taken the waters? Even at your young age you'd like it."

"Just once," I said, "in Aix-les-Bains."

I almost hoped that the son he'd obviously lost had been there too. I imagined saying, Yes, I did remember an Englishman from Essex. A wonderful fellow.

"Now, I've heard it's nice there. I have heard that." He turned to Edna and gestured for the horn, only to realize she was deeply asleep.

"Go ahead and lie on your side if you're tired," he said. "Edna will have me for a pillow over here, and I'll manage with this blanket."

"All right," I said, and I lay down. The temperature had dropped, and I fumbled with my coat and bunched my knees and tried to do as he said.

"That's it, get comfortable, young man." He leaned across the compartment and smoothed the coat around my legs. "Are you comfortable? That's it."

"Yes," I said.

"Now, really comfortable, young man. I mean it."

Dr. Bianchi was expecting me; even so, I carried a credential and a letter of introduction from Marcel, feeling very much like an imposter. It was warm and dry enough to go by foot, and from Bologna Centrale it was only a short walk into the old city, the dull red of the stone like rust on the afternoon. As it was a Sunday, the wide Via dell'Indipendenza was closed to all but pedestrian traffic. The arcaded sidewalks along the boulevard were so crowded that within steps I'd swung my suitcase into the backs of three separate pairs of legs. I cut out into the street, but there was hardly any more room there, the crowd flowing at a languid pace no one would have dared walk in Paris.

It seemed all of Bologna was out on the street: swarms of students in red scarves, prams shivering over the black cobblestones, men taking their jackets off in the sunlight, women donning sweaters as they strode into the shade. Later I realized no one was going anywhere in particular, having learned that the secret of Italians—their greatest strength and weakness—is that they *like* each other in a way the French, and especially the Americans, don't.

A few remaining medieval towers leaned over the red-tiled roofs. I turned onto Via Ugo Bassi, where shop windows were full of wedding dresses, yellow rolls of noodles, and big books written in Latin. I turned into Piazza Maggiore at the foot of an enormous brick cathedral without a façade. Half the old town hall's balcony was missing—from a Fascist bomb, I later learned. Its clock face bore huge Roman numerals, and, above the entrance, a sneering copper pope blessed the Marxists at the café tables. A man in a black field coat made a speech to no one in particular from a wooden platform, asking who had brought culture to all of Europe. The Romans. *Noi*. Asking what thanks they had gotten for it. *Niente*.

The hospital was on the opposite edge of the old town, through the university district on Via Zamboni. There, young men spilled out of cafés, chatting, or bent over books, or smoking alone. Broken glass glittered down the narrow street. In some windows, every pane was broken; other windows leered like fanged mouths; some had been boarded up, the boards pasted with posters on which Lenin and Trotsky stared into the middle distance.

Eventually, the old walls dropped away, and the street opened into a boulevard lined with newsstands shuttered for Sunday. The hospital sat on the other side of a honeycombed terra-cotta wall. Beyond that I could see a gravel path through a courtyard lined with trees, and beyond that I could hear an invisible fountain burbling.

Dr. Bianchi was at least a day unshaven. His hair, graying slightly at the temples, was uncombed. He had an almost Algerian complexion and was much younger than I had expected. His few age lines danced when he smiled.

It was late on a Sunday, and the courtyard was empty and quiet, but for the little table set with a bottle of white wine and two glasses. A strange welcome, I thought, all things considered. Bianchi handed me a glass and gestured to a chair.

"You've come at just the right time," he said. "There is no strike at the moment. And very little violence, at least in the city."

"I saw the broken windows."

"Most have been replaced, but around the university they refuse in protest." He sipped his wine in a way that made me wonder how many he'd already had. "You are from a French paper, but you aren't French, are you?"

"I'm American," I admitted.

This seemed to make him genuinely happy. "Then I must congratulate you," he said. "You have inherited the world. Be careful what you do with it." We laughed. "That is why you're interested in Douglas Fairbanks?"

"The actor?"

"The amnesiac. Our amnesiac."

"Why do you call him Douglas Fairbanks?" I asked after he had ordered our dinner at a small restaurant a few blocks from the hospital. The tables around us were crowded with generations of Bolognese. We sat under a ceiling of kitchen smoke as old men and young boys poured wine from straw-covered jugs. Bianchi's eyes followed mine. It had been years since I had spoken to a psychiatrist. What would he make of my eyes? Could he have guessed that I half-expected to find a woman I knew seated at one of these tables?

"The Sunday meal is for the family," he said.

"I hope I'm not keeping you from yours."

"No. I have a brother near, but it is difficult to see him. My parents are far away, in the south. Eating together, better food. Soon the waiter will put a bowl of tortellini in broth before me, and I will try, for you, not to burst into tears of disappointment. But I have not answered your question. It is very simple. A nurse named him. *Robin Hood*, you know?" He drew back an invisible arrow.

"Does he look like Douglas Fairbanks?"

He laughed. "He was the only American she could name. Fairbanks and Woodrow Wilson. But Wilson is not so popular now. I have to tell you, it is a pleasure to sit here like this, talking."

"For me as well."

"No. You are working. You don't need to say that. You see, it is difficult for me here in Bologna."

"Is it? I'd think you could leave tomorrow if you wanted. Someone with your reputation?"

"You're confusing me, I'm afraid. Our hospital has a famous reputation, and there *was* a famous doctor who ran this hospital, Dr. Consiglio. But he was replaced. And they chose a man from as far away as possible to replace him. If you want, I'll tell you why sometime. But that place was the Salento, and that man, as you see, was me."

He smiled, and indeed it was the smile of a man with too much responsibility. His eyes were bright, but the flesh around them had a bruised-fruit quality.

"You must forgive me. Sunday is my day to drink wine. I don't permit myself otherwise. In Leccese we'd say, *la Domenica sta bau fortissimo*. I go loud, or I go strong, something like this." He pounded the table, but meekly, and smiled sadly to himself.

The waiter put down our bowls of tortellini in clear shining broth. And huge pink slices of mortadella. I thought the food among the best I'd ever tasted. Bianchi waited patiently for me to finish.

"You're not too tired? I'll take you to my favorite place to drink," he said. "We can meet someone, if you want."

"Of course. Who?"

"Another journalist," he said. "I should have invited him to dinner, but, as you see, it is hard for me to eat this food even without an Austrian across the table."

I followed Bianchi through tunnels of sidewalk, past gated storefronts and tall doors with brass nameplates and buzzers. Lampposts breaking apart the darkness, corner by corner. Graffiti slashing down the stucco walls.

"Every street in the city center is arcaded," Bianchi explained. "Here, you could walk for an entire day without standing in the sun. A truly stupid idea."

Considering how far we'd traveled, considering how many cafés we'd passed with small tables outside, I was somewhat surprised when Bianchi ducked into a narrow storefront lit well enough to see brown grease stains on the walls and spiderwebs shattered in the pane above the door.

The mirror behind the bar was cracked, as was the glass in several shelves. In fact, there was still broken glass on the floor, and a tangle of splintered chairs pushed into one corner. Several of the remaining tables were taken by young men sitting alone, looking bitter and bored.

"Do you like it?" Bianchi asked.

"The décor isn't what I expected."

"Décor? Yes, funny. This was once a workers' club. Two months ago the *squadristi*—the Blackshirts, if you want—came to confront the men who gathered here. You understand, the Blackshirts came to intimidate their socialist enemies, but only a few of the men here were actually socialists. The others only liked to play cards. It did not matter. They were all *confronted*. Do you know what political confrontation today means, Tom? It means castor oil and cudgels to the little of the back. The broken chairs and glass were an afterthought."

"Who are these boys? What are they doing here?"

"They wait," he said, "for rapture."

"And us?"

"We wait for the Austrian. And for the man behind the bar to sing."

"I don't think I quite understand," I said.

"Some of the boys at the tables are communist lookouts. If the Blackshirts should return, it will not be so easy for them this time. I hope you don't mind that I've taken you to quite a dangerous place."

His eyes and voice suggested he wasn't serious, but I'd given up trying to tell. One of the boys did, in fact, seem to take note of us and left the café while Bianchi ordered drinks.

"In truth, all of Bologna is dangerous right now," he said. "One way or another I believe a revolution will begin here. What kind of revolution is the only question."

"What kind would you expect?"

"The problem is that the socialists can never agree on anything. But there is no ideology to Fascism, so it is easy to get people to agree. In that way, I must admit, it is a very modern political party. Anyway, we wait."

We didn't have to wait long. The Austrian came in as we finished our first round of drinks, apologizing for his lateness in perfect English. "It's a bit hard to know where you are on these streets, isn't it?"

"I told Tom," Bianchi said, "who would want to cover all of their sidewalks, to never see the sun?"

"Aside from Germans, you mean?" the Austrian said.

Bianchi laughed—impressed, I think—and introduced us.

I suppose my first impression of Paul was that he looked very German. I couldn't have said how exactly, but I remember thinking that faces like his broadcast a *terroir* in the way a good wine is supposed to. At the time, not such a strange thought, as many people believed that on certain hillsides, in certain valleys, the essential German, French, or Russian character grew like grapes. A war had been fought over those hillsides and valleys, after all. Of course, the awful consequences of such thinking were only too apparent in the next several years.

So Paul looked German. And he had a calm cheerfulness about him that is hard to fake. He said his name and we shook hands. He insisted on another round. He said that he had come from Vienna, that he wrote for a newspaper there; I didn't recognize the name.

"What interest do the Austrians have in our amnesiac?" Bianchi asked.

"Well, we did it to him, didn't we?"

In 1922 it was still all but impossible to have a third round of drinks without the war coming up. I bought us the third round and tried to answer their questions about Verdun but, as usual, found I couldn't say very much without portraying my experience as something that it wasn't.

"I was just an ambulance driver," I said finally.

"As was Douglas Foulbanks," Paul said.

"Fairbanks," Bianchi said.

"He's making a joke, I think," I said.

"Yes, isn't Foulbanks a better name for a man in his position?" Paul asked.

"Now I see," Bianchi said. "Yes, you're right." But he obviously didn't see the humor. It might have only been the drink. He hadn't needed the second round and certainly not the third.

"Was he an ambulance driver?" I asked.

Paul answered instead of Bianchi. "How many other Americans served in Italy? Not many, I don't believe."

"There *were* many Austrians, though, weren't there, Paul?" Bianchi asked.

Paul looked at Bianchi cautiously. "Are you asking if I served here? I did," he said. "I was almost everywhere."

"Galicia?" Bianchi asked.

"Yes."

"Serbia?"

"And Montenegro."

"Russia?"

"Yes."

"Then I must ask you a question," Bianchi said. "Where were the most beautiful women?"

We all laughed.

"If forced, I might choose Poland."

"Perhaps because they were the most frightened," I said. I was channeling Sarah, but they couldn't have known that, and the words sounded ridiculous, even alarming, as they left my mouth. Paul only smiled. He had a pleasant face, a resting expression that exuded well-being. People must either like him immediately or find him insufferable, I thought.

"I'm afraid I disagree," Paul said. "A happy woman is always more beautiful, at least to my eyes." He touched my shoulder as if to show there were no hard feelings.

"You ask at the right time. I only talk about the war on Sundays," Bianchi said.

In fact, neither Paul nor I had asked about the war. Obviously, it was only a matter of time before the doctor turned sour or sullen, and neither of us wanted to give him a push.

"On the subject of fear, everyone was frightened on the Isonzo River. My job was—I don't know how to say it—to un-frighten them. Is that how?"

"I don't think there is a word for that, exactly," I said. "Not in English."

"Whatever the name, it sounds like more ethical work than most did," Paul said.

"Yes, ethical work that I pay penance for now. Is there a word for that? There was a word for me. A name, if you want. They gave it to me in the field hospital in Caporetto. Caronte. That one I know in English: Charon. Do you know him?"

He pronounced it *Sharon*. I'd learned my Greek myths from Father Gaillard. The boatman on the River Styx was named Charon in French too.

"You couldn't have deserved that," I said.

"What did you actually do?" Paul asked quietly.

"Do you know how few psychiatrists we have in Italy? Not even two hundred. So you see, I was very important. I treated men who were compromised, suffering from hysteria and neurasthenia—shell shock—and got them back to the lines."

"How?"

"*Easily*. I was a wonderful hypnotist, but both of you could have done my job. Truly, you could have. A man who hasn't eaten or slept in three days, who has feared for his life for months, is very susceptible to suggestion."

"What did you suggest?"

"That fear is only a reflection of the less noble part of his soul, a weakness and an obscenity. These men, my god. Sometimes they absolutely refused to open their eyes no matter what was threatened. For me, it was twenty minutes only to cure them. Twenty minutes. But I had a record of twelve. Are you not impressed?"

Fortunately, before we could answer, the man behind the bar began to sing in a grumbling baritone. I didn't know enough about opera to have an opinion of his performance, but I suspected it was very bad. The voice had a strangled, sardonic quality, the runs sounding almost intentionally tuneless. He was short and practically hairless, with shattered-glass wrinkles around his eyes. As he sang he never stopped working—polishing the stemmed glasses with their gold rims, stacking white saucers on a high shelf.

"It's from *Falstaff*, I think," Paul said. "Though difficult to tell."

Bianchi shrugged. "Naturally. The great local nationalist. They say without Verdi there is no Mussolini. Perhaps you understand why the barman sings Verdi as he does."

"I might understand, but it's still criminal," Paul said.

"A fan of Italian opera?"

"Certainly. The Viennese invented Italian Opera."

"Yes. If only you'd been as generous with Trieste and Trentino, there would have been no war. Were you on the Isonzo, Paul?"

Paul nodded, but he must have sensed Bianchi was trying to bait him and wisely said no more. We listened to the singing, which seemed to grow only more sarcastically maudlin, more sour and grating. Something about a horse. Something about a river.

"Is there any use in feeling guilty now?" I asked Bianchi, a question I had asked myself often in the preceding months.

Bianchi smiled. "I'd like to say no, but, sadly, Tom, there is much use in guilt. If you want, I can say as both a psychiatrist and a Catholic: there is no civilization without it."

The barman finished the aria. We clapped and bravoed, but he never looked our way. Only three or four tables were occupied now; the young men sipped their drinks and stared off, just as they had all night.

"Do you think that boy will return?" Bianchi asked. "You remember, the one who left when we arrived? It's been too long."

The boy never did return, but later an older man with yellow skin appeared in the doorway of the café, and Bianchi got up to speak to him. They argued for what seemed a long time, leaving Paul and me to exchange glances, to raise eyebrows at one another, a bit too shy to speak without our chaperone.

Meanwhile, Bianchi and the man raised their voices, speaking in dialect. And though the other man's face was old and sickly, his shoulders were square and his knuckles were bloody. The longer I looked, the more the yellow of his skin—and the apparent wrinkles upon it—began to appear strangely uneven. The left side of his face seemed to have aged a decade slower than the right.

"I apologize," Bianchi said, when he finally returned to the table, "but we have been asked to leave."

"By whom?" Paul asked. "If you're in any trouble, certainly we can . . ."

"No trouble," Bianchi said. "No trouble. Just a matter between brothers."

As it happened, Paul's room was just above mine; we had the same view of a dark drugstore behind an iron grate, the same striped wallpaper, the same smoky blankets.

The wineglasses still bore the ten-lire tags from the shop where he'd bought them. It was warm enough to leave the windows open as we drank cheap Soave and talked the way strangers can when they're young and far from home. Paul lay on the bed, smoking; or paced, smoking. And I sat in the room's single chair, my wineglass on the windowsill, liquid shadows dripping down the walls.

His newspaper was a cultural weekly, not just edited but owned by his father. He had studied French painting—Bonnard in particular—prior to the war, a secret he'd protected with his life for four years.

"Now," he said, "may I ask about your roots?"

"You can certainly ask, but they've mostly been pulled up, so to speak."

"Perhaps that is a stroke of luck."

"Someone else told me that once," I said.

"Was he smart or stupid? I ask because I'm never sure where I fall."

"Very smart."

"That warms my heart. That's right, isn't it? The phrase?"

"That's perfect. He was a priest, actually."

"That chills my blood."

"What do you have against priests?"

He tried to explain the contradictory and destructive lessons of Viennese parochial education, but gave up because we were laughing so hard. He pointed to a scar on his cheek he'd received in a duel. At university, before the war. Over what? Over nothing. Dueling was illegal, but, due to a medieval privilege, the police had no jurisdiction over students in Vienna. Paul had leaned into the foil with his cheek, as was the custom. As was the custom in those days, he had worn a pair of gold-rimmed glasses without a prescription and ordered a beard tonic from an advertisement in the *Neue Freie Presse*. As was the custom, he was obsessed with looking older. "That's the mark of the end times, isn't it? When the young aspire to look old, instead of the other way around."

I smoked Paul's Gitanes, drinking the wine that much faster to wash away the taste. He produced a second bottle, and we talked politics with a moonlit intensity that often proves hilarious by daylight.

"Did you think it really was the end times?" I asked. "I mean, before 1914."

"Some did, certainly. When I was in gymnasium, I had a friend who was already at university, a friend of my older brother, actually. He could speak most of the languages in the empire, had read all the great Slovenian poets, could name every Turkish pasha going back five hundred years. He was so intelligent that—though I loved him—I was almost afraid at times. Do you know that feeling?"

No, I didn't know that feeling, just as I didn't know many of the feelings Paul described. We refilled the glasses with the yellow wine, swirled, and toasted with a cold click. No clock in the room, no light yet on the street. But his friend—he shot himself in the head one evening, leaving no note.

"I assume that's not something you ever considered?" Paul asked. "Suicide."

"I've been too busy trying to stay alive to think about it much. Have you?"

"My god, it's absurd to say yes, after everything I did to survive later. But at the time I trusted my friend's judgment completely. And he was far from alone. We had an epidemic, you know, quite egalitarian too: bankers, chimney sweeps, acrobats, even our crown prince. And I was sure, intellectually, that my friend had good reasons for what he did—he must have. But there were times when I simply loved being alive. At home with my parents and during the war too."

He looked down, embarrassed, but I wished I could have explained the affection I felt for him in that moment. I've since seen young actors return to the set with eyes red from highballs and Benzedrine, having spent the night talking themselves into an adamantine friendship. And the fact that I now see those mornings for what they are—the fact that I see the naïveté in those faces—only slightly diminishes the jealousy I feel at being too old for such things.

Santa Monica, 1950

The day after the composer's birthday party, I got off the phone with Max Steiner and listened to the entire Sunday broadcast of the New York Philharmonic. I couldn't have said what was played. I needed someone to talk to, but there was no one in particular I wanted to talk to. That's the best definition of loneliness I know. Work helps. The radio helps. Driving helps, but, when I looked outside, my car was not in the drive.

By midafternoon I'd stopped caring who I spoke to; all that mattered was finding someone who wanted to speak to me. But the phone stayed quiet, an austere black on the stand in the hall. Living alone, one encounters such flashes of non-existence, though they are mercifully rare. For me, they come on days like that one, when I feel regret. Days when I feel like being quiet and alone, but not *alone*. When effortlessness seems to matter a great deal. When the sight of a neighbor amid his dahlias would be a comfort.

And then Paul arrived near the golden hour, removing his tortoiseshell sunglasses when I answered the door.

"I meant to come earlier, so I could bring you something from the bakery, but I was ensconced in my book."

"Reading or writing?" I asked, trying to conceal my relief.

"I wouldn't keep you waiting just to read. This morning, I found I had a great many insights about Bierstadt's landscapes to put down." He smiled in that way of his—seemingly aware of the absurdity of his sincerity, completely sincere nonetheless. "It must be that seeing you again is good for my work. Or maybe it was the wine. Might I come in?"

"I'm sorry," I said, stepping out of the doorway. "It's only that you *haven't* kept me waiting. I wasn't even aware you knew my address."

"I assumed you'd want your car back."

I had to laugh. "You drove me home last night?"

"My god, man, were you that bad?"

"Well, it was quite an occasion, wasn't it?"

"Indeed. I was pleased to see you get on so well with Steiner. It isn't always easy with him."

"You didn't happen to hear us at the piano?"

"Of course. It's an event when he plays, you know. Even for that crowd. And you held up quite well. Singing, I mean."

Once he said it, the memory materialized, however dimly—the faces in the doorway of the tiny practice room; Steiner urging me to keep singing; I, stinking enough to oblige. Eventually, someone, thank god, had relieved me and begun a song in German with Steiner still at the piano. Had that been Paul?

"Was it anything you recognized? The song, that is?"

"Should I have?"

I wasn't sure whether I was relieved or disappointed. "Is my car still in your driveway then? Why don't we go?"

"Good. And if you'd like to have dinner, you'll be at my house anyway."

I couldn't help but smile. "I don't know I could survive another dinner like last night's."

"Don't worry. Tonight's birthday party is for a zookeeper. The crowd is much tamer."

"Tamer?"

"Yes, what do you think? Funny? I've been working on that one in my head all day."

CHAPTER EIGHT

Women in black shawls waited outside Ospedale San Lorenzo, holding bouquets. Around them, men in pale blue pajamas and straw slippers took the sun in lawn chairs, looking on shyly. Bianchi came out into the courtyard, clean-shaven in a white doctor's coat.

"Members of the international press," he said, smiling, "I welcome you."

He led us past a deserted nurses' station, and into the central hall with its rows of white beds, crisp as soldiers on parade. Meanwhile, patients wandered the ward in lazy shuffles. A typewriter was clicking somewhere. A man stood by a basin, slicking back his hair. We passed another man making the sign of the cross over his breakfast. We passed many men smoking and playing cards. There were white ceiling fans; and porticoes, dug into the walls, occupied by plaster busts; and fireplaces on either end of the room; and radiators under eruptions of sunlight from the big windows.

"Is that a bust of Bellini?" Paul asked.

"Yes, the hospital was a music school before the war. Someday it might be again. Or the country might abolish music entirely. No matter, it only makes sense to leave the busts and the pianos."

"Tuned?" Paul asked.

"The pianos? They are locked shut. Only *some* patients found the music therapeutic. As you see, I've chosen an open ward. More socialization, less faradization." Bianchi frowned when neither of us reacted to the flourish of language. "If you want, it is no secret that much of what is here is just for show."

"Showing what?" I asked.

"The progress of Italian medicine, naturally. Only it has been difficult to convince anyone to come to the show."

"Who are all the women in black?" I asked.

"Grieving mothers."

"But don't they know that this Fairbanks can't be their boy, that he isn't even Italian?"

"Naturally, I remind them of that fact each morning," Bianchi said.

Douglas Fairbanks did not resemble the actor. There was a trace of copper in his widow's peak, cut unflatteringly close. A dip in his right cheek tremored in code. One could still see the echo of a face that might have been striking if it were open in the typically American fashion. But everything about the man was closed. His shoulders pointed in, his cheeks caved in, his eyes were deeply set. He'd been given his own room—a former practice room, judging from the musical staff on the wall. There was no piano now, only a steel-framed bed and a night table covered in flowers. There were flowers on the sill of the single window, tinting the sun a sickening pink. Douglas Fairbanks watched the light on the wall.

"He is not always comfortable with visitors," Bianchi said. "Only the international press is allowed at the moment." He nodded at Paul and me.

"No one has claimed an identification?" I asked.

"No. As I say, many of the women you have seen already know that Mr. Fairbanks is not their son. They truly do know it, and still they come. They will have the chance to see for themselves, naturally, but I can only allow a few a week, so they must wait. That may sound cruel, but my responsibility is to Mr. Fairbanks, and the visits exhaust him. But I believe he feels well today. If you want, you may say something to him."

Paul said nothing. I introduced myself, and Fairbanks took a swing at me with his eyes.

"Try harder," Bianchi encouraged.

"I've come from Paris," I said to Fairbanks. "Have you been to Paris?"

Fairbanks said nothing. Paul said nothing. "Where *have* you been?" I asked. Fairbanks's eyes—the failing green of early autumn—stayed away.

Bianchi put a hand on my shoulder.

"I do not think to interrogate is the best way," he said. "May I?"

He scraped the chair toward the bed and sat down, smoothing the pleats of his pants. "I used to speak to him in Italian," he said. "He understands Italian, but he speaks English better."

"He does speak?" Paul asked. He had taken the seat next to mine, behind Bianchi. He squinted at Fairbanks.

"Naturally, he does," Bianchi said. "Mr. Combs is not from Paris. He's an American. Where in America, Tom?"

"Chicago."

"Do you know Chicago, Mr. Fairbanks? Can you picture this place?"

Fairbanks looked to the flowers in the window. He blinked at the wash of sunlight, as if he might find a shrunken city there. Perhaps in his riddled mind he could.

"You do not have to answer," Bianchi said to Fairbanks. Then he addressed us, "Naturally, he does not trust anything. He does not trust his own mind. He does not trust treatment. He knows not to trust because he knows he is beyond help. But perhaps he is *not* beyond help, and perhaps he trusts me a little now."

"What sort of treatment?" Paul asked.

"In Sienna, he was given, if I can use the term, the full arsenal. Faradization to every part of his body. Hot baths. Ice baths. Hot baths followed by ice baths in order to shock him back into consciousness. Exercise, both mild and vigorous. Extremely vigorous. Interrogation and intimidation. Purgatives, diuretics, and stomach pumping."

"Leeches?" I asked.

"You understand perfectly. I do not wish to insult my colleagues, but when he came here he looked very bad. You wouldn't think it to see him now." He must have seen the question in my face. "He looks much better, truly. If you want, you may write that my method is in part responsible."

And what was Bianchi's method exactly? He explained that there was, as yet, no term for it. Perhaps Paul and I could help him to invent one? What was the desired outcome? Naturally, for this man we referred to as Fairbanks to regain his personality, to return to the man he once was. And, in order for this to occur, Bianchi contended, he must be treated like that man. Here, Bianchi admitted, he made assumptions, but it was his belief that in his old life, Fairbanks was treated with dignity and respect.

"It sounds obvious, does it not?" he asked. Yet, he pointed out, even the famous Dr. Fenayrou of Rodez stripped his patient for examination before legions of strangers. He induced fever to occlude Mangin's resistance to treatment. "I refuse to use any of these methods. So perhaps this man's personality will be slow to return, but it will return. And he himself will be able to tell us who he is."

"You don't use therapy?" Paul asked.

"Naturally. But voluntary. Always voluntary."

"The diagnosis?"

"Like Mr. Mangin, Mr. Fairbanks is diagnosed with *dementia praecox*. He suffers from amnesia, severe disassociation, listlessness, what you might call paralytic melancholy."

"A fugue state?"

"Very nearly. He would starve to death if we let him, but, if asked, he will eat. If led, he will walk the grounds, and he will even seem to take some pleasure in the flowers and especially in the fountain. In certain conditions, he will speak."

"So you've said, doctor, but excuse me," Paul said. "I still haven't heard him say a word."

"No," Bianchi said. "Would you like to?"

He turned back to Fairbanks. "I will begin a process that will make you feel very relaxed, Mr. Fairbanks? Would that interest you, Mr. Fairbanks?"

Fairbanks's eyes stayed on the flowers. "If you want," he said quietly.

Bianchi unfolded a sheet of paper from the breast pocket of his coat and tacked it to the wall opposite the bed. The paper was blank except for a single blue dot, the size of an American penny.

"Please, the point, Mr. Fairbanks," Bianchi said. The man's eyes slid to it. "Can you see the point?" Bianchi's voice was almost narcotically kind. The light from the high window roared in. Fairbanks bridged his hand over his eyes.

"You are on stairs," Bianchi said. "The stairs lead into water. Please walk down the stairs into the water."

"I am," Fairbanks said.

"The water is unlike any you know. You can breathe and still feel the warmth of the sun, no matter how deep you go. Do you understand?"

"Yes," Fairbanks said. And I understood too. I thought of the newly literate mother from Jura who had come to Verdun with stories of magic boulders and mountain lakes.

"Let yourself sink into the water. Down. Now farther down. Now farther. Say my name if you can still hear my voice."

"Bianchi," Fairbanks said. His eyes were closed. The tremor was in his voice as well as on his cheek.

"Bravo. To begin, might you tell me about a time in your past when you were happy?"

Fairbanks said nothing. His face showed nothing, and I'm not sure I'd ever watched a man's face so intently. Bianchi's pen scratched in the silence.

"You must not worry, Mr. Fairbanks," he said. "I am not disappointed. Just tell me what you see now. What is before your eyes?"

"The lock is high up," Fairbanks said after a moment. "I have to reach with the key." Was his accent American? Perhaps, but the voice wavered and shook. The window light blasted across his mouth. He was missing most of his lower teeth.

"The lock to what?" Bianchi asked.

"The front door," he said.

"Why do you say the *front* door?"

"There's a back door too. I have to lock it too."

"Naturally, if you must," Bianchi said.

Outside the hospital room, nurses crossed in white flashes. The flowers smelled like a trap, honeyed bread in the heat. The living are not meant to be surrounded by so many flowers. Fairbanks locked the back door; he had to reach up for the lock again.

"Do you see anything else in the room?" Bianchi asked.

"There are jacks on the floor."

"A ball?"

"It rolled away. But I don't have time to find it."

"No? Why is that?"

"I need to lock the windows."

"If you want, please. Where are the windows?"

"Upstairs."

Fairbanks's voice warbled up the stairs, and I thought of a night during the war when I'd sat down beside a French girl at a bar. Everyone else had gone home, the waiters were stacking the striped wicker chairs, and I thought perhaps she'd stayed for a reason. But when I introduced myself she answered only by wetting the tip of her finger with her tongue. Then she circled the rim of her glass—the wine inside was so pale that perhaps it was only water—until the glass began to emit a warbling, shrill tone.

In Fairbanks's hospital room, that memory was suddenly so vivid I could smell the grease of the girl's lipstick, and I had to scribble in my notebook to return the feeling to my hands. Meanwhile, Fairbanks described the room he saw. Naked windows, closed but unlocked.

"What is outside the windows?" Bianchi asked.

"Night," he said.

He locked the windows one by one, five in all. It was difficult because he had to climb onto the sill to reach. Then he continued upstairs.

Bianchi's pen scratched, the dry sound of it more unnerving in its way than the image of the black windows in the empty house. Bianchi's face was unreadable. Paul had pushed his chair back into a corner, and he was blinking as if into the light. Three faces, and I didn't know what to make of a single one.

The tremor in Fairbanks's cheek traveled to the lines around his eyes, and across his forehead. His shaking voice was picking up speed, his breathing coming faster and heavier—I could almost hear his footsteps on the stairs, faster, heavier; I could almost hear those footsteps moving through the blank rooms, past blank doors.

I glanced once more at Paul. He was shaking his head, slashing his pen at his notebook.

"I have to climb onto the sill," Fairbanks said. "I lock the first window."

"How many windows this time?" Bianchi asked.

The patient's mouth spasmed, his shoulders collapsed. He made a terrible sound—part gasp, part shriek.

"What did you see?" Bianchi said, his voice not quite alarmed. "Something at the window. An explosion?"

Fairbanks was crying, strange sobs falling from his half-ruined mouth.

"No. No," he said. "A lion. A lion's face at the window."

I hadn't thought of the French girl with the wineglass in years. I was on a repair detail in her village near Reims for weeks afterward, and I thought I might see her again in the café, but I never did.

Once, after I had moved to Los Angeles, I saw a woman on Montana Boulevard dragging burned curtains across an intersection. Knowing full well how she might interpret my offer, I asked if she needed a ride. We drove to a professional cleaners that she thought—wrongly, I imagine—could help her. She offered polite responses to my observations about the weather.

"Obviously, I set them on fire," she said eventually. "But I didn't mean to. I only wanted to burn her letters, especially her stupid poems."

My car smelled of kerosene for days, but I never saw her again either.

On the afternoon that Fairbanks saw the lion at the window, Paul raced from the hospital to type and file his story. But I walked from Dr. Bianchi's office at a pace that seemed right—a slow pace—thinking of the lion's face; and the face of the woman in the bar; Bianchi's face, full of something resembling love as he calmed Fairbanks, as he congratulated him on a job well done.

Outside, the fountain burbled, and an issue of *Avanti* crackled in the breeze, and Sarah was standing in the courtyard. I saw her in three-quarter profile. I saw her wearing an appropriate black dress. I saw her raise her left hand, touch her ear. I saw her a moment before she saw me, and another moment passed before she recognized me, which gave me the chance to arrange my face into a look of surprise.

She looked the same as she had in Verdun, exactly the same, which, I suppose, did surprise me. I thought her hair might fall past her shoulders instead of just to her shoulders. I thought her eye shadow might be a tick more blue. I thought there would be some tiny change, visible only to me.

I crossed to her, passing the mothers and the mental patients. She looked at me just as she had when I'd last seen her. It seemed a long time ago, and yet, there it was: that same wooden expression, still but not serene; trapped.

"Don't explain why you're here," she said. "Not yet." She took my arm, and we walked into the old city.

We found a café near Piazza Maggiore: red brick, gray birds. She put her hat on an empty chair. We looked out at the square in the throes of midday desertion. The big doors of the cathedral swung shut. A fruit cart rolled away. A young girl crept after it, storing dropped grapes in the hem of her dress.

"I didn't think it was actually possible to be speechless," she said. "But truly, I'm finding words hard to come by."

"Why don't we try something simple? To talk about, I mean."

She took a breath. "This is a nice enough city. But it needs a river."

"Dr. Bianchi told me there were once canals from the Po, but they were built over. Apparently you can still see them in a few places."

"That might be something to do one day," she said. "If we're bored."

I studied her face, afraid I'd misunderstood. She sipped her coffee and looked at the birds. I could almost see her trying to believe in me. A very pleasant feeling, as it happens. "All right," she said. "Now I think it's safe to tell me what's become of you."

It was easy to tell her. In Paris, I had often imagined she would eventually ask such a question: my *quartier* was in the Marais, my office near the Palais-Royal. The city, though far bigger than Verdun, was still oriented on a river; there was still a right bank, still a left.

Most days, I told her, I'd eat lunch on a bench in a little courtyard off Rue Sainte-Anne. There, I'd always find cigar butts between the cobblestones. I always wondered who the man was, how he sat where I sat nearly every day without my ever seeing him, how city life meant sharing space with the unseen.

"What I like most about the story," she said, "is that it could have been a woman. In almost every other city in the world you'd assume it was a man, but not Paris."

"What was your brand?"

"I don't happen to smoke cigars," she said. "Did that miserable paper really send you here?"

"So you do know why."

"It took me a moment to put it together. You remember that I wrote you there."

"I haven't forgotten that. But I don't think it's so miserable. I suppose I shouldn't be surprised you know it."

"At one point I likely even knew the editor's name."

"Marcel certainly knows your name. I spoke of you often."

I signaled the waiter for the check with a swirling pantomime she laughed at and imitated. We drifted through the shuttered arcades near the square. Newsstands closed, butcher shops closed, fishmongers closed, the streets still a wet pink below the cleaning tables.

The group she had met in Trieste—the group she'd mentioned in her letter—had turned out to be something more than swindlers, but something less than the miracle workers for which she'd hoped. The records they'd found for a considerable sum were incomplete, and, though Lee's name had appeared on an intake list in the summer of 1918, the corresponding identification number didn't match.

Far more troubling was the fact that, for the first time, she found herself too exhausted to contemplate the possibilities. She'd been on the verge of leaving Italy many times. On the verge of returning to Paris. On the verge of returning to America. On the verge of missionary work in the South Seas. On the verge of giving up.

We seemed to be wandering aimlessly, though I already had a sense of the streets. To this day, there isn't a city I know that feels more desolate than Bologna when the shops are shuttered.

"My imagination," she said, "is destroying my life. I can imagine anything, and I can do nothing." Well, not quite nothing. She still followed all the papers and bulletins. She still wrote patient letters of inquiry to the few prisoners in the Austrian camp whose names she'd been able to learn. But was that pure inertia? Would she know Lee now to pass him on the street? Of course she would, but the very fact that she could ask the question terrified her.

"Then you heard the amnesiac here might be an American?" I asked it like a question, but how many times had I imagined her coming across the item in the bulletins, her face flushing with hope?

"I did. And I was excited. But only because—for a few days, anyway—there would be something I knew to be the right thing to do."

"How many days?" I asked.

"Well, I arrived this morning to find that he isn't even allowed visitors. The nurse I spoke to said it may be weeks before I can see him. But perhaps that's for the best. Fate or not-fate, as it were." She took my arm at the elbow with gloved fingers. "When I asked you before what's become of you, I thought you'd know what I meant. And perhaps you did, you just don't want to say. Did you fall in love?"

I thought of the Americans in the Chevalier Vert, Rose's long hair, the bright river at night, the darkness of narrow streets in the afternoon. The answer was: almost, but not quite.

I pointed up at the dark green shutters on the second floor of the hotel.

"This is my room," I said.

We kept the shutters closed. In the dim light she lay on her stomach and I watched her shoulder blades as she breathed.

"It's hard to believe," she said.

"I know," I said, but really everything that had occurred that day—finding her in the courtyard within the sound of rushing water; our walk through the empty city and the near wordless way we'd gone up to my room and undressed—was so like I had imagined it, as to take on a sheen of déjà vu. Getting what you want, however improbable, is almost never a surprise.

"What I'm surprised by is how I feel seeing you." She flipped over and sat up in bed. There was sweat on her forehead and around her mouth. I'd never been with her, or with any woman, in the daytime, and I wanted to open the shutter, to see what she looked like in natural light. Under the sheet I could see her legs crossed at the ankles. She placed a pillow in her lap, resting her elbows. "I'm going to embarrass myself, but what's the difference? I tried to convince myself not to come to Bologna at all. It's not possible—no, it's possible, but it's certainly not healthy—to keep hoping to find Lee like

I have. I know that. I *mean* to stop. I've meant to for a long time. But do you know what I felt when I recognized you? Joy. Honestly, joy. I came here looking for that feeling, and there it was in your face. Isn't that a surprise?"

The poorly lit room seemed unbalanced, asymmetrical. It felt as if the desk and the bed and the woman in it could all slide away.

"I should have gone with you to Udine, even if you didn't want me to," I said.

"Perhaps, but this is better. It's hard for people like us to talk seriously about how we feel, isn't it? Perhaps in order to do it properly we need to be somewhere unfamiliar, somewhere neutral."

"Are we there now?"

"I don't think so. Someplace neither of us has ever been."

"And change our names."

"Yes, that. I'd love an alias. I have one for you: Tom Morrow. How does that sound?"

"Tomorrow? We could make you Esther Day."

"At the hotel I'd have to be Esther Morrow."

"What hotel?"

She made a face and fell back on the pillow. Suddenly I was grateful the shades were closed, the murkiness protecting us from the other's eyes.

"It's a nice thing to think about anyway," I said. "Would you like to come to the hospital *tomorrow*?"

"You haven't been listening, Tom. Or perhaps you just don't believe me." She sounded almost angry. "I don't need to go to that hospital at all. Not anymore."

CHAPTER NINE

"When he arrived, Fairbanks saw only fire," Bianchi explained.

Paul and I dutifully scribbled in our notebooks as Bianchi roamed his office, banging open windows already warped in the morning's heat.

"And now, with your help, I suppose he sees ice too," Paul said.

He'd been that way all morning, impatient with my questions, dismissive of Bianchi's answers. It was as if there were somewhere else he'd rather be, and yet he also couldn't seem to stop talking, to stop arguing. A day before, it might have bothered me, but I felt, at best, half-present.

"I do not understand," Bianchi said mildly. "Again, please."

"I mean that one hears so many theories about war neurosis," Paul said. "Microscopic lesions in the brain. Unmetabolized adrenaline in the blood. They all begin to sound ridiculous, don't they?"

"And you are forgetting pure group suggestion." Bianchi, unfazed, returned to his desk, which was strewn with case histories detailing the madness of at least a hundred men.

Paul blotted his brow with a handkerchief. "And I suppose I can't help but mention Freud."

"That is stamped in your passport, I think." Bianchi laughed a little too loud. He switched on an asthmatic desk fan and pointed it in Paul's direction. "But certainly you do not believe sexual conflict is the only cause of neurosis. Could it not be true that the sexual instinct, if you want, is only a biological imperative?"

"Reproduction, you mean?"

"Naturally, and when the instinct is frustrated, the mind must cope, in dreams, violence, hysteria. If you want, the Viennese—I use them only as my example—have been more repressive of the instincts of women than men. This is why hysteria has been seen as a woman's disorder."

"What of Italian women?" I asked.

"An interesting case. In Italy, most women—especially in the south—do not have the freedom to be ill. But during the war they did not have husbands to care for and finally they could go out to the squares and cafés at night. The war was a great crime against the men, but the women, actually, did well. Maybe illness cannot be far behind."

"Are you teasing me?" Paul asked. Bianchi made an apologetic, almost ashamed, face. Still, Paul's ill temper didn't bother me. The heat didn't bother me. I'd left Sarah asleep at my hotel. Despite what she had said, I wasn't entirely sure if she would be there when I returned, or how to find her again if she wasn't.

"I only mean to say," Bianchi continued, "that the need to reproduce is descriptive of a more basic need: to live. If repression of the sexual instinct leads to hysteria, imagine what might happen when you are told that your duty is to lie in a trench under a barrage or advance into machine-gun fire."

"Or drive an ambulance through a barrage, I suppose?"

"Naturally. Men like Fairbanks were asked to repress the very desire to live. I myself helped them to do it. *This*, I think, is the true meaning of trauma."

"And you think someone like Fairbanks can be . . . I don't even know the word. Healed? Cured?" Paul asked.

Bianchi raised his eyebrows in sincere surprise. "Have we not witnessed trauma on a scale once thought impossible? Perhaps we must consider recovery on such a scale too."

I pictured Fairbanks sitting on his bed, hands under his chin, frozen and hollow. On the other hand, hadn't I led a baby into a tunnel of corpses? Somehow, hadn't I recovered? I imagined taking Fairbanks to Paris, helping him find his own hotel with bugs in the wallpaper, his own café with arsenic dye smeared on the bar. His own Rose. His own Sarah.

"In any case, it is everyone's right to believe or disbelieve." Bianchi shrugged. "Perhaps you can allow your readers to make up their own minds? How many readers do you have, may I ask?"

Though it was still early in the day, his pomaded black hair was already sliding out of place, and sweat blistered his nose. He gave a nervous laugh, as if there was some impression he feared he were failing to make. In fact, I'd begun to notice that his English—when he was on the subject of Fairbanks, anyway—seemed more fluid, more sophisticated, as if he'd written the words out beforehand. "One thousand readers? Five thousand? Ten thousand? I am only curious."

"I honestly don't know the number," I said. "And we've taken too much of your time, haven't we?" I meant it in the way it's usually meant: too much of *my* time had been taken.

"Just a minute, Tom," Paul said. "We were hearing about his dreams, and then I interrupted. The doctor might like to finish."

"If you want," Bianchi said, but cautiously now. "When we began, all he saw was fire. To say it another way, there was nothing within reach but faceless, inhuman torment."

"How can one confront fire and darkness?" Paul asked.

The fan continued to *chink*. Paul continued to blot his forehead.

"Naturally, you are right," Bianchi said. "A man can neither relate to nor influence a void. And for months a void was all Fairbanks would describe. But one day he found himself in a burning *room*. Then, slowly, the flames extinguished. And yesterday was a masterpiece."

"Of what exactly?"

"You must understand that the dream always ends with a return to terror. He reaches the last window to find the fire and darkness that was once his entire world. Then, later, he finds explosions at the windows—grenades, artillery. But, yesterday, the lion."

"The lion can be confronted," Paul said.

"Exactly that," Bianchi said.

"Has he always had to reach for the lock, to climb onto the windowsills?"

"No," Bianchi said. "And this is also encouraging."

"He's a child, isn't he?" I said. "The height of the windows, the toy in the corner, the lion. It's a child's terror, not a man's."

Bianchi nodded, almost proud. Paul leaned forward and fumbled with the fan until he found the switch. "Enough now," he said. "What can you tell me about *him*?"

Bianchi's face changed; all at once he was so alert as to seem almost clairvoyant. "I am telling you what I can tell you," he said. "But tell *me*, what is the matter, Paul?"

"What sort of uniform was he in when he arrived in Udine?"

"Rags, naturally."

"Can he drive?"

"An automobile? He can walk on his own only a little. You members of the international press ask very strange questions."

"How do you know he's American?"

Bianchi hesitated, twisted his lip in thought. "He dreams of America. The room is in America. Two or three times he has said that."

Quite unexpectedly, Paul began to laugh.

"The Italian amnesiac dreams of America," he said. "I'm sorry. It sounds like the title of a bad poem."

* * *

When I returned to the hotel I found my bag packed on the bed. Sarah sat at the window, smoking. She crushed her cigarette and put her arms around my neck.

"We'll take the overnight," she said. "I've spent the day planning it."

"To where?"

"La Morra. They grow grapes there, for wine."

"And?"

"And? I asked the agent where he would go—within limits, obviously. In fact, I thought the less we knew about the place the better? Because of what we said yesterday." Her eyes dimmed, and she took a step back. "I wasn't joking," she said, "if you were. If . . ."

"Not an if," I said. "Not a single if." I was pleasantly surprised that she was at all unsure I'd go.

"Good. But *if* you need to work . . ."

I could hold on to the story I'd just typed up until the following day, and then write something to file as soon as I returned, and Marcel wouldn't even know I'd left Bologna. I'd need Paul to file my story for me, however.

"I'll need to ask a favor of another reporter," I said.

"Do that," she said, "and, if you'd like, invite him to dinner to say thank you. If we eat with him tonight, we'll feel that much more alone when we leave. Don't you think?"

"Alone?" I asked.

"Alone together. But there isn't a word for that, is there?"

Paul dressed for dinner in an English tweed jacket. The temperature had dropped, and he'd accepted my invitation without asking any questions.

"Mrs. Hagen," he said, as we took our seats, "I acted like a fool today. Such a fool that I must apologize not only to Tom but to you as well."

"I accept your apology," she said, "and, in my experience, Tom's very forgiving."

"I am," I said. "You were harsh with Dr. Bianchi, though. Is there something he did?"

"Hardly. Purely my own frustration. I had to promise my editor quite a lot to come here. No one in Austria wants to read about the methods of an Italian psychologist. That sounds arrogant, perhaps, but we have little else to take pride in these days. My own methods were clumsy, I admit. Of course, he is the one to whom I must apologize."

"What did you say?" Sarah asked.

"I was rude. It seems one has to be careful in those places that you don't catch the madness."

"I disagree," she said. "The real danger is catching it at one of those rallies in the piazza. Did you know yesterday I heard a man say that the Soviet flag was the color of menstrual blood?"

Paul blushed, just as, I imagine, Sarah had hoped. I liked that she was testing him. I liked that side of her.

"The Fascists aren't courting the woman's vote, I suppose," he said.

"I also saw a boy's teeth knocked out for passing around pamphlets," Sarah said. "Tell me, whose vote *are* they courting?"

Da Poeti was an old restaurant, famous for its version of the meat sauce the city was known for—but it was early, and the dining room was only half-full, the front windows shaded, most of the candles yet to be lit. Every time the waiter left the kitchen, a welcome fringe of light brushed the table. While we waited for the food to arrive we tried to talk about pleasant things, but that never lasted. Paul's studies before the war. Bonnard. The Princesse de Polignac's salon. Paris.

"And what did you do there, in Paris, Mrs. Hagen?" Paul asked.

"After my husband left I worked for my aunt with the CFFD."

"Did you? The artists' charity?"

"Painters and musicians mostly. I'm not certain that they were the most deserving, but everyone said we were fighting to preserve our culture. Someone had to keep the painters drunk. My aunt's joke, not mine."

"Your aunt must be Maud Monroe?"

"You know her?" Sarah didn't seem the least surprised.

"I certainly admire her writing."

"She'd be pleased to know she's won the esteem of a real live Hussar. Quite impressive, isn't it?"

Paul laughed and blushed again. "Not at all. I spent most of the war requisitioning horses. I was bored and lonely far more often than I was in danger."

"How awful," Sarah teased. "How did you pass your time?"

"Of course I looked for love, Mrs. Hagen. It was very instructive for me."

"In what way?"

"In all ways."

The pasta arrived, white and red in the shadows. Did I feel a twinge of jealousy? No. Not then. In fact, it was a pleasure to listen to them talk, to see that Sarah and I liked the same people. And Paul's manner was simply too earnest to seem flirtatious.

"I didn't realize anyone could know all the ways," Sarah said. "You must at least tell us one of them."

"I could," he said, "but the minute I try to talk about love I'll use conventions that may cheapen and dilute it. That is the danger, isn't it?"

"I suppose so," Sarah said. "But we can stand a little risk."

"You'll find this to be the case too," he said, "when you try to tell the story of the three of us here in the future."

"And how do you know we'll want to tell this story?" she said, laughing.

"Tom will," he said, smiling at me, "because you are in it."

Sarah and I shared a glance, and shook our heads at his old-world manners.

But here is what he told us.

He saw footprints in midwinter, in a Silesian town called Radun near the Prussian border. It was a town of good horses and streets of frozen mud, smoke leaking from the doorways of chimneyless huts. In the single tavern a single game of *Taroki* had been played nightly between four brothers for thirty years.

Paul did not play *Taroki*, and, so far as he knew, was not related to any of the players, so after dinner there was nothing to do but walk. But he liked the blank snow, the strange things he noticed etched there. Once he'd seen hundreds of black birds—crows, he assumed—asleep on the ground, wings folded, pressed shoulder to shoulder as if for warmth.

And then he'd seen footprints beyond a broken fence that surrounded a white garden; the steps traced a pattern that gleamed in the moonlight. After studying the yard for some time, he saw that it wasn't just a pattern but a crudely drawn picture: to his eye, a vase of flowers. He tried to recall the last time he'd seen a real vase of flowers and couldn't.

Paul returned to the fence the next night to find that the vase had blown away in the wind. Strangely disappointed, he was just about to turn back toward his billet when a woman in a fur hood—a girl, really—stepped from the garden door and began to cross the snow.

"Hello, Lieutenant," she said in French. "I saw you through the window. I wondered how you liked our little town."

Paul said it was charming.

"Please," she said, "there's no need to be polite."

She explained that she had been home from boarding school in France when the war broke out; her parents felt it was too dangerous for her to return, and she had been shut up with her mother without anyone to talk to for more than a year. Her name was Ilona. She took down the hood to show her gleaming brown hair.

"What I really wondered," she said, "is why you paused at this house, of all places?"

"Were those your footsteps? Was it a vase of flowers you drew in the snow? Or was that my imagination?"

"Those were my footsteps," she said, softly, "but I was just dancing."

For ten nights they met that way, speaking of the friends she had left behind at school; her father, called away on business in Opava; her mother, who had become forgetful of late, confused.

"She *collects* things," Ilona explained. "We all do now, we must, but she collects things she shouldn't. Disgusting things—I can't even tell you. And last week she seemed to think I'd put some drug or poison in her milk. She didn't quite accuse me, but . . ."

"A doctor could help," Paul said.

"Yes, but medicine in this town is medieval. If I could somehow get her to Prague."

"Would she permit a military doctor? Would you?" Paul felt excited, almost elated, at the fairy-tale simplicity of the solution. "Once we've gathered the horses—a few days from now—they'll send an officer to check them."

"A horse doctor? Those we have."

"In normal life he's a medical doctor, a good one. I could ask him to look in on your mother."

She squeezed his hand; he could feel the strength in her fingers through his fur-lined gloves. She opened the gate and led him through the garden. He stepped in her footprints, trying not to leave a trail. Her mother was in the front parlor, lost in her needlework. It was safe enough, she said. And they sat, shivering together on a hard sofa in an unheated back room, breath puffing white as they talked, white as the words trickled away.

"My mother can't know we've already met," she said later, at the fence. "She'd tell my father. And if he knew . . ."

"What's he so afraid of?" Paul asked.

"Of exactly what has happened," she said, smiling. "We must find a way to make it seem as if you and your doctor friend have met us by chance. Can you come to Saturday tea at the hotel? It's practically the only time she leaves the house now, other than for mass. Introduce yourselves? Flatter her? I'll make sure you are both invited to the house." She kissed him on the cheek with freezing lips. "And perhaps then she will be well again, and perhaps after that . . ."

He walked home, imagining Ilona's face in daylight, imagining the words he'd use to charm her mother, imagining the words he'd use in the future to tell his own mother he was engaged to a Silesian girl. But the orders were waiting for him when he returned to his billet. He was expected to report in Lemberg—for god knew what reason, practically no reason at all, as it turned out—by eleven the following day. He'd already missed the night train and his only option was another that left at five in the morning. There was no way to tell her, no way even to send a note. There was no way to sleep or eat for days after. All he could do was imagine her eyes looking for his amid the crowd outside the hotel, distracting her mother, giving him time to find her. All he could do was imagine the moment she put up her hood, her slow walk home, and, later, the cruel image of him she would dance into the snow.

* * *

In Da Poeti the plates were cleared, the restaurant had filled, and we could see a family in the foyer that had likely been promised our table.

"Well," Paul said, "have I risked enough?"

"The story's compelling, but I don't know that I fully believe it," Sarah said.

"Too romantic, is it?" Paul asked.

"I'd say it feels a hundred years old."

"Perhaps," he said, "but you must remember that in Europe progress always comes slower in the east." We laughed at that. And drank and didn't worry that we'd overstayed our time at the table. In the end, I didn't care if anything he'd said was true or not, even though it felt imperfect in the perfect way that true stories often don't.

"You could look for her now, couldn't you?" I asked.

"Perhaps I could," Paul said, "but there are many wrongs one might want to set right, and, unfortunately, one must be very selective about which he chooses."

"That sounds rather ominous, Paul," Sarah said.

Paul smiled and began to laugh at himself. "It is ominous," he said, after a time. "Of course it is."

Santa Monica, 1950

Paul's address on Rockingham Drive was only a few streets from the first house I'd slept in when I arrived in California in 1927. I had been working as a bank teller in Chicago—my third job in as many years since returning to the United States—when I decided there would be no harm in writing a letter to my grandparents, my father's parents. For years I'd been curious as to what the response to such a letter might be, but I expected little—certainly not the first-class train ticket to Los Angeles folded in with their ecstatic reply.

Once I arrived, they bought me clothes and gifts, and presented me with my father's tattered boyhood copy of *Tom Brown's School Days*. Several times they apologized tearfully for the fact that it had taken us so long to meet, and, once, at the end of a long dinner drowned in better French wine than I'd ever had in France, they shyly told me they loved me.

They were kind, confused people who had clearly saved the sentimental phase of their lives for their twilight years. In short, they were the fulfillment of every child-orphan's dreams. But I was almost twenty-eight by then, and, no matter how kind they were, it was hard to forget that only my parents' deaths had washed the shame from my existence.

My grandfather, who went by Duke, had been an investor in a film company in Chicago that had followed the free light to Southern California. But by 1927 he was retired, and both he and my grandmother, who went by Tina, devoted themselves to what they called "the causes." They seemed thoroughly pleased to have an actual cause by blood relation. When I told them I'd done some work as a reporter, it was all but settled on the spot that they'd arrange a trial as a script and scenario writer. Was there a particular studio I liked?

Where does Douglas Fairbanks work? I asked.

In those first years, I arrived at my desk in the Writers' Building at Columbia by nine every morning; most of the other writers came in after ten, complaining. I tried not to make enemies. I tried to make sense of what people wanted in a picture.

Hollywood, then, as now, was in the pleasing business, and the great secret was that the dictators who ran the studios—Mayer, Zanuck, Jack Warner, and the rest—were slaves to the whims of preview audiences in places like Santa Ana, to people who came straight from the laundries or machine shops, exhausted but emboldened by the fact that they had a *say*.

And what did they say? What did they want to see magnified in light and nitrate? Strangely enough: anguish. But anguish disguised by humor or brawn, by wit or wisdom. By guns and ships and speeches and speed. By song and dance too, but all the better if the disguise was a bit more fragile. Naturally, anguish is best disguised by beauty—in faces and bodies, above all else. But beauty that is purely happy will never play in Santa Ana. Many people still don't realize that.

Once one knows the formula it's not difficult to follow, and I have earned a comfortable living doing so. Only, somewhere along the way, I ran out of ambition. Perhaps the copious sunlight bleached it out of me. I don't know exactly, but I never made any secret of this—least of all to Faye when we married. Nevertheless, ambition was one of the many things we fought about. She was a writer too.

She started out as a script girl and, as a woman, had a far harder time of it than I did—I realize that, of course. She never felt that ambition was a luxury.

A number of ugly things occurred before it was clear that it was better for us to part, but the decision, once it came, was surprisingly easy. It wasn't that I didn't care for her—quite the contrary. It's just that the sentimental phase of my life came early rather than late.

It was too cool to eat outside that night, so Paul and I took our dinner of cold chicken on trays in his study.

"With some friends you don't want to stand on ceremony," he said. "This is how I usually eat when I'm alone."

"How often is that?" I asked.

"More often now that my children are away."

I don't know why it surprised me that he had children. Most people do, after all. "I didn't realize. Did you mention them before?"

"Haven't I? Usually I can't stop talking about them. Lilly is in her third year at Berkeley, and Stephen just started boarding school. My wife has strange New England notions about that sort of thing. I insisted that he at least stay in California. Thatcher. Not far." But the expression on his face suggested that the school felt very far indeed.

"He's what then, fourteen?"

"Yes. An age when you might want—you might not want, but you might need—your father. Isn't it?"

"I'm sure it is, but I'm probably the last person to ask."

"Did you and your wife ever consider it, children?"

I shook my head. Part of the reason Faye and I never had children was that I feared the responsibility—not of caring for a child, exactly, but of curating a childhood. I felt I had no idea how to do it, and, as it turned out, that was one of the few questions on which we agreed.

"I might as well tell you, Paul, that I'm separated from my wife," I said.

He nodded sadly and pushed away his plate. "I was beginning to guess that might be the case," he said. "Would you care to tell me about it?"

I told him. About our public arguments, our private infidelities. I explained how odd it had been to *like* someone so well, even at the end, to be charmed still by the traces of Texas in her accent, the outraged face she made at the price of bananas, the religious discipline with which she approached her writing. I explained that, unfortunately, fondness wasn't enough, that what ultimately did us in was our inability to comfort each other. I explained that we were both surprised to learn just how much comforting the other needed.

"But enough of that," I said. "I'm sure you've been wiser in love than I have. When does your wife return? You met her in Italy, I heard?"

"I did," he said. Was there something to detect in how his jaw tightened as he said this? "Did Steiner tell you? I did, indeed."

I tried to make my voice sound light. "Anyone I know?"

CHAPTER TEN

In La Morra the air was thick with insects and the particular green light of valleys. Mr. and Mrs. Tom Morrow stayed in a family-run hotel without hot water, but in the evenings the family—the Donatis—cooked bright yellow pasta they called *tajarin*, or simmered risotto in the local wine.

In the afternoons Mr. and Mrs. Morrow sat with the truffle dogs on the terrace above the vineyards. Across the valley they could see the other hill towns—Barolo, Cherasco, Verduno—in the greenish haze. They could see Nebbiolo grapes planted in long lines on the hillsides, little roads penciled between the square fields. The dogs followed at a respectful distance everywhere they went.

The Donatis had their own vineyard at the foot of the property, the vines as old as Italy. They had their own patch of forest where once they had found a white truffle the size of a man's head. The family home had stood for more than four hundred years. Turning the old house to an inn must have been quite a humiliation, but they never let it show.

Mrs. Morrow spoke to them in Italian, and Mr. Morrow chipped in when he could. *Questo è interessante, questo è terribile*, he said when the family matriarch, Marisa, explained that the grapes were of such value it had once been a crime to cut them down, punishable by amputation or death. She explained that, as children, they were forbidden even to go into the vineyards.

"Did you have a forbidden place when you were a child?" Mrs. Morrow asked Mr. Morrow later that evening.

She meant some place rife with both terror and possibility, but the truth was that most places had been forbidden to him: stores, restaurants, the lobbies of the buildings downtown. And of course the place he most wanted to go: the flower shop where his mother worked. He didn't tell Mrs. Morrow any of this because he was embarrassed. He wondered which questions she answered with half-truths.

He had feared it would feel different to take her hand, to steal a kiss, to make love when it was no longer forbidden. But it didn't feel different, at least for him. Then again, they were only pretending it wasn't forbidden, weren't they? He said this to her one night, her hair sticking to his cheek.

"Perhaps we were only pretending it *was* forbidden," she said.

They learned that they found some of the same things funny. She told him about a trip she'd taken to Sicily with her aunt, a pilgrimage to a Greek amphitheater where plays by Aeschylus had premiered more than two thousand years before. In Siracusa, there was a cathedral built on the remains of the old temple to Athena, Doric columns still visible in the Christian marble. Maud sat in the café on the other side of the square and wept.

"When I asked her what was wrong she said that she was 'just so moved by civilization.'"

Mr. and Mrs. Morrow laughed on the terrace.

One of the truffle dogs was named Victor Emmanuel. Without quite meaning to—the wine came in big clay carafes, so there was no way to know how much they'd drunk—Mr. Morrow began to speak for the dog. "Would you mind, Mrs. Morrow, sneaking me a truffle?"

"It seems only fair," Mrs. Morrow said. "Where did you learn such good English?"

They joked about stealing the dog, taking him with them when they left. In that way they began to talk about the future.

She wondered if he wanted to return to Chicago. He said that someday he'd like to see the headstone inscribed with his mother's name in the cemetery on Milwaukee Avenue. But, otherwise, as far as he was concerned, there was no more Chicago.

Did she want to go back to Boston? No. Though Boston—Wellesley—was very much still there. She could feel it, feel the old version of herself shut up in her room. What would they do?

He said he'd learned that he could be happy doing almost anything.

"I'm not sure I believe that," she said. "Maybe you could once, but is that still true?"

"No," he said, thinking about it. "In fact, it isn't true at all anymore."

He had another week left in Bologna. Should they look further ahead than that? Let's try, she said. One evening, when the sun was yellow and low, she turned to him on the terrace and closed her eyes. In this light, she said, I can almost see you through my eyelids.

Bologna Centrale again. Sarah and I walked arm in arm through the overflowing arcades. I carried my typewriter, having just written a profile of Bianchi that I would need to send on to Marcel that afternoon. She hadn't slept well on the train, and we'd planned to go to her hotel near the piazza—a far nicer room than mine, she assured me—and lie down.

"I'm not a person who naps in hotel rooms in the middle of the day," I said.

"Yes, well, no one is who they used to be," she said.

But the hotel and the hospital were in opposite directions, and I hoped to check some of the terms with Bianchi before I filed the story. I could picture Marcel in the *La Voix* office, laughing at my misspelling of *dementia praecox*, shaking his head, calling me back to Paris.

"I won't be long. I'll meet you."

"How many hours straight have we spent together, do you think?" she asked. "Let's not ruin it yet."

Perhaps I believed she was too tired to mean anything other than exactly what she said. Certainly I believed she was too happy.

"I won't be long."

"You already said that." She looked at me, her smile only just slipping. "And I already said that the hospital doesn't matter to me. I'd just like to stay with you now."

We passed a cart heavy with green tomatoes, purple lettuce, and white radishes. I lagged a few steps behind.

"Keep up. I don't know where I'm going," she said. "I might lead us into the river."

"But there is no river," I said.

It was early enough that many of the patients at San Lorenzo were still in bed, in various states of undress. One man was stripping his sheets with rubber gloves. Others lay with pillows over their heads to block the squeaking of nurses' trolleys, or the light from the big windows. A strange sight, but certainly there had been times when I couldn't tell day from night myself. We arrived at Bianchi's office to find the door locked.

I pecked her cheek. There was a black padded bench—a piano bench—in the hall.

"Can I leave you here while I look for him?" I asked. Trusting her? Testing her?

I found Bianchi in another office, deep in conversation with a much older doctor with enormous eyes.

"Sit down, sit down, Tom," Bianchi said. "Dr. Boccioni would like you to tell him how the Italians are getting on in America. In New York City, for example, what is life like? He has a nephew who wants to immigrate, but he doesn't trust what he hears. I will translate."

Boccioni looked surprised, but with eyes like his he probably always did.

"I don't know much about New York City," I said.

"Then tell us about Chicago. He won't know the difference," Bianchi said.

The truth was, I never fully believed in Lee Hagen. I knew abstractly that he existed, but I was never jealous of him. I continue to wonder how this was possible, exactly.

Once, when Father Perrin and I had stayed up late in his office, when we had drunk too much wine and talked for too many hours for the question to feel offensive, I asked him how he still managed to believe in God. The day had been particularly upsetting. A couple from Nîmes had come to pay their respects to a dead son and to inquire about a missing one. During the course of the conversation they told us that two more sons had survived the war, but one had come home blind and the other deaf.

I often wondered what exactly Father Perrin did believe in. He quoted Charles Darwin as often as Paul of Tarsus. He once told me that if I wanted to see the proof of the devil on earth it was in the fact that the two ideologies that dared to help the poor—Catholicism and Marxism—should find themselves opposed in so many other ways.

Father Perrin drained his glass and plucked his mustache sardonically, like a movie villain.

"I don't believe in God anymore," he said. "Not in the way you mean, if I understand it. That is: I don't *think* He exists. How could I?" And yet, he continued, when he prayed, when he said mass, when he dreamed, he still did believe, and, above all, he still did love. "And I must tell you, Tom, for the first time in my life, truly, I don't find myself in despair."

If Father Perrin had given up on God in his rational mind, but still felt him in his stomach, my belief in Lee Hagen followed the opposite pattern. As did my relationship with despair.

It feels almost needless to say that when Bianchi and I returned to the hall outside his office, my typewriter had been orphaned on the bench. He raised his eyebrows and unlocked the door. I hadn't told him any of the lies I had considered—that Sarah was my fiancée, or my sister. I'd only said: friend.

"Your friend should not be walking around alone." Bianchi looked at me with more disapproval than I'd thought his face could muster. "These men live here. And to tell the truth, it may not be completely safe for her."

I was about to apologize when I heard a woman's voice. She was crying. I shot from the chair, afraid that one of the patients had confused her for someone else—touched her, frightened her. And I saw that panic flash across Bianchi's face too. I followed him down the hall.

We found ourselves in a familiar room, Fairbanks sitting in his familiar position on the bed, cheek agitated by its familiar tremor. There was a woman sitting in the chair beside him. She had black hair just to her shoulders. Pale skin and blue eyes, crying—I could see now—tears of joy.

Countless pages have been written on the varieties of melancholy, but precious few on the varieties of happiness; most people, I think, simply want to leave the happy alone. And when we don't leave them alone we talk down to them. There's something stupid-seeming in happiness. It's false most of the time, and, even when it is sincere, we think of it as bereft of the complexities of sorrow. But in her face I saw an expression as concentrated as sun off a mirror. It took even Bianchi a moment to find his voice.

Should the parting of lovers be shot from below to maximize, or from above to diminish? Through the window to offer distance, or close-up to offer intimacy? No one ever thinks to ask a writer's opinion, but, obviously, the camera should go in the veins.

The story takes place in the body. Happiness flashes across the brain. Sorrow ripples through the arteries. Joy and fulfillment are real, but they're quiet and they're slow. They drip like relief from an IV. And the devastation, when it comes, is usually quiet and slow too. Because the real story is not one of dramatic instants, but of the gradual reversal of expectations over many days in the dark when hope is slowly abridged. As often as life is difficult, it is just as rarely sudden.

Later, I told myself I was a fool to be surprised. But, in the moment, I felt the sense of sublime shock that one turns to great forces of nature to explain—avalanches, storms, and the like.

I kept thinking: it's not real yet, not until someone else speaks. If we walked from the room we would erase the scene inside it. Why not just admit that at one of the critical moments of my life I reasoned like a baby playing peek-a-boo? Why not admit that for a moment I actually believed—and I believed this more strongly than I ever believed in Lee Hagen—that if Bianchi smiled kindly, if he laughed and sat down beside her and took her hand and said, Signora, that can't possibly be, it would make a difference.

Bianchi caught my eye, curled the corner of his mouth in a question mark. But what choice did he have?

"If he is your husband, tell me who *you* are, please," he said. I could hear only the blood in my ears. I don't know how she answered the question. There was paint peeling on the ceiling. An empty portico, wanting its composer's plaster head.

"Tom," she said.

"What?"

"Tom. Didn't *you* recognize him?"

In the late afternoon, Santo Stefano was empty and damp, the chapels lined with dark paintings of grime-soaked angels, a dented brass altar plate left as a decoy to thieves.

I wandered into the deserted cloister, ringed with pencil-thin arches of red marble. I envied the monks this space, so perfectly proportioned. I envied that, for them, there was nothing to see; this was simply the place to walk on nice evenings, to think on awful evenings.

In a square off Via Maggiore I watched five boys play *Terremoto.* The game worked like this: The boys pantomimed baking bread, sweeping out storefronts, threshing wheat. Then one boy yelled, *Terremoto!* They pretended the earth was shaking—bending their legs to keep their balance, twisting their faces in terror. Eventually, the four larger boys collapsed onto the smallest and lay there, stone-still, as he tried to dig himself out.

On Via Ugo Bassi I found two women in tears in front of a shop window. The bridal shop. All the white dresses had been dyed Marxist red.

* * *

I crept into a *vinteria* near my hotel. Paul was at a table reading a newspaper, the only other patron. As I waited for my glass of wine from a boy no older than fifteen, I watched Paul snap the pages, section by section. No one ever taught me to read a newspaper like that, I thought. But when he lowered the paper his eyes were bloodshot. The ashtray was full of mangled butts.

"You don't look well," I said.

"Oh, I never look well," he said. "I am a bit surprised at how *you* look. How was your trip?"

"The trip was wonderful. I suppose I can at least say that."

"What's wrong?"

Sarah believes she found her missing husband in the hospital this afternoon. You see, Paul, the language of suffering is seldom literal.

"I drank too much wine, I think. By the way, I brought you some."

The shelves were crowded with hundreds of bottles; some looked a hundred years old. The tables were a clean, white marble, and behind the bar the boy shaved ham with a sharp knife.

Sometime later—it was true dark and I'd finished my dispatch to Marcel—there was a knock on my door. The bed was unmade, I hadn't put on a clean shirt or so much as looked at a mirror. I hadn't at all decided what to say to her—still, it was no relief to open the door to Dr. Bianchi. I pushed open the window, all too aware that despair has its own smell.

"I now understand what happened today," he said. "You should not be embarrassed."

"What should I be?"

"You should have a drink," he said, pulling a bottle from his doctor's bag.

"I've already had a drink."

He smiled. "I don't permit myself any day but Sunday. I'm making an exception for you out of friendship. And perhaps you are not the only one who has problems."

He poured the Fernet into the dirty wineglasses, and sat in the chair by the window. In the single lamp's yellow light he looked quite unwell. God knows what I looked like.

"Did you recognize Fairbanks?" he asked.

It would have been easy enough to tell him that I couldn't possibly have recognized Lee Hagen, that I'd never seen him in my life—not even a picture. That I'd lied to Sarah from the beginning. Bianchi would have understood, in his way. But the truth—that version of the truth—no longer seemed to apply. It may be best to say this: I knew the story I'd told Sarah was a lie, but I no longer felt it as such. I only felt my hold on her slipping—palms, to fingertips, to nails.

"No," I said. "I didn't at all. She's wrong."

"You are certain?"

"Your friendship comes in a very strange form," I said. "I already told you I didn't."

"I know," he said. "I needed to ask. Now, what do you need to ask me?"

"What has she said?"

"She wondered where you went."

"I'm sure she understood."

"What else?"

He poured more Fernet. I wished I could make the ceiling, the whole world swirl, the way I did the glass.

"Is it possible?" I asked.

"We both know there are many false identifications."

"I mean is it *possible*? Do you understand?"

He sipped the drink. "Perhaps I say it is possible only because I would like to believe it."

"Out of friendship again?"

"I must admit, I find her perseverance moving."

"What perseverance? She said she loved me this morning. *This* morning." I was speaking much louder than was at all dignified, but I'd left dignity behind the minute my lips had touched hers a year before. Love brings wonderful things, but seldom dignity.

He smiled again—a tired smile he'd probably practiced, a smile meant to express sympathy without revealing what he actually thought. Whatever the truth, couldn't I understand his sympathy for her, hadn't I felt some version of it? And didn't he likely have somewhere to be, someone to be with, aside from me? I decided it might be more pleasant to feel bad for him instead of myself for a few minutes.

"Are you worried about your brother tonight?"

"Every night."

"But particularly tonight? Is he in danger?"

"Yes. I fear for his life. I would like to convince him to leave the country, but how can I? I have never left the country myself."

"Perhaps there is something I can do to help," I said. There was nothing I could do to help that I knew of, just words. "Does he speak any French?"

Bianchi laughed loudly. "He hardly speaks Italian. He is very intelligent, but not a man of letters, so to speak. If I am to convince him to leave I must find a new life for us in some other country. He's a true believer, if you want. I must find something else for him to believe in to save his life, I think. He's only eighteen, did you realize?"

"I wouldn't have guessed that."

"Because of the iodine he applies. Someone told him the Bolsheviks used it as a disguise."

"You've never said—do you share his politics?"

"I can't say yes, exactly. Perhaps I've studied the psyche too long, but I have no confidence that man will ever do the right thing, no matter the belief. What's the use of a political party?"

"If that's the case, what's the use of anything?"

"A question worth asking. You look tired," he said. "Have you slept?"

"I can't even imagine sleeping."

"Lie down at least." He walked around the room, tidying up. "It's a cruel situation. If you want, I could help you. I promised to tell you how I came to this hospital, didn't I? You may find it instructive. Amusing, at least."

"Tell me anything. As long as you refill the glasses."

The patient's name was Giuseppe Anglani, and, like Bianchi, he came from the south. From Calabria or Basilicata, no one quite knew. He was in the Thirty-Fourth Infantry or the Twenty-Third. No one quite knew. He'd been a field hand or a fisherman. No one quite knew, but it *was* known that he could neither read nor write. He survived the third battle of the Isonzo without much distinction; then the fifth and the sixth; then in 1917 he appeared at the flap of a field hospital near Tarcento with a blistering fever.

"You must be tired," Bianchi said to me. "Lie back on the bed. I don't mind." There was warmth in his voice like light through a shade.

Anglani's ambulance made many stops in Vicenza. He was the last man in the back; when they finally dropped him off, they lay the stretcher on the floor of a black room. There, he waited for a nurse to assign him a bed, but no nurse ever came, and when a slab of light slid under the door—daylight—he was able to make out the blue faces of the corpses stacked around him like firewood.

"I nearly put living men among the dead myself," I said. "Pure exhaustion made it hard to tell."

"Nobody slept," Bianchi said. "For five years nobody in Europe slept. The consequences are obvious. How do you feel now, tired?"

By the time Anglani was brought up to the ward his fever had reached nearly 40 degrees. For the second time in as many nights he was left to die, and for the second time in as many mornings he woke up alive. The doctors found him sitting up in bed, his skin cool to the touch, counting quietly on his fingers.

What are you counting, they asked.

All the men who have died, he answered.

That's nothing to think about now. How do you feel?

Better, he answered, but afraid.

The worst is over, they said.

I'm afraid, he said, because it is my responsibility to stop the war. I'm afraid I might fail.

"That's quite an idea," I said. "What could he possibly do?"

"Nothing but get himself shot. Which is why the doctor in Vicenza, Dr. Ursi, took pity and sent him to the mental hospital in Bologna, to the famous doctor there, Consiglio."

"Your predecessor."

"Yes. How do you feel? The story might be better without the lamplight. Do you mind if I shut it?"

I was too tired to object. The walls of the room rose up in green blurs.

"Was he a friend of yours?"

"Consiglio? We never met in person, but under no circumstances would we have been friends. When I arrived I had years of his notes to read. He treated illness like a priest would treat a devil. Often, his only recommendation for treatment was a return to the most dangerous parts of the front. He called this approach, in English, something like 'a fatally beneficial solution.'"

His prescription for Anglani, however, was faradization. Three sessions a day: electrodes to Anglani's throat in the morning, his groin in the afternoon, and his temples before dinner. It was all in Consiglio's notes.

Question: Do you plan to return to the front and fight for the redemption of Trieste and Trentino, for the unity of Italian peoples in Europe?

Answer: No, I do not. I plan to stop the war in any way I can, save further violence.

Somehow, despite the thousands of volts he faced day in and day out, despite the welts from the electrodes and the infection in his tongue where he had bitten it, Anglani stayed both lucid and resolute.

Quite the feat, Bianchi explained. A body can be trained to withstand such therapy, and a mind can be trained as well, but each course of training takes its own lifetime. The body will often let down the most resolute mind, and vice versa. After a month, Consiglio was forced to concede. He abandoned the electrodes, and cordially invited Anglani into his office.

"For hypnotism?" I asked.

"Doubtful. Talking, in Consiglio's opinion, was for Jews, not Italians. To be honest, I do not know what they did in that office. But it seems that the faradization must have been effective in some way, because, shortly after Consiglio conceded, the miracles began."

"Miracles? Please, I've had enough of those."

It is all in the notes, Bianchi said. There was a man in the next bed who felt lice crawling through his hair and over his skin. He could only sleep for thirty minutes at a time. He would snap awake and scratch, picking the invisible nits from the hair on his arms and at his groin.

"One day," Bianchi said, "Anglani said to him—and there were many witnesses—'Why don't you stop scratching, friend? I've combed all the lice away.' And immediately the man *did* stop scratching. He slept for a full day, and when he awoke he went for a peaceful walk in the courtyard."

The bed seemed to liquefy below me.

The notes reported that even Anglani was surprised at what he'd done. He spent the evenings by the fountain with his face in his hands, hiding tears. But a week later a patient who had not spoken in a year began to sing passages from *La Traviata*. A patient who had been absolutely terrified of the moon asked for a telescope. Another patient who had arrived at the hospital with every strand of his hair standing on end was found with his head in Anglani's lap, brush in hand.

Are you *him*, the other patients began to ask.

"Are you who?" I asked.

"You know. *Gesu*. How do you feel, Tom? Relaxed? You can close your eyes if you want." I did close my eyes, and felt Bianchi lift the glass from my chest. I heard him pacing as he spoke, the floor creaking, almost a music.

Are you Jesus? He never claimed to be. Nevertheless, the patients asked for blessings, for relics. Then the orderlies asked, then the nurses. They stole clippings of his hair, his nails. And one day Dr. Consiglio was found eating from Anglani's bowl and ripping pieces from his sheets.

I tried to raise my head. I found I could no longer move.

"He believed?"

"You must understand that, until recently, the most hard-hearted Italians were also the most devout Catholics. Consiglio was so convinced that he wrote to the military board suggesting he had stumbled upon a man who would change the course of the war. He suggested they see for themselves the incredible things of which this man was capable."

"What did they see?" It took most of my strength to ask the question.

"Naturally, they saw nothing. They transferred or fired the nurses, the doctors, even the kitchen maids. They transferred Consiglio to a tiny hospital in Sardinia and replaced him with a man from the south who could not have been more of a stranger to Bologna, to the patients."

"And Anglani?"

"By the time I arrived the armistice had been signed. And I was told that I could do with him what I wanted. Naturally, I had already heard all about him. But he was not at all what I expected. I asked him: Did you really think you could stop the war? Of course not, he replied, but what was the harm in trying? What was the harm in telling his suffering bedmate he was clean? Nothing, I thought.

"And I asked him: What of the claims that you are *Gesu*? 'Oh, not you too,' he said. I ordered his release. To me, he simply seemed like a man who had a small compulsion to do good in the world, nothing more. The next month he died in a fire in a brothel outside Naples."

"That isn't very cheerful." I heard my voice, but was not conscious of deciding to speak. My eyes felt too sticky to open.

"It is a very sad story, in fact." Bianchi spoke from far away—perhaps the door, perhaps the hallway. "But I only promised it might be instructive."

"And what does it instruct?"

"He deserted. This is how he got to the field hospital in the first place. He walked right off the mountain. And I asked him, how did you manage to survive? If you were thinking like a rational man who wants to live, why would you do such a thing? He was delighted by my question. He said that he had come to a conclusion during the sixth battle of the Isonzo. His battalion had been ordered to advance up the side of a mountain, into a slaughter so pointless and thorough that eventually even the Austrian machine gunners began to shout from their trenches that they'd killed enough men already, begging the Italians to retreat. The only way to survive under such circumstances, to find peace of any kind, Anglani realized, was to give oneself fully over to the irrational, even the impossible."

"Everyone says that."

"Yes, but how many of us can actually do it?"

The following morning I left early enough to see the fishmonger on Via Cartoleria pulling up the iron grate of his storefront. He spun at my footsteps, a clutch of eels hanging from his fist.

I'd slept so well that it was almost possible to imagine the day before had not happened. But then the image—the tremor in his face, the beaming look on hers—would return, relentless. I'd never seen that face on her, so I knew I could not have made it up. All the same, I decided to go to her. It was simple, in the end. I had one choice: whether or not to be a coward. And I could always be a coward later.

I met her at the restaurant in her hotel, just as I had in Verdun. Polished marble pillars; stained glass and frescoed ceilings. A love affair so dependent on hotels is probably not meant to last. Still, my chest fluttered at the sight of a place set for me at her table.

"I was happy to get your note," she said.

"I should have waited yesterday."

"No, you shouldn't have."

"I see."

"I mean that anyone would have left. I hope it's all right that I ordered for you."

We ate pastries. Drank off-white foam from white cups. It took a long time before she pushed away her plate.

"I keep wanting to say, 'Let me explain,' but there is nothing to explain, is there?"

"I understand that."

"And if I apologized that would only demean things between us."

"I understand that too."

"But there is one thing I do want to say: I imagined yesterday so many times. And of course I thought I'd feel unconditional happiness if I ever found him. But I didn't. I think, perhaps, that's the price I have to pay to get him back. You are the price, and it is a great price. Truly."

Her face was absolutely open, her voice absolutely sincere. She met and held my eyes. But I'd seen her face the day before also, and I knew she was lying.

"Also, I wanted to tell you that I would have gone to the hospital to see him eventually. Even if it hadn't been yesterday with you. I know I said I wouldn't, but I would have. I assume you already know that too."

The thought hadn't actually occurred to me, but, yes, I did know it.

"It's truly him?" I asked.

"Yes," she said. "It's truly him. It's him."

I tried to think, tried to come up with some argument. But there was simply nothing to say. Sometimes the right word at the right moment makes all the difference. Sometimes not.

"Have you cabled his parents?"

"Dr. Bianchi has asked me to wait."

"Just a precaution, I'm sure."

"I understand why he's skeptical. Obviously, I understand why you are." She tried to sip her coffee, but the cup was empty. "That's why I need to ask you a favor. Would you look at him again? Would you tell Dr. Bianchi if you recognize him?"

She must have known what she was asking, but she didn't hesitate; her eyes were so clear, so unembarrassed. There was only a subtle shift in them—it was frightening just how subtle—as love gave way to utility.

I suppose as I left the hotel and drifted toward the hospital that I thought I was doing something noble. I could have told her I'd been lying the first day, lying all along, that I'd never seen her husband in my life, but I didn't. Why not? I still wanted to have some use. Self-sacrifice, after all, is the only consolation of the sacrificed.

I had to wait for Bianchi a long time, with nothing to do but attempt a few headlines in the Italian papers. The socialist mayor of Prato had been hung by his feet from a tree while police officers assaulted his wife. Blackshirts laid an ambush in the hills above Florence, and set fire to Fiesole. Bianchi burst into his office, apologizing, shaking my hand, asking me how I slept.

"You asked me yesterday if I recognized him. For what it's worth, I don't."

"You already told me that, Tom."

"And now I'm telling you again. It's not him."

I spent the rest of the day looking for the old canals. Something to do.

* * *

From the street I could see Paul smoking at his hotel window, the yellow lamplight at war with the sunset on the pink buildings.

"Do you still have my wineglasses?" he called down.

He answered the door in his undershirt. His bedclothes were twisted, and empty wine bottles—my Donatis included—lined the dresser. I handed him the glasses, but had no intention of going in.

"I hope you've made good use of these with your lovely Mrs. Hagen. I apologize. I bought other glasses, but they've broken. Join me? It would be a favor."

The armoire was open, six or seven stiff suits hanging on the rod. The little mirror inside was cracked, and Paul's razor rested on a shaving bowl brimming with white water. He poured wine that I drank but didn't taste. The glow outside had turned a thin, blood-in-the-water red. It was easy to imagine hurling myself through the window in such a light. I decided I had better sit down.

"Have you been to the hospital today?" I asked.

"Not in several days, actually. What's become of it?"

So he didn't know about Sarah. I wasn't sure if this was a relief.

"I couldn't face it either," I said.

"Oh?" There was something bordering on bitterness in his expression, but then it passed. "What can you face?"

"What can *you*?"

"Just what you see." He lit a cigarette. "I know you deserve better company. If you drink faster I might not seem so bad." He let his head fall back against the window frame and crooked a leg on the sill. There were white scars weaving between the braces of his sock.

"You might be better company if you told me what's wrong with you," I said. "What happened while I was gone?"

"It occurred before you left. It's just that I'm still coming to terms, if you like."

"If you want," I said in Bianchi's singsong.

Paul snorted. "Yes, if you want."

He began to answer my question, but I wasn't listening. I was trying to convince myself there was a future: I would live a long life after I left Bologna. There would be Rose, perhaps. There would be work. There would be America someday. And yet all of this was impossible to want. I wanted nothing more than to sit with Paul because once we had both sat with Sarah.

"I'm sorry. Start over," I said.

"The best I can explain it is that all day I've imagined a man I never spoke to passing under this window. A Russian or perhaps a Pole."

"Either would do?"

He looked up at me. His eyes were shining with tears.

"I'm sorry. Start over again, please."

"I always felt guilty," Paul said, "sleeping in a stranger's home when we billeted. I suppose privacy is far from the worst thing one loses during a war. All the same . . ."

All the same, there was a certain pleasure in having the run of someone else's house, of fashioning a picture of a life based on the clues left untouched by looters. It was a pleasure antithetical to army life: imaginative, artistic, childlike.

In July of 1915 the Second Regiment of Austrian Hussars took the town of Suwałki in Russian Poland and requisitioned a grand house on the main street. The wine cellar glinted with broken glass. The library shelves were empty, the books ashes on the hearth; but a diamond-patterned Turkish carpet still covered the floor of the great room, and several fine paintings still covered the walls—portraits of an old family with dimpled chins.

One evening Paul noticed grooves in the floor, the ghost of a grand piano, no doubt long since split for firewood. In a nearby cabinet he found—amid the expected Chopin and Beethoven—a piano sonata written by a composer, hardly known outside Vienna, who had been a friend of his older brother. Paul explained that he had once been invited to the composer's apartment, that he had heard the composer himself perform the piece. Paul explained that, so far as he knew, that was the only occasion on which the piece had ever been performed. But apparently not. Apparently a Polish or Russian family had once gathered around a piano playing obscure Viennese music. And now they were gone and an obscure Viennese lieutenant was in their place.

Paul often tried to remember the melody of the sonata as he stared out the big front windows at Suwałki's ghostly river, at the thousands of prisoners—literally thousands—who lurched through the main street on their way to the camps in Galicia. Thin columns of thin men, hazy in clouds of summer dust. A beating of feet against hard earth, the occasional snap of a crop or pistol. A long low hum of exhausted, ashamed words.

Only on a single occasion was he able to tell one man in the line from the next. Only on one occasion did a Russian officer, just as gaunt and gray as the others, somehow find the energy to shout. In fact, he began to point with both arms at the window in which Paul stood. He seemed desperate for his fellow officers to look at it, and perhaps one of them flicked his face that way before the whole throng slogged past and vanished utterly. Or not quite utterly, because Paul was sure he had recognized the shouting man's face. He had seen that face many times, in fact, in the portrait on the wall in the great room.

"He was the owner of the house?" I asked.

"Think of it. To be captured, marched a hundred kilometers,

only to pass by one's own home? And then to see a stranger in the window. I still can't fathom what that might feel like. But it *did* happen."

There were footsteps in the hall. They paused outside Paul's room and continued on. Night had fallen.

"And you think this man will pass below your window now?"

"Only metaphorically."

"I'm afraid I don't understand."

"Truthfully, I don't quite want you to understand. I only want you to believe me."

"I do believe you," I said. He looked genuinely relieved, and still I continued. "People do tend to see what they want, though. I could give you a hundred examples."

"I *don't* want to see it." He raised his voice, then waved his hand through the smoke, as if to say: Why argue? "I'm flattered that the question even matters to you. I've talked all night, after all. You understand, I would only permit myself with a friend. Please, you say it's never really what you want. Give me a hundred examples of what you mean. Give me one, anyway."

"You can't write anything about what I'm going to tell you. Can you promise me that?"

He nodded. The wine had softened my pride. I'd meant to tell him only of Sarah's delusional notions about Fairbanks, but I found myself circling back to the fish in her purse. Keep going, he said. The pelvic bone in her hand, her step echoing down the Meuse. Keep going. Keep going. The dancing bears in Bar-le-Duc. Paul listened and smoked. Her letter to Paris. The lean dogs in La Morra. Fairbanks's face. Her face.

And at some point I realized that I was finished and it was only once I had said all the words that I understood what they meant. Bad fortune, that was all. And, comparatively speaking, not even so bad.

But at the same time I also understood that I deserved some special pity, and I suppose I expected Paul to offer it.

He said nothing, only sat at the window, his cigarette flickering in the dark, the ashtray on his knee, the moonlight on his shoulder. There was a car outside, its poorly oiled engine squealing up the street. When the car passed it was quiet enough to hear the murmur of the crowd outside the *vinteria*.

Santa Monica, 1950

I once met the owner of a chain of theaters in Nevada who admitted—bragged, really—that he'd sliced the opening titles from a gangster picture I'd worked on and run it as a double feature. Without the titles to tell them, the audience didn't realize they were watching the same film twice in a row.

"How does that strike you?" he asked, as if the only response was pistols at dawn.

"I'm not sure I would have noticed either," I said.

Though I enjoyed stamping out this particular man's fire, my answer was almost honest. Most of the time my work was beautifully inconsequential. The majority of what I wrote was never made, and I seldom felt much gratification when it was, or much frustration when it wasn't.

There was one script I'd badly wanted to see on the screen, however. The setting: a secret government lab in Northern California. There, a chemist named Wilson Lloyd arrives at work one morning to find that a colleague—Colleen Hill, a brilliant scientist with large coffee-brown eyes—has gone missing. Wilson immediately feels he may be responsible. In fact, Colleen and Wilson shared a kiss only the night before, amid the beakers and burners, before she guiltily pushed him away and rushed home to her husband and children.

Wilson asks Colonel Chambers, his supervisor, if Colleen is sick. The colonel has a neatly trimmed mustache and an eye patch he got in the Pacific. Is who sick? he asks. Colleen. That is, Mrs. Hill. That is, Dr. Hill. The colonel appraises Wilson with his remaining eye. I have no idea who you mean, he says at last. Are you feeling quite all right? Pressure here isn't getting to you, is it?

Wilson asks the other chemists about Colleen, and all peer at him through thick glasses before answering in thicker accents—how many of these colleagues were recently Nazis is a question left up to the audience—that they have never heard of anyone by that name. He asks the toothless lady at the canteen, who, just the day before, ladled them both Stroganoff. No, sir. He asks the janitor, who nearly mopped his way into their tryst (thank god he whistled as he worked!).

That night, Wilson drives to Dr. Hill's home, drunk, and rings the bell. Her husband and daughters are eating banana cream pie around the dining room table. Where is she, he demands, sounding unhinged even to himself. Where is your mother, he yells at the two frightened girls. They begin to cry. Of course they both have Colleen's coffee-brown eyes. It's time you left, their father says.

Wilson walks the deserted streets in a light rain. The kiss in the lab, quite frankly, had not meant a great deal to him. It was a lark with an intelligent, attractive, but obviously repressed woman. He ought not to have done it. In fact, he's always been a bit of a cad, having already broken the heart of a blind hatcheck girl and countless second-shift nurses. But through the process—the agony—of trying to remember every detail of Colleen simply because no one else can, he finds, of course, that he loves her. He dwells on the taste of her lipstick in the lab, a violet-red—finally remembering that they had mixed a cocktail of rare enzymes that flushed violet-red in the beaker. The beaker broke. Colleen was clumsy, one of the qualities he now realizes he loves.

He races back to the lab, half-drunk, fully desperate. He remixes the compounds. He re-smashes the beaker.

The following morning, he finds Colleen at her desk, chatting with one of the former Nazis about slalom, her left arm in a sling. He runs to her, embraces her, confesses his love and so forth.

I'm sorry, who *are* you? she asks.

It took the producer I was working for at the time—Tim Tweller, a man well known for that type of melodrama—several months to get back to me about the script, so I knew his answer already.

"Just who do you think is going to believe this?" he asked.

"Which part?" I answered.

"Obviously we could work around the magic beakers. Problem is, why would this Wilson even care? We'd need a female lead much too beautiful to be a scientist."

I felt completely crestfallen and couldn't fully explain why. Faye and I had just separated; no doubt that was part of it. It didn't occur to me until much later that both the script and my disappointment might have had more to do with my feelings for another woman entirely.

As it happened, Tweller was the producer who had asked me to work with Max Steiner on the spy picture. And so he was the man I went to see in Culver City the Thursday after Max called me at home. But, by then, seeing Tim Tweller meant seeing his wife, Alice.

It had been an open secret for years that she was the one who made the decisions. No one complained. Tim was a drunk, and Alice was better at his job than he'd ever been sober. In fact, it had been several months since anyone had talked to Tim at all. It was assumed he had checked into a hospital and was having a hard time checking out, but no one really knew. Of course, his name was still the one that appeared in the titles.

I liked Alice. She had been a middle-class girl from western Michigan, and, though her circumstances had changed dramatically, that's exactly what she still looked like. She wore flower-print dresses with cap sleeves, and smiled at everyone from Jack Warner to the security guards on the lot with the same thrifty warmth.

The office was just as Tim had left it, with autographed pictures of various Detroit Tigers on the walls, and a detailed model of a P-47 one of their sons had flown in the Pacific. Alice sat behind her husband's desk—a glass and metal thing that looked like a collapsed skyscraper.

"Goodness, Tom. How lovely to see you." She may even have meant it. We'd always gotten along. She killed with kindness. The people I disliked were the ones who wouldn't let you be nice.

"I came about the spy picture," I said.

"Obviously you did," she said. "We didn't know what we had there. That's always how it is with the really good ones, isn't it? Tim is ecstatic. He asked me to thank you for pitching in. To kiss your feet, actually. But you don't mind if I just say it, do you?"

"I don't mind at all," I said. "And I'm glad you like the lyrics, but I have something embarrassing to admit." I tried to make it funny. I set the scene of the party, the chocolate cake and balloons, *The Threepenny Opera*. The strong, sweet wine. I'd been drunk. And a bit in awe of Max Steiner, and, because I'd wanted to impress him, I began to sing lyrics that . . . were already spoken for by another picture. Would she explain to him that we needed to try something else?

She listened politely, laughing in the right places, encouraging, but her eyes narrowed as I finished, as she realized just how egregiously I'd been wasting her time.

"Which picture is that?" she asked. I began to answer. Her eyes flashed to the clock on the desk and then back at me. "Actually, it doesn't matter. There's weight behind this little thing now, Tom. I was trying to explain that to you. Anyway, it's already been shot."

"The song's been shot?"

"Max wrote it up on Monday. Today is Thursday. You are aware we have a budget? I was just on my way to look at the dailies. Why don't you come? Once you see it I'm sure you won't change a thing."

"That's all right," I said.

But she was already up, her skirt swishing. She put a friendly hand on my shoulder and squeezed with the strength of three men. "It's your job, after all."

The projector light flared. The reel began. A wrinkled mouth in close-up. A German-accented voice.

Arthur Bradley—the former major leaguer programmed with the radio codes—has arrived in Ghent after a devious route by train, rowboat, and ski; dodging communist agents, slowly falling in love with the dead psychoanalyst's beautiful secretary. He has long since become aware of the dangerous knowledge implanted in his brain, but has no better idea how to access it than the Soviets. The secretary, Inga, has promised that another doctor, the analyst's mentor, might extract the codes. But they missed him in Zurich, and again in Cologne.

Now Bradley sits in a comfortable armchair on the third floor of one of the Flemish houses that line the Leie River. You can practically smell the wool, leather, and pipe smoke in the office.

The wrinkled mouth and accented voice belong to the old doctor, the last person alive who might dig out the secret. He has a beard, and a pocket watch that ticks like a branch tapping at a window. The camera shifts to Bradley's face, relaxed for the first time in two reels. He's a good actor and very handsome. More naturalistic in approach than most. It won't be long before he's a star, everyone knows that. The shot switches to his point of view. The doctor's pen light flashes.

His voice is soothing and low. Bradley's eyes droop, and the camera follows him into the dark.

He wakes to the thin sound of a whistle, to the doctor shaking his head, slowly, sadly.

My student was clever, wasn't he? he says in the phony accent. Too clever. We now know the trigger. It is a lullaby your mother sang. But there is a problem. *I* cannot pull this trigger, nor can Inga, nor can the Soviets. It must be your *mother's* voice. That's the only way. You *must* reach her.

As far as Bradley knows, his mother is in Iowa, in the same house she has lived in for most of her life. The problem is: he has not spoken to his mother in ten years. She is a proud and cold woman. He had no father, and she wanted him to be a doctor, but he gave that up to play baseball. There was a terrible parting, during which he said things he can scarcely believe. It was just that streak of cruelty he came to Vienna to understand and slay.

Inga spots the Soviet spies through the window. In fact, she herself has been their agent the entire time, but now—in love with Arthur Bradley—she realizes she is through with her former loyalties.

They're coming, she says. Is there another way out?

No, the doctor says, but we still have a few minutes, and I do have a phone. It is worth a try, is it not?

The phone rings in a house on Market Street in Mount Vernon, Iowa. A woman, played by a silent film star whom audiences have not seen in years, puts down her morning coffee and paper. She wears a flannel robe. It's very early. She has no reason to be up other than habit.

She hears her son's voice, tinny and distant, panicked, and on her face we see the buckling of a stubborn pride. The actress can do a great deal with her face. Hard bones go soft before the camera.

They're in the building, Inga whispers.

Do you remember the lullaby? Arthur Bradley asks. There's no time to explain. Can you sing it?

Yes, his mother says, but . . .

There's no time to explain, he shouts. Footsteps on the stairs. His mother takes the receiver from her ear. Her nostrils suggest that she is angry, the rest of her face looks stiff and disappointed. She makes a gesture as if to hang up the phone, then doesn't. Then sings.

I fled to the sea, the sea was too small
But I still had a ball, I still had a ball

I kissed my girl out in the park
There's better light, now that it's dark

I stumbled home at the end of the night,
There's better dark, now that it's light

The snow covered the window and spread to the mirror
The perfect end to a perfect year

Steiner's melody is far more delicate and difficult than a man behind the wheel of an ambulance could ever dream up, but it fits. You can *just* hum it. The mother's voice does not match her hard face.

Then the camera cuts to Arthur Bradley's face. The actor plays this moment well. His eyes slip into a trance, even as they well and tear. You can see all he wants to say to his mother, all he has wanted to say for years—it was just the two of them, for so long she was his entire world—but all he *can* say are the mechanical and cold radio codes: 2, 33, 7, 908, 1004, 2, 1919, 13 . . .

Alice Tweller sneezed as the lights came up. Some people are like that, apparently; the abrupt shift from dark to light makes them sneeze.

"Well?" she said.

I didn't say anything, but that didn't appear to bother her.

"There will be an arrangement for the credits as well. We may even spring for a name to sing it." She squeezed my knee, not quite so hard this time. She was a talented woman. Her touch could say so many different things, and so unmistakably. "Your angle here isn't money, is it? I can ask Tim, but you know what he'll say, and I don't see your leverage."

"I don't see my leverage either. I agree, it's good."

Alice smiled, as relieved that she could get on with her day as anything else. "Isn't it? We're even considering it for the title now."

"Which part?"

"Tim likes *Better Dark, Now That It's Light*. Or maybe just *Better Dark*."

"Don't do that," I said. "It's *The End of a Perfect Year*."

CHAPTER ELEVEN

Notions of duty were unfashionable in the years after the war, and with good reason. Nevertheless, I convinced myself that duty kept me in Bologna. Marcel had wired to say that our series of articles had been received with enthusiasm. He offered me another week to observe the amnesiac before I even asked.

For several days I managed to disappear into my work, interviewing the women in black who came to see Fairbanks, writing up their deluded hopes. I sent Marcel a profile of Marisa Donati, our kind host in La Morra. Her son, I wrote, had gone missing during the Fifth Battle of the Isonzo. Marisa had been in the family chapel, lighting a candle for him when the wick and flame flew off as if shot by a rifle. A nub of white wax lay at her feet, the flame still flickering in the half-dark of the church. She heard droplets, as if from snowmelt in the mountains. She scooped the flame into her palm, and still it burned. She knew then that her son was wounded, but alive.

Later I changed the battle from the Fifth to the Sixth, for reasons of sibilance. In truth, Marisa Donati's only son was twelve years old. He juggled pickle jars to entertain the guests. I felt more than entitled to my cynicism.

* * *

I saw Sarah crossing the hospital courtyard, but we never spoke. I did not see Paul for the next several days. The key to Room #9 dangled in the hutch behind the desk, but the clerk informed me that he had not checked out.

I might have begun to lose my sanity, but somehow Bianchi found time to walk the hospital grounds, to drink *caffè correttos* with me in Piazza Maggiore. From under the big umbrellas we watched pigeons scatter across the bricks and teenage revolutionaries shake their fists. We watched squads of Blackshirts march into the square—as they did most afternoons—goose-stepping and drilling in formation. The tight salutes and solemn turns seemed harmless, even ridiculous.

"Do not be fooled," Bianchi said. "The theater is in the cities. The violence is in the countryside."

He tried to explain the real violence, the riot in that very square the previous year when the socialists had swept the City Council elections and the Fascists opened fire on the inauguration with revolvers and homemade bombs. He explained that a Fascist leader had been killed in the fight, and described the reprisals at Workers' Clubs in the countryside, communists dragged behind trucks while Blackshirts urinated on them from the roadside. Kangaroo trials and quick stabbings, while the police looked on impassively.

Needless to say, all I really wanted to discuss was Sarah, which Bianchi was not able to do. Though he was willing to describe what *generally* happened in such a case.

An identification had been made. How would the case proceed? The attending doctor would offer the claimant an opportunity to prove her identification. What did that mean? It meant the doctor would ask the claimant to present keepsakes, photographs, letters. It meant the doctor would look for hints of recognition, of agitation, shades of attention or inattention relative to the patient's typical state.

Then he would write to the war office for—hypothetically, let's say, Lee Hagen's—military records, moles, scars, the date he went missing, to put against all that was known about Fairbanks. He might, in time, ask for a handwriting sample, even though Fairbanks had yet to write.

It was up to the attending doctor then—hypothetically, let's say, Bianchi himself—to decide if there was enough evidence to put the claimant's case forward in court. An especially complicated matter, as the very facts of the case determined its jurisdiction.

What a vision this all was: Sarah's eyes pleading with Fairbanks's, her mouth trembling as his tremored. Bianchi impassively jotting it all down. What did the doctor know of her now that I didn't? I was afraid to imagine. Already I had every story she had ever told me about Lee to cast with Fairbanks's face. Fairbanks touching her elbow in just such a way in the Tuileries. A teenage Fairbanks dressed as the Pauper in purple tights, his shaking hand offering her a Linzer heart. Fairbanks with his trembling mouth at her mouth in a banker's apartment in the 2nd arrondissement. His trembling tongue on her tongue in a banker's bed, her left arm flung back behind her head, as she always flung it back during sex.

How was it possible to feel jealous of a man with half his mind—most of his mind—gone? Yet there were times—when the light came through the shutter slats and I recalled the shape of her body on the bed; the violet of her perfume, now nowhere in the room—when I would have traded places with Fairbanks.

On Sunday, I hoped Bianchi would be at the café with the opera singer, but I didn't expect to be able to find it again on my own. Likely, he didn't expect me to either. Certainly his face suggested as much when I came in, but he welcomed me over. His hair was uncombed, a slick of beer shaped like the Baltic Sea spilled on the table.

"Tell me about America," he said. "Do you think I'd be happy in America?"

"Some people seem to be," I said.

"But could I be a doctor there? I would not slice meat or sell fruit."

"You're a doctor here," I said.

"For now, yes. But if the Fascists come to power, my career will be finished. And then there's my brother. I wonder if we could do better in America."

"I don't know how popular communists are in America."

"But you have no Mussolini yet, do you? Perhaps I could be a doctor still?"

"You must know more about that than I do."

"I do. There is very little hope, in fact. The truth is, Tom, I know if I emigrate my brother will go with me. And I know that he may die if we do not emigrate. But I have worked hard to be a doctor here. I cannot go somewhere else. I don't want to. Unless I was famous . . . and then . . . Have you been writing? Have you been filing your stories? How have they been received?"

I had my opening, and I only realized later that he must have planned it for me. "Perhaps you can help me with all of that. How has Fairbanks reacted?" I asked.

He waved his hand and finished his glass before answering in a low voice. "Fairbanks is a negativist, in psychological terms. If you want, he reacts adversely to almost any kind of stimulus. He doesn't *want* to be found. He is terrified of being identified, of being asked to remember."

"Why?"

"Why? Perhaps because he is smarter than the rest of us. But this is not what you really want to know."

"Not entirely," I said.

"Oh, I'll tell you. Why not? He's had no response to Signora Hagen. No response under hypnosis. No interest in her gifts."

"What gifts?"

"French chocolates. The sports pages from a Boston newspaper. Novels by Mark Twain."

Where had these items come from? She couldn't have bought them in Bologna. She must have carried them wherever she went. Had her suitcase in Verdun been packed with *Tom Sawyer* and the *Globe*? On the off chance?

"What does she say?" I asked.

"She holds his hand and whispers."

"And what else?"

"She weeps. Sometimes with frustration, I fear. She sings to him. She sings well. She feeds him chocolates. He eats the chocolates. But that means very little."

"But what does she say, to you?" His eyes met mine again, and he wiped the foam from his lip.

"She is undeterred." Bianchi rubbed his hand over his face. And just then, to our mutual relief, the barman began his aria.

When I returned to the hotel that night, Paul was just rising from one of the shabby chairs in the lobby, crushing a cigarette. We shook hands.

"It's quite late," he said. "I've been waiting for you."

"I've been waiting for *you*. Have you been in town?"

"Not for a few days. Just up to Cortina. I was there some years ago."

"Happy memories?"

"Hardly. But that doesn't matter."

"And what does?"

"That tomorrow, if you're free, I'd like to take you and Mrs. Hagen to dinner."

CHAPTER TWELVE

The osteria Paul had chosen was already crowded when I arrived, a storefront with tall windows left open in the heat, brown butcher paper on the tabletops, white candles in round glasses. I was drinking a second Campari when Paul arrived. She arrived later in a familiar blue dress. I stood when she came to the table but didn't trust my voice to hide how stupidly pleased I was to see her.

"Thank you for accepting my invitation, Mrs. Hagen," Paul said.

"Well, they won't let me stay on at the hospital in the evenings. And I was curious. I wonder if I should also be worried?"

"Not at all. I've been told this is an excellent restaurant for game," Paul said.

She gave a weak smile in reply. Paul refolded his napkin and commented on the heat, rain finally expected that night. The waiter came and went with our order. Words were hard to pick out in the din. Outside, dusk slipped over the street. She still hadn't so much as looked in my direction. But I knew what to say if I wanted her attention.

"How is he? Is there any progress?"

Sarah hesitated, likely wondering if it was safe to answer.

"There's progress. Slow, but it means a great deal to me."

She didn't sound very much like a woman in love, but I knew better. She was only hoarding the details.

"He's said something?" I asked.

"He reached out for my hand."

"Did you know that he took my hand too, Mrs. Hagen?" Paul asked. "A few days ago."

"Did he?" No smile, not even a pretense of politeness.

"I wonder, what has Tom told you about me?" Paul asked the question as if I weren't sitting beside him. "I imagine he has already realized that I did not come to Bologna only to report for a newspaper."

She glanced at me. I tried to seize her eyes, but her expression was too smooth to hold. "Tom and I have not had much reason to speak of late."

Paul took a breath, and for a moment I thought he might be able to explain just how wrong she was. Just how crucial it was that she listen to me. But he didn't. He said: "Like you, Mrs. Hagen, I have been looking for someone. For a very long time now."

Sarah nodded. She turned to the windows as if plotting an escape. Then she looked at Paul again, with much softer eyes. She seemed to feel no need to respond, not until she was absolutely ready.

"Someone you cared for?" she asked.

"No."

"I'm sorry," she said, as if she hadn't heard him. "And I think I can say I even understand, if that doesn't sound patronizing. It's no comfort to see others' good fortune, I realize, but you may still find him."

Paul took a sip of water. "Mrs. Hagen," he tried again, "it's difficult to explain, but I don't especially want to find him now."

She narrowed her eyes. "I don't really understand what this has to do with me."

"If you heard my story I believe you'd understand."

"I'd rather not, honestly."

"Wasn't there a time, Mrs. Hagen, when all you wanted was for someone to listen?"

She glanced at me once more. I wondered what she actually saw. I tried not to look disappointed. I tried to look like her friend. The waiter returned with wine, with a plate of meats and brown bread. The door was propped open on account of the heat. A few steps and she could have been outside.

"Yes," Sarah said, finally. "Actually it was a very long time."

Well, Paul said, there was no single place to start, but he could begin with the day he lost his horse, the day the emperor's army finally accepted that the cavalry was just a pageant, the age of pageantry passed. As a rule, officers who grew sentimental over their horses died early. Yet he could begin with how angry and careless he became, how he made powerful enemies. How his enemies sent him to Italy, how he made additional enemies on the Isonzo—over what he could no longer even recall—who sent him into the Dolomites.

But truthfully—did we already know this?—if he were to tell it from the very beginning he would have to start some years earlier. He would have to begin with the night that Franz Conrad von Hötzendorf, the Austrian supreme commander, met a beautiful Italian woman at a ball in Trieste. She touched him with her fan. They bowed and waltzed and Conrad fell dangerously in love. How dangerous can love be? Very. In 1914, it was Conrad who pushed for a decisive and immediate response to the archduke's assassination, Conrad who demanded an invasion of Serbia, hoping that glory in the Balkans would sweep away the obstacles that stood between him and his true love.

"What obstacles?" Sarah asked.

"One husband. Five children. And one thousand years of

Habsburg tradition," Paul said. "But he knew that if he couldn't have her he would be unhappy for the rest of his life."

"Why *her* in particular?" I asked in a voice that might have sounded comically bitter had anyone been listening closely. Paul shook his head. So began the World War.

But perhaps it would be better to begin when the Italians broke out of the Falzarego valley to the west of Cortina and occupied the summit of Mount Tofana. The Austrians withdrew to a promontory of rock to the west, a second peak, separated by a narrow screed ridge of approximately five hundred meters. They called it the Kinderhaus.

"The children's house?" I asked.

Paul snorted. "It was *called* that, yes." But imagine, he said, one of the red towers of medieval Bologna. Imagine if this tower were approachable by a single bridge hundreds of meters in the air. Imagine trying to slither over this bridge, looking for cover among pebbles and sharp limestone. Imagine scaling the face, toehold to toehold, hacking the stone for purchase. Even by Italian standards such an attack would be insane, though the Italians did try—several times, actually, in the last months of 1916—and were slaughtered.

Paul reported to his post on the Kinderhaus in late January, 1917. He found rock trenches ringing its summit, an officers' dugout chiseled into the stone where a predecessor had hung a portrait of Franz Joseph in red robes and ermine. Under the emperor's bemused gaze the wind lashed white ice across the lower Dolomites. Paul's cold feet and fingers moved as if by levitation. And even two thousand meters above the sea there was always something to dig. Pockets in the rock to be chipped into dugouts and field kitchens, where thin potato soup would simmer. Snow to be cleared from the narrow paths, from which mules fell to their deaths routinely.

They dug tiers in the mountain, already white as wedding cake, and climbed iron ladders bolted into the rock. They climbed through the wind with sandbags strapped to their backs; or belts of ammunition for the Schwarzlose machine guns; or explosive shells; or packages from Zagreb, Bolzano, and Vienna containing thick socks, cured ham, and news from home.

Paul commanded twenty men, not including his valet, many of whom had grown up in Bozen or Tyrol, natural mountaineers. A good bunch, on the whole. They showed Paul how to avoid snow blindness by making slatted goggles from old shell casings. The nights were long and quiet enough for slivovitz and grappa. He was easy on their letters and did his best to learn their songs in Ladin and Friulian.

Nevertheless, each man was alone in the snow. Snow, invisible and visible, pink snow in the dusk, black snow during night watch. Snow that smelled of cordite, that tasted of limestone. Snow that fluttered from the swaying clouds, through the daylight, through the moonlight and wind. Through their boots and greatcoats, through the bent legs of a dead sergeant who lay frozen to the eastern face of the summit. *I am alive*, Paul wrote to his mother, *but alive inside a ghost*.

In the osteria, Sarah lit a cigarette and watched the smoke drift to the windows. Evening waited for her, the rest of her life waited. Paul waited too, politely.

"Tom loves ghost stories, if that's what this is," she said. "I myself . . ."

I'd said that, yes. Another dinner where I had no business.

"Believe me, in this story the dead are dead," Paul said.

Sarah flicked her eyes up in apology.

Still, Paul continued, the Kinderhaus was very much a haunted place. The creak of old rock, old ice. Wind so unrelenting it seemed to carry a grudge. And if in France they joked—how hilarious—that the trenches were merely graves already dug, in the mountains it seemed as if the shroud had already been laid.

The only relief was that the war had frozen over too. In the autumn the Italians had attacked the Kinderhaus with artillery, and there were still powder burns like black flowers on the cracked rock. But the Italian guns were never able to properly target the Austrian positions, and by January the two sides exchanged only half-hearted fire. Paul watched for spring through field glasses, the Italian field glasses glinting back from the opposite peak.

But here was the real beginning: mid-March, the snow melting in rills, Paul censoring letters. The work was dull, the men reticent to a fault. He felt the first tremors in the soles of his boots. His imagination? An avalanche on another peak? He swept his field glasses across the valley. Nothing. But the buzz continued, a mild churning, almost possible to ignore.

"Do you feel that?" he asked his sergeant, a man named Tretta who came from a valley in Badia and whose first language was Ladin.

"A drill, I'd think, Lieutenant," he said.

"Drilling what? A tunnel?"

"What else?"

The previous year a peak on the Asiago Plateau had disappeared in a shower of rock, the emperor's soldiers garrisoned there along with it. Turned to dust by an Italian mine.

"My god, anything else," Paul said.

That night Paul sent Tretta across the saddle to listen. Tretta reported the grind and whine of the drill, twenty minutes on, then ten off while the bit cooled. He reported clinking shovels scraping away the rock. The tunnel was roughly a third of the way across the saddle separating the two peaks, Tretta reported. They should be very worried, Tretta reported.

The major at the Fifth Division headquarters didn't look nearly as healthy as most officers of his rank, and this led Paul to trust him. He offered coffee and asked Paul to join him on a walk through the gardens of the requisitioned villa outside Cherz. There were freshly trimmed topiary dogs at the crest of a sloping green lawn, still wet with the melt and fringed by bright yellow laburnum.

"Are you married?" the major asked.

"No," Paul said.

"I hope you don't have children then."

"Of course not."

"And how old?"

"Twenty-two."

"Twenty-two." The major nodded. "No one told me the truth about anything when I was twenty-two. Have you found that to be the case?"

"That's difficult to judge," Paul said.

"It isn't, actually. For example: we can't abandon your position. It's too important, strategically."

"Sir, I wasn't asking for that," Paul said.

"I know you weren't. But the truth is also this: I can't give you relief, or reserves. The truth is that the Italians will have to blow up fifty more mountains if they expect to reach the Brenner Pass. This mountain will do them no good. It's simply not worth the resources to defend it. Not at this moment. Now you know what the truth sounds like."

The major did manage to provide two sappers who began work

on the countermine at once. If they could find the Italian tunnel under the ridge, they could lay their own charge and collapse the Italians' work. But there was no drill, so all of the digging had to be done by hand at exhausting and almost pointless expense. At such a pace, they would find the Italians only by blind chance.

"Before you ask, Mrs. Hagen," Paul said, "there are many stories about blind chance, but this isn't one." The tortellini had arrived. Paul took a drink of the red wine. The rain had begun, heavy and sudden. The waiter hurried between tables, banging shut the high windows with a hooked pole.

"If it isn't about chance or ghosts it must be about love," Sarah said, mockingly, but Paul didn't seem to notice her tone.

"Do you know any love stories that don't include chance and ghosts?" he asked.

"I think I do," I said.

Sarah cut her eyes at me, a sympathetic glance at last. "Go on, Paul," she said.

The story was about how Paul stared into the hole the sappers had dug in the rock, claustrophobic and vacant at once. It was about the light at the *beginning* of the tunnel. And about how the sappers told him not to expect much.

"What should we expect?" he asked their sergeant, a man no taller than five feet with black hands that looked too big for his wrists.

"An explosion, Lieutenant."

"Can you be more specific?"

"This Kinderhaus is a large position. I would expect a large explosion."

"You're a cold one, aren't you?"

"Aren't *you* cold, Lieutenant?" There was not a trace of irony in the sapper's voice. He had, however, discovered one useful piece of information: the Italians were working on two tunnels, not one. Two tunnels with two drills, the first and larger one under the Austrian position, the second on the face of their own peak. He guessed that they planned to blow the western face so they could attack directly across the ridge.

"But perhaps their plan of attack won't matter very much to you," the sapper said. "After all . . ."

"On the contrary," Paul said, "now I know not to hope I somehow survive the explosion."

Paul called the sappers off after a week. The men who remained oiled their rifles and dug an extra few inches into the limestone. But it was all for morale, to keep busy, to keep from thinking too much. One day the mountain would crumble beneath them. Paul thought about the kind of voice he would have to summon to tell them that they were all going to die, and soon. Well, it was 1917, he need only use his normal voice. And they already knew, anyway. All the while the Italian drill buzzed under their feet, the shovels chipped and clinked.

Tretta snuck back across the ridge to report every midnight, and afterward they stayed up in Paul's dugout, listening and drinking slivovitz. Tretta imagined aloud the life he would not have, a girl he liked in Badia, the children he wanted.

"I'd put them over my knee and give them five of the best," he said.

"The best?"

"With the belt."

"You dream of punishing your children?"

"What do you dream of? Kissing them?"

That was how they always joked after that. If we survive we'll give the major five of the best. We'll give General Conrad five of the best. We'll give the emperor five of the best. They stared up at the portrait on the rock wall one night when the slivovitz was gone.

"We could give the old man his share right now," Paul said. But neither of them was willing to go quite that far. The ground shook as the drill drew closer.

"How much longer?" Paul asked.

"Probably not tomorrow," Tretta said.

In the meantime there was terror unlike any Paul had ever felt. It wasn't like fear at all. It was more like delirium. He'd forget the names of his men, if he had eaten, how to write a cursive letter. Sometimes he counted his breaths, wondering, quite literally, how many more he might take. Sometimes he felt the rock as a burning cold pulse through his body, he felt he could vomit powdered limestone. *Chink, chink.*

He knew the Italian sappers were just men—probably illiterate, certainly poor—from squalid places he had never heard of. Still, he pictured them with flaming claws and fangs, or, just as often, as angels in white silk, halos lighting the dark tunnels. Power over life and death. *Chink, chink.* Shovel blows; drilling needles, colder than the wind. How much longer?

He sent away what men he could, asking the same questions the major had put to him in the villa. Wife? Children? Perhaps we can move you into reserve. Some refused. Some thanked him in tears. To Paul's surprise, his valet clicked his heels and left without protest. It was only then that Paul realized how little they had always liked each other.

"How much longer, Tretta?"

"Please stop asking, Lieutenant."

That night Paul awoke in the dark. For minutes he heard nothing and lay breathing in the smell of the field stove. Only when he felt the drill reengage, felt the ground convulse under him, was he able to fall back asleep.

Then, drinking with Tretta the following night, suddenly he could hear the drill itself, the whining motor. He could smell the scorched oil, not unlike the smell of tar on the Vienna rooftops.

And he could hear men singing, spectral voices, voices of the afterlife. It was almost a relief to realize that he had finally gone mad. What were the voices telling him? Something about ancestors, descendants? The truth in the hearts of women he thought he had loved. His brother's heart on a bayonet in Russia, his mother with her hair up at a window. His father, black-masked at the Industrialists' Ball. What were the songs saying? That might be worth knowing, but he didn't recognize the melodies. When he was able to pick out a word, he didn't recognize it either.

"Is that Italian?" Tretta asked. "Do you hear that?"

Paul laughed. Tretta had tears in his eyes. No afterlife. Just the Italians singing as they dug. They could hear cursing and shouting too. Shovels passing from man to man. They could smell the tobacco smoke and the coal smoke of the field stove, the simmering barley soup. They could hear the spoons rattling in the bowls. All of this drifted up through fissures in the rock.

"What would happen if we called out to them?" Tretta asked.

"They would hear our voices and become conscious of our shared humanity. Then they would stop digging."

"Mamma mia," Paul and Tretta yelled into the dark of the dugout.

"Ciao, bella!"

"Prego! Prego!"

The following afternoon the portrait of the emperor was shaken from the wall. Full pots of soup slid from the stove. That night, as they sat in their quarters trying to steady the bottle to their lips, Paul heard a tap on the table and looked up to see that one of Tretta's gold fillings had fallen from his mouth.

And still the digging made them feel safe. Lying down that night in a hammock that shuddered beneath him, Paul slept through the calm, waking only with the explosion.

Limestone between his teeth, in his gums; stinging pebbles blown in *through* his eyelids. The candles snuffed, the lamps shattered. Paul fumbled for the canteen at his belt and poured it across his face. There was some air still in the dust, enough to breathe. The ground swayed as he searched for the mouth of the dugout. There. A sooty sheet, pathetic light.

Outside, there was moonlit darkness to the morning. His watch had been blown from his wrist. Three men he didn't recognize staggered in the ash. Another man was dumping soup into his eyes.

Where was he, exactly? Half the peak had turned to fog. Their artillery had been washed into the valley, their entrenchment carried down the slope. He called roll: nine voices answered. He put his field glasses to his eyes and one of the lenses fell to pieces in his hands. On the opposite peak the Italian field glasses glinted and winked through clouds of dust, as if to say, We both know none of this is real, don't we?

Over Paul's shoulder I could see the waiter consoling the chef. The entrées had arrived, but we hadn't touched them.

Paul finished his glass and poured more. "I'd like to get a better bottle next if you'll join me. Certainly I'm paying, for boring you this way."

"Not at all," Sarah said. "It's even a little interesting."

"We should have ten more bottles," I said, "to celebrate that you survived."

"I've probably celebrated too much already," Paul said. "The Italians just underestimated. Or the charge must have gone off only partially, or some other miracle."

"Do you call it a miracle?" Sarah asked.

"Only when I'm speaking English."

But where was the Italian attack, where was the second explosion the sappers had promised? Paul's remaining men surrounded him, bleeding from their ears, spitting bits of rubble into their hands. They reported the field telephone gone. Their best hope was to descend the western side of the ridge to where reserves waited, and from there dig in again to halt the Italian advance. It would not even be a retreat exactly, as the position that Paul had been charged to hold no longer existed.

Then the second explosion hit, flinging them all to the ground. The rock face of Tofana, adjacent to the ridge, dropped like a curtain, and Paul knew they were as good as dead. The Italians would be on them in moments, have clean shots across the ridge in moments. There was blood on his fingertips. He couldn't hear his own voice, but somehow he heard the Italian whistles, signaling attack. Black smoke poured from the hole in the face of Tofana, and then the Italians in their green-gray uniforms were surging through the black smoke. They made the first twenty meters across the ridge. Then they began to fall.

One man went down, then the next. They dropped their rifles and put their hands to their throats. Paul looked through the glass to see eyes bulging in their sockets. It looked like the work of an invisible and silent machine gun, except that they dropped almost at once.

The wine had come. Paul put his nose in the glass and breathed. "In English it's called 'white damp'—more of a miner's danger than a soldier's. The carbon monoxide from the explosion was sucked out in such a concentration that the Italians all suffocated on the spot. Amazing, isn't it?"

"My god, yes," Sarah said. "You say white damp now, but at the time . . ."

"At the time, I didn't know."

"What must you have thought . . . ?"

"Now I know I survived only because of an error caused by exhaustion or poor training. But, yes, when one sees something like that, one can't help but feel . . ."

"Protected?"

"Yes."

She brought the napkin to her mouth. "You felt that you deserved to survive?"

"Deserved? I don't think *deserved.*"

"That you were the only real person in the world. Obviously you would survive what seemed like certain death."

"You've felt this way, Mrs. Hagen?"

"It's something Lee said to me once before he disappeared. Anyway, you haven't mentioned Tretta at all."

"No."

"But you have reason to think he survived the explosion?"

"I know he survived. As I gave the order to fall back, and as we were scrambling down the summit, I stepped on one of his hands. It was as if he had just appeared there. Right at my feet."

They began the retreat, eleven of them now, with Paul supporting Tretta himself. Looking for footing on the mountain paths, coughing up the powdered limestone and descending the ladders. But then the Italians began their barrage, and with half the Kinderhaus at the bottom of the valley the Austrians were now fully exposed. The Italian guns hadn't found the range, so the shells flew high, but this was little comfort as they struck what remained of the summit. A chunk of bone-white cliff the size of a car fell. Then another. Landslides rumbled like applause in an opera house. Explosions. The mountain melted.

They reached another ladder and clamored down, Tretta hopping rung to rung. They scuffled onto the narrow path below, the collars of their field coats turned up against the dust. Another explosion, and an iron ladder scuttled past and dove into the valley. A shell landed twenty meters ahead, sending up blinding clouds, and Paul and Tretta limped forward, somehow avoiding the edge of the road as it twisted down the mountain. When Paul's vision cleared, there was no one else in sight. He clutched Tretta, and they continued on.

"I had lost any sense of where I was. I had lost sense of anything other than the fact that I was moving," Paul told us. "That was all. And eventually we were past the range of the Italian artillery, and still we kept going, as fast as I was able. And eventually Tretta said, 'Lieutenant, I think we have to stop, I have to.' I don't know how many times. Many before I heard him, I think.

"What?" Paul asked Tretta. "What? What? What?" It was all he could say. "What? What? What?"

"My foot," Tretta said.

"What?" Paul said. Tretta no longer had a foot. The sole of his boot was gone, the leather looked like a bloody sponge.

They stopped, and Paul lowered Tretta to the ground.

Tretta was stocky, and both his bald head and face had the permanently flushed red of too much cold, heat, or drink. Paul sat at his side and tried to belt Tretta's thigh, tense with pain.

The road had widened, passable by car now, but there were no cars in sight. No smoke. The limestone was chipped and scorched. Phantom dugouts, eroded, green with lichen. The sun seemed to be setting, though that was only an effect of the dust. Paul's muscles squirmed in the aftershock. He had no chart.

They stumbled into a dugout at the roadside, Tretta's eyes bubbling open and shut. Paul lay down and immediately began to dream. When he awoke it was night and Tretta had managed to raise the mangled foot on a lip of rock.

"What are you doing?" Paul asked.

"Waiting."

"You can't walk, can you?" Paul asked.

"I can't *walk*, no."

"If we find a crutch? If I carry you?"

"If. If," Tretta said.

"I don't know where we are," Paul said.

"Not where we're supposed to be," Tretta said.

They should have already arrived at the Austrian positions. Somehow Paul had taken them east instead of west—but how was that possible? Weren't they just walking down the mountain road?

Paul closed his eyes again and saw a ball in Vienna before the war. His father was wearing the black mask he'd worn at every ball since 1888, the year the crown prince killed himself. He'd tied it around his shoulder as a mourning band and still wore it twenty-five years later, though the silk had rubbed through in many places. His father had invited Paul to take the mask—it was his first ball, he was sixteen—but Paul dressed as an Arctic explorer instead.

"Lieutenant?" Tretta said. "I've been calling your name."

"What? What?" Paul tried to rub the dream from his eyes but couldn't keep his hands still.

"We should leave while it's still dark, shouldn't we?"

"Yes. Yes."

But then he was back at the ball. His first. An Arctic explorer with a white fur collar and gold-tinted goggles. The Steinhof Hospital Ball, wasn't it? Yes. Only Steinhof wasn't just a hospital, it was an asylum. An orchestra was playing familiar music. Fake white trees hung upside down from the ceiling, and dancers swept around the bare white branches. A woman dressed as a mermaid hung on Paul's arm. And his father—he was on the hospital board—peered at him through the old mask from across the room.

Paul missed a step, and a man dressed as Jack the Ripper cut in on his dance and spun the mermaid. He stood alone. None of his friends had arrived as they were supposed to; they'd gone to a better ball, one he'd been invited to, but his father had made him attend this one. A girl dressed as a nun approached him. She whispered something in his ear.

"Lieutenant, it's almost dawn," Tretta said.

Paul knew they needed to get up. He knew. He could see the moon through the rough arch of the cave, yellow, boiling over into the clouds. Her face, framed by the habit, was gentle as moonlight.

"Would you put your tongue between my legs?" she said in his ear, and touched the lobe with her own tongue. He looked away immediately and, by mistake—of course by mistake—caught his father's eye. His father caught the eye of someone behind him, and a moment later there was a hand on Paul's shoulder. It was one of the doctors, dressed as the kaiser in Prussian blue, left arm hidden at his side. He escorted Paul away, gently. And gave him a drink of water.

"What did she say to you?" he asked.

"I can't repeat it."

"She's a patient," he said. "You realize that, don't you?"

"What?"

"Oh yes, they deserve one dance a year, just like the rest of us. But what did she say?"

"Lieutenant. Lieutenant," Tretta said.

Paul tried to sit up. Tretta's leg drooped from the rock lip, looking withered and swollen at the same time.

"What time is it?"

"I don't know," Tretta said. "It looks like the moon outside."

Paul managed to get to his feet. Tretta's face was not the gaunt white he'd prepared himself for but a glowing yellow. His good leg was swollen, and Paul bent down to rub it. He could feel the leg shivering under his fingers. Tretta's eyes had gone somewhere else. There was sweat across his brow, his cheeks, his lips.

"If that is really the moon out there I can still walk, Lieutenant," he said.

"It might be the moon. Why don't I check?"

Tretta closed his eyes. Paul stepped from the dugout. There was a smear of orange in the eastern sky. The mountains were still a cool white. They all had names, but he'd forgotten them. There was an impassable drop and a silver ribbon of river in the distance. That was all he knew.

Tretta's eyes flicked open and closed through the rest of the morning; still, he was the one who heard the engine. At first Paul thought his friend was having another fever dream, but then he heard it too. Paul told Tretta to be quiet, but already he was breathing raggedly, deeply asleep. Paul let the vehicle pass before inching out to the road, praying for the Habsburg double-headed eagle on the back of a staff car.

Instead he saw a Red Cross ambulance with the Italian *Tricolore* on the tailgate; it was twenty meters down the road, driving slowly, even given the incline. Paul had only a moment to make the decision.

"Stop," he yelled in English. He couldn't remember how to say *please*. He ran a few steps and almost fell. The ambulance stopped, the engine still running, and Paul put his hands in the air.

The light in the sky had gone from gray to silver, bright enough now to make out a skull and ribs on the side of the road, a screaming mule's probably. The driver stepped from the vehicle, coughing into his hand—a tall man, tanned, with the reckless smile of a child. His hands were dirty-red from infection. A thin mustache on his lip looked like a practical joke.

"All right, I've stopped," the driver said in English.

"Thank you," Paul said. "I know you didn't have to."

"I don't *have* to do anything," the driver said. He had the petulance of a child too. But then he looked at Paul with sensitive, blinking eyes. "Are you surrendering to me, Lieutenant?"

Paul hadn't spoken English in months; the language made his tongue feel heavy and slow. He tried to explain himself and found he couldn't.

"That's all right, Lieutenant. You don't *have* to do anything either. But how long do you want to stand out on this road?"

Paul took a breath. He said words in English he thought made sense, but he could tell from the driver's face they had been gibberish.

"Where are you from?" Paul tried then, hoping a few easy words would help him find the rest.

The man smiled, rather sardonically. "New York. The state, not the city. I always have to add that before anyone asks. And you?"

"The city of Vienna," Paul said.

"Oh, not the state?"

"No."

"I'm only joking. I know all about Vienna. My favorite college professor was from Vienna. He was very proud of your city. 1683 and the Turks. Charles V. I know all about it. Dr. Szeps? By any chance?"

Paul shook his head.

The driver shrugged. "Well, it would have been too strange if you had known him. Why don't you just show me what it is you want?"

Paul led the driver to Tretta, still asleep in the dugout. The driver nodded and knelt to listen to the breaths.

"Can he survive?" Paul asked carefully.

"Not really my territory," the driver said. "I've been surprised. Either way. I'm on my way to triage now, though. That's certainly his best chance."

Paul nodded. Tretta would be put in a camp after that, but the chances of someday giving his children five of the best in a mountain valley were much better. Perhaps they could even save the foot.

Tretta opened his eyes. "What is it, Lieutenant?" Tretta asked. "Who is he?"

Paul knelt down so that he could speak into Tretta's ear. "Red Cross. He'll take you to the Italian doctors. I think you should go, but it's your choice."

Tretta bit his lip but didn't look the least bit afraid. "Obviously I want to go."

Paul nodded to the driver.

"Help me get him to the ambulance then," the driver said. "I could take you too. No doubt there's something wrong with you, if we were to look."

"Yes, I'm sure there is," Paul said. They both managed to smile.

"You survived the Italian mine, didn't you?"

"How did you know?"

"Because that's what you look like," the driver said.

Later, Paul would think about that line. He would think about every inflection in the man's voice, in the way he had said *New York*, *Vienna*. Later, he would see the man's face in the windows of butcher shops and in the round mirrors of carousels in the Prater. And he would see it in Bologna five years later.

Why?

Paul had been surprised to find the back of the ambulance loaded with two other men, unconscious on stretchers; surprised that the driver had been going so slowly; surprised that he had stopped at all.

"Thank you," Paul said. And the American looked away and smiled, as if something in Paul's voice had embarrassed him. He nodded once and slammed the door and drove another forty meters, to where the road began to vanish around the mountain. Paul remained in the middle of the road, watching, reckless with relief.

But there the driver stopped the car again and got out and saw Paul, still standing in the road. He held up one finger—just a moment, he seemed to say—and opened the back of the ambulance, as if there were something wrong inside. And indeed it seemed there was something wrong; the driver pulled Tretta's stretcher from the back of the ambulance, and holding half of it up to his shoulders, walking backward so that Tretta once more faced Paul down the length of the road—he was almost upright; his eyes discernibly open; his mouth open, speaking to the driver, though the words were impossible to hear. The driver dragged him like that to the narrow shoulder of the road and, under the broadening light of midmorning in the mountains, dumped Tretta over the side and into the valley.

The restaurant had almost cleared; outside, a boy beat the rain from the awning with a broom handle. The chef stood at the bar, drinking wine and wiping his brow.

"He died," Sarah said. "He died?"

"He certainly did," Paul said.

"But why?"

"I've gone to considerable lengths just to ask that question. Now, perhaps I can."

At Paul's signal, the waiter brought a bottle of grappa and three chilled glasses. Sarah poured one for herself, carefully, then threw her napkin on the plate and shoved it away.

"You think my husband did that?" she asked. "You think he did that?"

It was almost touching how she could so thoroughly miss the point. Paul tried to look her in the eyes, but she batted away his gaze.

"Fairbanks—the man in the hospital here—is not your husband. His name is Drummond Green. He was born in Albany, New York, and left Cornell University to join the AFS in 1915."

"That's the name of the driver?" I asked.

Paul nodded.

"How on earth did you find out who he was?"

First he had to survive. Would we indulge Paul in that part of the story too? He really was almost finished. He traveled west at night across the Italian-held roads and arrived at the Austrian position in the middle of the second day, where he was brought before the major from Cherz. You'll be pleased to know, Lieutenant, the major said, that our counterattack was successful. *Pleased*, Paul thought, what does *pleased* mean?

They sent him to the rear with nervous collapse, then back to Vienna for treatment at the Steinhof Psychiatric Hospital, where, in another lifetime, he had attended the ball as the Arctic explorer. He would spare us the details of his treatment—his nightmares, his stammer, his eventual recovery—other than to say that he looked up from his bed one day to see the face of the girl—she was not wearing a black habit now, but a nurse's white cap—who had once spoken to him at the ball.

The rain began again. Every table was empty except ours, and the entire staff sat on stools under the awning outside, smoking, cooling in the spray. Sarah drank off her glass and poured another.

"Drummond Green," she said. "You truly are still trying to find the man who killed your friend? Weren't there a lot of men who killed your friends?"

"True obsession, I suppose, bears no real explanation. Why him? I've already given you my best answer."

"Then try the easier question," I said. "How did you find him?"

"It wasn't difficult, actually. I had a name to start with that he'd given me just by happenstance."

"Szeps?"

"I found a Rudolph Szeps who taught at Cornell University. I learned later that there was in fact a unit of Cornell men—isn't that the phrase?—in Italy. I found the list of those names—there are lists of names everywhere to be had now, as you both know."

"Yes," Sarah said. "But I also know that names are really worth nothing in the end."

"And what of faces? I looked at hundreds of American faces, all doing their best to look optimistic."

"What faces?"

"In Cornell yearbooks. I sent away for all the recent ones. And, eventually, there he was. Drummond Green. I knew him immediately. Even dressed as he was."

"Which was?"

"As a geisha in *The Mikado*. Drummond Green, History, class of 1913. Once I had his name I was able to request records from the AFS. Drummond Green went missing around the time of Caporetto. According to his parents, he'd been suffering from war neuroses. They even suspected he'd taken his own life."

"That wasn't enough justice for you?" Sarah asked.

Paul laughed. "I admit my story paints me as a fool, Mrs. Hagen. But not the kind of fool who believes in justice, I hope."

"You kept looking?"

"Obviously, I did."

"Planning to do what?" she asked.

"Fairbanks has nothing to fear from me, if that is what you're wondering. Mrs. Hagen, I give you my word."

"Did you say 'his parents,' Paul?" I asked. I knew I should be happy, or at least hopeful, but I only felt all the more alone.

"I wrote them too. They were devastated, of course."

"And told them what?"

"The same lie I told everyone I wrote. That in 1917, in the mountains, Drummond Green saved my life."

The young man in the picture wore a sweater and a crimson-striped tie. He was not handsome, exactly, but cute—boyish, as Paul had said—and his smile was so guileless and broad I almost felt sorry, knowing what would later become of him.

But was this man Fairbanks? At first I thought not—the bearing and mien of the man in the photograph were so at odds with the patient's. But what of the shape of the face, what of the deep-set eyes and the slightly crooked nose? And what was a *bearing* anyway? What was a *mien*?

"You can see, can't you?" Paul said, as he picked the photograph up with his fingertips.

"What am I to see?" Sarah asked.

"That there's a chance you might be wrong, Mrs. Hagen," Paul said. "Have you considered that you might be wrong?"

She opened her purse. She found her own photograph and pushed aside the bottle of grappa and placed hers next to Paul's, with a look of something like triumph on her face.

But it wasn't clear what she thought she'd won. I'd never seen a picture of Lee Hagen before, and he looked little like I'd imagined.

He was in his AFS uniform, one arm at his side, the other self-consciously holding his belt. His face was mild and even a bit chubby. The close-mouthed smile was far more mischievous than I would have guessed.

Clearly I was not the most objective audience, but, the more I looked at the two pictures—the more I thought of the tremoring face in the converted practice room—the more I did see a resemblance between Fairbanks and Green. If you cropped the hair, if you sunk in the cheeks and wrecked the teeth, if you haunted the eyes, they might very well have been the same man.

I studied those faces—the sanguine expressions held too long, smiles decaying at the mercy of the shutter. I studied until I grew tired of looking, and I was somewhat startled to realize that I had grown just as tired of the faces at the table—Paul's and even Sarah's face.

It felt as though all I knew of the world was grief, and yet I knew nothing of grief—not their kind of grief, anyway. My own when my mother died was private, personal, and, for that reason, just bearable. I had felt the streets crumbling under my steps, the clouds falling from the sky, but no one else seemed to, so I was able to preserve my sense of the world, more or less. But for Sarah, for Paul, for the families I'd met at Verdun, there was no such levee.

How do we know a man cannot return from the dead? Scientific fact, I suppose, but what is fact but agreement? In Europe, in America, in many other places in the world that year, nearly everyone was grieving. Might they then agree, as Paul and Sarah did, that the dead *can* truly rise, not to demand atonement from the living as they do in *J'accuse*, but to return to beds and tomato gardens, to slip behind newspapers on trams? To appear, disguised, in mental hospitals? It was nice to think so, but wasn't it the responsibility of those of us left relatively untouched to hold the doors open for the rest of the world, in the hope that the madness would someday fade?

Once, in Verdun, I ran into an old couple hurrying down the Voie Sacrée, each holding an end of an old steamer trunk. They were both dripping with sweat, arms trembling with the effort.

"Can I help you somehow?" I asked. The man gave me a look—asking for pity, or offering it, or both. The woman seemed to catch this expression because she turned to him, then turned fiercely back to me.

"We don't have any more money to give you. We've paid it all to the gravedigger."

"What gravedigger? From where?"

"Thiaumont."

I knew I should stay silent, but I was full of scalding anger toward the greedy man who'd sold this woman the bones of a stranger, probably, for all the money she had in the world.

"You must listen to me," I said. "The graves in Thiaumont are all unmarked. There are no names. There's no possible way . . ."

"That's what the gravedigger said too," she answered. "But don't you think I know my own son?"

I let them flee down the road—god knows how many more miles they had to go—without saying another word. Why didn't I know as well years later, in the restaurant with Paul and Sarah? Outside, the rain came in sheets. One of the busboys ran into the downpour and back again to the safety of the awning. Everyone laughed as he wiped the wet hair from his eyes. I could hear the laughter of the hostess above the rest.

I thought a long time about what I wanted to say, how I wanted to say it, but it still came out wrong.

"Fairbanks is neither of these men. Don't you see that it's impossible? It's impossible, and it's a little insane."

The restaurant was dead quiet, and I'd spoken much louder than I needed to, but I almost thought they hadn't heard. Sarah began to cry, and Paul put his hand on hers for comfort. She didn't recoil. He looked at me in the manner a parent looks at a child who is trying but simply doesn't understand.

"You haven't seen me cry, have you, Tom?" Sarah asked.

I'd seen her cry many times, but I didn't say so. She dabbed her eyes with a monogrammed handkerchief that Paul had handed to her. He tried to smile.

"I suppose it *is* impossible, Tom. But don't you know by now that impossible only applies to other people?"

Well, I should have known, but it was too late. "Perhaps we'd better let them close up," I said.

"They don't expect us to go anywhere," Sarah said. "Not in the downpour. I'd very much like another drink. But go if you're tired, Tom. Paul can walk me back."

And the way she looked at me, I couldn't help but stand up and leave without even offering to pay for anything.

I sheltered under the awning for a minute or so, waiting to make a run to the arcaded sidewalk on the other side of the street, hoping one of them would call out to me, wondering if there was some way to go back in. There wasn't.

I'd assumed that the busboy and hostess were siblings or cousins, but now I wasn't so sure. The busboy pointed out into the downpour. The hostess laughed. *Non posso*, she said. *Non posso*. But then she did run out into the rain, just for a moment, and came back laughing with her arms crossed over her chest.

CHAPTER THIRTEEN

"What is it you want?" Bianchi asked. We were in his flat near the hospital, a young man's apartment in an ancient building, every wall painted blue. He poured me Puglian wine and explained that he'd had a terrifying dream once—he'd wanted to scream, but instead a bluebird flew from his mouth. The walls were painted the color of that bird. He was trying to pay better attention to his dreams, he said. Did I pay attention to mine?

Far too much attention, I said.

There were books in French and German fluttering on the windowsills, open on the unmade bed. He crushed garlic on an English dictionary, closed on his kitchen counter.

"You sleep with your books," I said.

"Oh yes. You don't mind the mess, do you? A man only cleans for his enemies. My father's words."

It was one of many evenings I spent with Bianchi in the week after my second dinner with Sarah and Paul. Most days I walked all morning so that I might be tired enough to sit still and work on dispatches to Marcel in the afternoon. And when I couldn't work, I loitered in the courtyard of Santo Stefano, trying to remember the music I'd heard over the phone line in Verdun.

It was easier to hum, certainly, than to decide what needed to be done, to accept that perhaps nothing could be done. And I hummed because there was music in the streets I preferred not to hear. Blackshirts singing "Giovinezza." Singing "All'armi." Singing about fighting until the last drop of blood had dripped from their hearts. It seemed obvious, looking at the callow faces of these boys, that most of them would not actually fight until the last drop. I'd seen the last drop of blood fall from several men. I wondered how many Blackshirts would fight after the first drop.

Still, they sang to the slap of boots on parade. Sometimes, more menacingly, their songs seemed to well up from nowhere, to reverberate from window to window, to flood the arcades, faceless, fearless. Over the music rose the sound of speeches, delivered from balconies, from benches in the parks. Every morning there was news of fires in the countryside. A paper plant near Cremona had burned down. The house of the socialist mayor of Ponticella had burned down. And I passed the café in Piazza Maggiore where I had once lingered with Sarah to find Paul sitting across from her, in my old chair. I hurried past, using every last drop of my own blood to stay on my feet, to keep walking, but not before they saw me.

I found myself increasingly desperate for Bianchi's company. Still, I was surprised when he invited me to dinner at his apartment. There, he cooked pasta he'd rolled himself, some of which he fried in a pan and tossed with chickpeas and oil. A Puglian dish, he explained, closing his eyes as he tasted at the stove, chewing slowly, giving me time to look at the paintings on the walls. A woman in a green dress and black beret at a café table, dark circles under her eyes. A man in a deep-sea diver's suit, helmetless on a pier. His hair was wet, his brow furrowed as if he had no idea what to do now that he'd surfaced.

After dinner Bianchi served iced coffee sweetened with almond milk. We switched back to the wine, which made him sentimental.

I was happy to let him talk. He described his hometown of Lecce, its baroque cathedrals carved from the local soft stone, Roman ruins preserved in the main square. His father, he explained, was a clerk for the prefect, a lawyer by training who spoke beautiful French and German. But he touched his testicles whenever death or disease was mentioned, and refused to smile at strangers so as not to expose his teeth to black magic. He had good reason to rely on irrational precautions, Bianchi explained, because the irrational ills were legion.

Puglia was a land of earthquakes and shipwrecks. Of wildfires and tidal waves. Of one-square towns so poor the churches were carved into caves in the hillsides, Peter and Paul painted on the rock like prehistoric horses.

His father thought it important that Bianchi and his brothers—Mauro and Gabriele—understand all of this, Bianchi explained. So they often traveled with him in a horse-drawn carriage through scrub fields partitioned by low limestone walls, the air thick with the smell of burning olive wood. They watched as their father struggled to explain the tax laws to peasant families in his administrative charge, many of whom spoke dialects barely intelligible to their neighbors one town over. Many of whom, when informed in 1915 that their sons would be drafted into the Royal Italian Army in order to redeem Trentino and Trieste, confessed that they had never heard of these places.

The government in Rome had hoped Italy's entry into the war might complete the *Risorgimento*, not just by reclaiming the so-called ancestral lands in Istria, Dalmatia, and Alto Adige, but by finally unifying all the peoples of the peninsula as *Italians*. But Bianchi's middle brother—Mauro, who fought with distinction on the Isonzo—came home not as an *Italian* but as a Marxist.

He set about organizing workers' councils in Nardò, a town just south of Lecce where Puglia's only socialist mayor presided. And in early 1920, Mauro was at the vanguard of a nationwide Marxist revolt, helping the day laborers and peasants occupy Nardò. They put snipers in the campanile, built barricades of oxcarts, and held the frontier for nearly three weeks as they waited for word that the revolution had spread. Word never came, but eventually the carabinieri did, shelling the town to pieces. Mauro died in the assault.

"Is he the diver in the painting?" I asked.

Bianchi refilled his glass and looked out the window into the empty street. "You could tell I was the artist? Is the work so bad? No. The truth is that I don't recall Mauro's face well enough. I hadn't seen him since before the war, and we were forced to burn all our photographs of him when he became a revolutionary. I refuse to paint my brother with the wrong face. The painting is of Gabriele, whom you saw in the café. Before he took the foolish iodine cure. He talked of being a diver before he too became a revolutionary. It is useful, I think, to introduce our wishes to our senses, if only in paint." He shrugged and drank as if he didn't fully believe his own theory. "Gabriele followed me to Emilia-Romagna. I should have taken better care of him. His troubles are my fault."

"How is he?"

"Safe, for the moment. As long as he avoids the Fascists. No more beatings, no more castor oil. They'll kill him if they find him. But I have said too much and am ruining my own dinner. I hoped we'd talk about *you*. I should tell you," he said, taking up my plate and bringing it into the kitchen, "Paul has accompanied Mrs. Hagen to the hospital these last several days."

"He's told you why?"

"Drummond Green." Bianchi looked over his shoulder, then turned back to the sink. "You already know this, I think."

"Does his story have credibility?"

"As much as hers."

"What does that mean?"

"That it will become a legal matter soon."

"Couldn't that take years to resolve?" I could hear the panic in my voice.

"I would think so."

"Who will that help?"

"I hope that it will help Mr. Fairbanks."

"I wish that you would do more," I said.

Bianchi returned to the table with two little glasses and a bottle with a homemade label. "More of what, exactly?" He put a hand to his mouth, perhaps to hide his disappointment. "It was nice not to talk about the hospital for a few moments, wasn't it? The mistake is mine, not yours, Tom."

I knew exactly what he meant. He'd invited me into his home—had shared his past, his fears, his guilt—and he was warning me, pleading with me, really, not to use this vulnerability against him. But I had to.

"You've been hoping all along that your treatment of Fairbanks might give you enough fame to work in America or another country. Isn't that true?"

He sipped his amaro and looked out the window. "Perhaps. But I've come to realize there are too many famous people already. I don't think anyone can help me."

"I have a friend who can help both of you in France."

What friend? Help how? The more pressing question was why such a look of dismay had settled on Bianchi's face.

"Tom," he said eventually, "do you really think Mrs. Hagen will return to you, no matter what we find?"

"No, but she may return to herself someday," I said. The lie was obvious to us both.

"I see. Then it is noble to offer, Tom," Bianchi said. "You would like me to use more coercion?" His smile was still intact, but I could tell he felt betrayed. And I cared very much about that, just not quite enough. "Tell me what you'd like me to try. Electrodes to his temples? To his throat? Strip him naked? Castration? It is true that I have invited your friendship, and it is also true that I have bent ethical rules. I have also decided to treat one man, one single man, as if he were a human being, not a . . . a . . . *lavagna*. I can't think of the English word. What the teacher writes on in school."

"A chalkboard," I said. "I'm sorry. Don't be angry."

Bianchi shut his eyes and took a drink. "What right do I have to be angry?"

So, I waited. Carried by crowds flooding from church doors. Past bunches of garlic hanging in market stalls like little clouds, and whole pink pigs' heads laughing at the narrow streets from butcher shop windows. I waited as a new general strike was called, as the streets filled with uncollected garbage, as the porters at the train station waited and the cab drivers waited.

But not everyone was waiting. I watched a boy fire a rifle at an owl on a balcony. I watched the red banners in the square cut to ribbons, watched the wedding dress shop window smashed by cobblestones pried from the streets.

I passed them again at the café, bent into the sunlight, napkins sticking from their cups. Talking close. Sharing a cigarette? I sat down at their table. No one spoke—not until the waiter came, and I said, "Campari and soda."

"We've seen you walk by. I suppose you know that," Paul said.

"We wondered why you hadn't stopped," Sarah said. There was no malice in her voice, only exhaustion.

Obviously the notion of the two of them—the sudden "we"—had forced me to keep walking. But now, despite the fact that she'd used that word, it was clear there was no "we"—not in the way I had feared. There was, in fact, a stiffness about both of them; if they shared anything it seemed to be a deepening chill. Paul tried to smile but the chill stilled his face.

"It was just a surprise to see the two of you together," I said.

Sarah nodded. "Not least for me. Paul informed Dr. Bianchi about his claim, about Drummond Green. So now we're waiting together."

"You deserve what comfort you can find, I suppose."

"I wouldn't have guessed it would be a comfort, but you're right, *it is*." She said the last two words in Paul's accent. And they both laughed.

"Mrs. Hagen wastes no opportunity to mock," Paul said. Though he didn't seem to mind. "Occasionally we even talk about matters aside from the hospital."

"Such as?"

"Well, we haven't written it all down, Tom," Sarah said coldly.

"Try it. You might not forget things so easily," I said, realizing, at first with real surprise, and then with real relief, just how angry I was at her. Suddenly it was obvious that the only thing to do was to walk back to the hotel, pack my bag, and get on a train. In truth, that had been obvious for weeks, but for the first time I could picture myself actually doing it. I began to get up, but before I could she brushed my knee with her fingers and the picture dissolved.

How many more times could her touch have kept me bolted to a chair, a city, a country, in which I had no business? There must be a limit, I thought, a moment when sense ceased to yield to desire. And, though I clearly hadn't reached such a moment, I felt that perhaps I could see it somewhere in the distance, and it occurred to me then just how terrifying it might be to fall out of love.

"I'm just exhausted," she said. "And someone in my position can only be cruel to the people that deserve it least. I'm sorry."

"I don't think I deserve it least," I said. "There are many children in this town."

"I hadn't thought of that. Perhaps we should look for some." She smiled, briefly. "In the meantime, let me catch you up, Tom, if you'd like. What *was* I saying, Paul? Just now?"

"About the funeral procession?"

"I'm only joking," Sarah said. "I remember."

In late March of 1918, Sarah awoke in her old bedroom in Maud's apartment to an explosion up the street. The smell of cordite drifted in through an open window, but she wasn't afraid. The streets below were deserted in the gray drizzle, but she wasn't afraid. In fact, the girl who had arrived in France afraid of trombones in Le Havre and headless mannequins along the Champs-Élysées was no longer afraid of much of anything. Her worst fears had already come to pass.

"Lee was missing by then?" I asked, feeling it would be easier if I said his name first.

Yes. He'd made it through service in France with only an occasional stammer, the usual thinning of hair. But something had changed once he was sent to Italy. What? She never knew, most likely she never would know, but his letters were written in a shivering new hand. Rats had stolen his father's pocket watch, he wrote. There were parasites in the blankets. Insects in the engine of the ambulance. His hands were infected. The river—what river did he mean? the Isonzo probably—had been electrified by the Austrians, and rippled with blue sparks.

His clothes always smelled of smoke, he wrote. He watched three Italians hung for insubordination, their bodies tossed into a bonfire in the main square. What town? Could that possibly be true?

"Like effigies," Paul said.

"Like witches," Sarah said.

They said it would taste like berries, but it doesn't, Lee wrote.

Don't worry so much, he'd said to Sarah on his last night of permission, just before Christmas 1917, the last time she saw him before he disappeared in Italy. His hands *were* red and infected, that much was true. You think I'm going to die, but I can't die.

Why not?

The world would no longer exist if I died. He looked at her. It was impossible to tell if he was joking.

But it wasn't all like that, even at the end. There were still glimmers. On their last night together they drank two bottles of Pol Roger 1910. A friend of Lee's had confiscated them from a *maison* in Épernay. It was shocking that there was still champagne to steal. Lee had heard that the head of Pol Roger had been the mayor of Épernay in 1914, that he'd met the Germans in the middle of the street when they invaded, that he'd threatened to destroy all his stock if they went a meter further. Lee and Sarah laughed, as people had begun to then, at the quaint ideas of the old century. "Still," Lee said, "it will be a long time before there's much good champagne again." Sarah was surprised at the observation—his taste was too Protestant for champagne—but she was pleased he still thought in terms of *long times*.

No, Lee didn't want to talk much, but there were glimmers. His puttees hung from the shutters, drying after she'd washed them in the sink. He hadn't wanted to go to a restaurant and she didn't press. The wine had affected her. It was difficult to see him—well, not difficult, exactly, but exhausting, and she fell asleep sooner than she would have liked. Well, no, she only pretended to sleep. She was awake to hear his watch ticking on the bedside table, to notice him turning on the light every hour to check the time. But there were glimmers, still. He kissed her on the mouth when he turned the light out. She pretended to be asleep, afraid that he would freeze—as he often did—at the sight of her open eyes.

Three months later the notice from the American War Department arrived just as Sarah was choosing a coat for a charity event where a gas-blind pianist was to play nocturnes. *Missing, believed dead.* She read the notice twice to make sure she understood it, chose the lighter coat, and ran to catch the metro to Passy.

She didn't tell anyone about Lee that night or the following day. She didn't cable her parents or Lee's parents, whom she still had not met as an adult, still had not met as his wife.

"Do you remember what it felt like to pretend?" she asked Paul and me. "When you were a child. To pretend that your stuffed bear had a personality, or that your family was in the circus. You must have. Everyone does."

Sarah had given herself two days to pretend. At the end of those two days she would cable her parents and tell them. She would cable Lee's parents. She would tell Maud and the friends she had made in Paris, of which there were surprisingly many. Two days to pretend that he was still alive somewhere in the northeast of Italy. To imagine the pressure of his hand holding her ring finger and pinky. To imagine she might feel that pressure again. That she might wake in the night to find him reading under the green desk lamp.

What she was really trying to do was put her memories of Lee in order. Because these memories were now among the most precious things she possessed, and the most deadly. Surprising, wasn't it, what mattered? The first time they'd bathed together after they were married, watching his ankles warp in the water, feeling someone else's skin prune. The heat rash on Lee's forehead in summer, the *one* summer, anyway.

Pigeons had descended on the square in Bologna, preening in the golden evening. In that kind of light even a pigeon can preen. Sarah sighed.

"Well, I only meant to tell you about the funeral. Let me go back to that. It was complicated, because of the barrage."

"Operation Michael," Paul said. "That was the German name for it."

"Oh, we were already on a first-name basis," Sarah said.

On the twenty-second of March—two days after the notice from the War Department arrived—a shell struck the Place de la République in the early morning, after the prostitutes had gone to bed and before the men selling tip sheets for the races at Longchamp had arrived to take their places. No one was hurt. But more explosions followed. Near Place Clichy, a dentist and his patient were killed when the office crumbled around them. In the Marais, not far from where I would later live, three Jews died during services when the temple was grazed with a shell. In Montparnasse, a cinema collapsed, killing ten.

The barrage came in spurts lasting approximately two hours, between three and five times a day, a shell falling every five to fifteen minutes. The papers were exact in their numbers, so as to underscore that the odds of being hit were not especially high. Still, many left the city altogether, and even the government made plans to evacuate to Bordeaux. For those who stayed, Paris became a place of lonely statues and empty trams. Those who stayed rose early, in the cover of half-light, to search out a day's worth of butter and news.

Sarah was one of those who stayed, though she did let Maud persuade her to move from the apartment she'd shared with Lee in the 2nd arrondissement back to her old room in Montmartre. When the air-raid sirens screamed and the artillery rumbled overhead, Sarah and Maud spent their evenings together in the cellar. Two days became eight and Sarah still hadn't told Maud about Lee. Sarah still hadn't told her parents. Or Lee's. Or anyone. But on the ninth day after the notice arrived, Maud handed her a black dress.

"What's this for?" Sarah asked.

"It's a funeral, after all."

"What funeral? Today?"

"Inconvenient, certainly," Maud said, as if she knew about Lee.

Did she? Sarah thought she must know, and that was part of why she put the dress on, why she sat in the taxi that sped west through empty streets and gray March drizzle, past the Arc de Triomphe to the Bois de Boulogne. There, a small group of mourners—ten, twelve—milled beneath umbrellas. A carriage waited with two veiled figures inside.

No one seemed in a hurry, despite the rain, despite the air raids. Eventually, a black coffin was slid into the hearse and the procession began, east along Boulevard Haussmann. The storefronts were either boarded or barren: the mannequins naked and ghost-white. Sarah's heel caught in a tram track, and Maud helped her along. It was quiet enough to hear the soft flap of the crop on the funeral horses, to hear their steady plod over the cobblestones, cracking the shattered streetlamps underfoot. They still had a long way to go.

There was the whoosh of a shell overhead and an explosion in the distance. Had anyone discussed what was to be done if the barrage began? Sarah looked to Maud, who continued at the same pace, refusing to meet her eyes. Sarah looked to the horses, as if they might make a choice. She looked to find someone in charge, but if anyone was in charge it was the dead man—whoever he was—and he had nothing to fear from the artillery.

Two dogs wobbled into the street, tongues spilling from their mouths. The mourners acted as if they didn't notice, waiting, perhaps, for another explosion to scatter them. But even after the next shell hit, closer now, the dogs kept to a cheerful trot, and there was nothing the mourners could do; everyone knew a true Parisian could never hurt a dog.

Eventually, the boulevard narrowed, and the streets began to take on more life, even as the quality of the *quartier* deteriorated, garbage left in the gutters, shop awnings left to fade. The poor couldn't make themselves as scarce. Three boys looked on from a doorway, angry with hunger. Sarah watched their eyes follow the procession in the reflection of an empty bakery window. Another shell hit, and the image rippled on the glass.

It seemed to her they must have taken a wrong turn. The street, lined with half-timbered houses, was so narrow that the carriage had trouble squeezing through. The shops on the street were apparently so old and familiar that they no longer required signs; it was impossible to tell what was what: cafés, laundries, cobblers. But each window was full of faces, watching them pass. A boy ran out from one of the storefronts, and his father caught him by the arm; but he was laughing at the boy, not angry or afraid, it seemed. There was no threat in any of it, only a queerness.

Then another shell hit. Sarah looked at her feet because she thought she might have lost a shoe; she felt her balance give. She looked up in time to see a white storm racing up the street. There was just time enough to hold her breath. To register the horses finally crying out in fear. To bow her head. And to wonder what else might be hidden in the dust. Her imagination moving faster than the explosion.

Her eyes were closed, but somehow she saw perfectly through the squall. The horses reared into the blast, which struck the hearse with such force that the coffin shot from the back and skipped once down the street. There was no slow motion at the time, so Sarah did not use the term, but I certainly imagine it that way. How else to imagine a dream in the waking world, the hollow knock of box to stone, the singe of white flowers on the coffin. Black gloves over everyone's eyes. The coffin bouncing a second time, seeming to ride the explosion as though on a lip of surf, and, on the third bounce, breaking open and hurling out the body inside—a body whose eyes had blown open as well, who was riding that surf too, pushed by the momentum, still managing to land on his feet and to stay on his feet, nimbly running the first few steps, then slowing to a walk, as if he'd stepped off an arriving carriage too early, testing himself in the pointless way men do, especially if a woman is watching.

Well, she *was* watching. She could hear the tap of his shoes on the street, the pat of palm to shoulder on the beige summer suit as he tried to beat back the dust hurtling by. She saw his chest heave. He walked past her; she was close enough to reach out. He walked past, and paused, smiling shyly, his expression asking if they knew each other. Of course they did. But when she opened her mouth she began to cough and she realized that her face was just noise under the dust, that he couldn't really see her at all. He smiled again as if to apologize for the misunderstanding.

And then the dust was gone, the body with it. Sarah came up coughing. She had lost her hat. Her hands were gray-white. There was a dry feeling in her mouth, the burned taste of a drilled tooth. She wasn't alone. Everyone was coughing and wiping their eyes. The driver had a made a valiant effort to calm the horses. The dust stuck to Maud's face where it was wet.

There were many rounds of are-you-all-right-yes-fine. What

about the horses? Yes, fine. Several men came out of the café and inquired. They brought carafes of water and everyone drank. They brought a little carrot for the horses. And then it was time to continue on to Père Lachaise.

But first one of the men from the café—he had a badly groomed mustache, a sickly belly that wouldn't have fit a uniform—touched Maud's elbow.

"If you don't mind my asking," he said, "*who* is this procession for?"

The waiters put candles on the tables, little outposts in the falling darkness. The square had filled, as it often did in the early evenings, couples and friends out walking after work, the shop lights going on, seeping onto the stones. The moon rose low and big, like another shop opening for the evening. The hour of *passagiato*, of people going nowhere, their voices echoing across long shadows and off the old buildings. From far away, the sound of car engines.

Sarah leaned back in her chair. She twisted her mouth, then her napkin. And Paul and I waited, because it seemed there was still more to say.

"I'm not sure why I told you any of that," she managed, eventually. "Saying all that out loud has only made me feel foolish."

"How long before you told anyone about Lee?" I asked.

"Another day, maybe two. I had known for almost two weeks by then. I changed the date on the notice with a pen when I showed Maud. With a pen. You see, I've never told anyone that, and it doesn't make me feel any better."

"Maybe you wanted us to feel better," Paul said.

"That's possible."

"But who *was* the funeral for?" Paul asked. "Surely not Lee."

Sarah smiled. "Claude Debussy."

"Claude Debussy, my god, really?"

The waiter appeared and began to ask us to pay the bill before breaking off mid-sentence and crossing the square. Only then did I notice the swell of panic in the voices at the tables around us, the chair legs scraping cobblestone, the whimpering of shushed children, suddenly afraid. But soon enough the frothing of engines wiped away the other sounds. And the song reached us, the melody surprisingly mellifluous, though there was nothing pleasant in the words or in the timbre of hundreds of voices singing, "*All'armi! All'armi! All'armi o Fascisti.*"

Headlights seared the piazza, scattering families and lovers. At the same time, more people poured in, emerging from the twist of streets, looking for room to run. But we didn't run, not at first. Gunshots popped. You could always tell by the whistle of a shell if it would fall close enough to hurt you, but you couldn't tell whether a bullet had struck its target from the sound.

The first of the Fiats followed the burrow of headlights and spit into the square, the back loaded with men, pistols pointed at the moon. There was none of the military order of daylight. Rather, they slunk from the back of the lorries like wolves, which I suppose was part of the idea.

My first feeling was closer to regret than fear. They were nineteen, twenty maybe, and the uniforms did nothing to age them. Some were handsome, some homely; they had acne scars and crooked teeth, cheekbones from statues, noses from antique coins. They seemed confused about where to go. They were looking for the telegraph office. There were accusations and recriminations.

"What should we do?" Paul asked.

We continued to do nothing—imagining, I suppose, that remaining at a café table would spare us—until a boy peeled off from the squad and began to smash the tables with his cudgel, toppling ashtrays, wineglasses, and the money left in the little silver clips.

His grim gratification was something to watch. You could almost smell the countryside on him, the thatch of his old roof, the boredom of life in a town with no square and one tavern he wasn't allowed in. You could almost see the beauty of the stars through his childlike eyes, then the greater beauty of the headlights blazing into his valley, a distinguished-looking man in the black uniform of the *Arditi* stepping out and offering him a piece of the new country. His paper doll come to life. I was reminded of the bear with the white eye who had charged Sarah and me in the tent in Bar-le-Duc. I'd been far more afraid in that moment, but this boy probably wasn't as well-trained as the bear; he was probably less capable of restraint.

"We should get off the street," I said.

The crowd in the piazza churned and twisted as if wrung out like a rag, and, still, panicked faces flooded from narrow streets, as the Blackshirts swung cudgels to clear enough space to light fires.

Sarah and I were separated from Paul in the crush of the crowd. I heard him calling our names, but there was no time—it felt like that, anyway—to turn my head, to stop. I pulled Sarah through the frenzy, out of the piazza and onto Via Ugo Bassi.

"Where's Paul?" Sarah said. We didn't see him. We saw high school boys pressed against one of the old towers, watching boys not much older throwing punches at college students. We saw three old women in black shawls at a window like a row of tombstones.

Every street had its own fire. We saw two Blackshirts trying to light a pile of bicycles. Cobblestones pried up and hurled at roofs, roof tiles hurled down in the streets. Typewriters splashing into fountains. We saw boys in their black hats, eagle feathers protruding. The glow of fires on their night-dweller faces.

We kept running, past the post office on Via dell'Indipendenza. We saw hatboxes smoldering, a rocking horse kicked on its side, still half-wrapped in brown paper. A Blackshirt confetti-ing letters from a sack. We saw flames scratching out windows.

We kept running, turned another corner—I had no idea which—and found ourselves in an unfamiliar courtyard where two Blackshirts stood amid a shambles of gurneys and operating lights. A metal basin came hurtling out a second-story window, and scalpels clattered on the stones. The boys had taken off their belts and were whipping a withered and naked old man, who lay facedown on the ground. He didn't cry out, so the only sound was the lash on the frail shoulders, the boys' laughter as they reared back, turn by turn.

I took Sarah's arm and began to pull her away. "*Basta*," Sarah said. Then, louder, "*Basta.*" It took me a moment to realize she wasn't talking to me.

They did stop. They couldn't see us at first, coming from the shadows as we were. Sarah stepped into the light. The boys exchanged shy, shamed smiles, full of peasant teeth.

The old man didn't move or make a sound.

"You've killed him," she said in Italian.

They shook their heads emphatically.

"No," one of them said. "No, signora."

She knelt down, touched the old man's shoulder and immediately drew back her hand.

"Can we help him?" I asked.

Her back was to me. She got to her feet, turned, and looked one of the boys in the eyes. As he watched, she nudged the old man with her foot. The body rolled over to reveal eyeless sockets and an open incision across the abdomen.

"It's a cadaver," she said to no one in particular.

"Naturalmente, signora. Cosa hai pensato?" one of the boys asked.

* * *

I'd hoped we'd find refuge at Santo Stefano, but the doors were barred. We caught our breath in the strangely deserted square.

"We'd better go to my hotel," I said.

"I don't think so," she said.

"I didn't mean . . ."

"We'd better go to *mine*. The police certainly won't be protecting yours."

She was right: two men in uniform leaned on rifles under her awning. Soon we were in her room with the door swinging closed.

The shutters were closed. I sat on a sofa of soft leather. She mixed drinks in bare feet. She left the lights out, except for one in the attached bath, giving the room a late-sunset quality. My drink tasted of formaldehyde. We could hear rain on the roof. Sarah peeked out at the street, then closed the shutter again.

"Anything?" I asked.

"What do you mean?"

"I don't know. Do you see anything?"

"It's raining."

"That's lucky."

"It's disheartening."

"It's good for the fires."

"Obviously I don't mean the rain."

It would be nice to think that she or I might have read the tangled medieval streets below like lines on a palm. Later I would learn that the Chamber of Labor was torched, the post office torched, the town hall firebombed. I learned that communists were rounded up, tied to the statue of Neptune in the piazza, and flogged. That the old man who tended bar in Bianchi's café was burned to death.

Later still I learned—everyone learned—that the Blackshirts broke the strike in the Po Valley. That they marched on Rome, took the government, dissolved Parliament, and declared the death of liberal Italy. Later still, in the closing days of World War II, Mussolini was shot by partisans and hung by his feet outside a petrol station in Piazzale Loreto. But not before his brutally incoherent brand of politics captured the minds of any number of influential admirers. In retrospect, a good deal of the future became visible that night, particularly in the faces—orange and sweating beside the fires—of boys who had come of age just a few years too late to understand what they were doing.

But at the time I saw only her silhouette against the storm shutters.

"I'm sure he's all right," I said.

"Paul? I hope so."

"Your husband, I mean."

She sat on the edge of the bed and rubbed her feet.

"I've hardly thought of him tonight," she said. "I think you're the only person I could admit that to."

The drink was helping despite the taste. My heart had finally slowed, then it was at a sad gallop again.

"It's no admission," I said. "You were running for your life." She crossed the room, a shadow changing into a robe.

"I know. But it feels like, somehow, now that you're here, I'm supposed to admit something."

"You're not supposed to do anything. Nothing you don't want to."

"If you think that, women must not make a bit of sense to you."

"They don't. You, most of all."

"I'm sure. You've been quite a good friend, considering."

I actually laughed. Perhaps it did say something that we were still friends. Romantic love can endure nearly any degree of shame. But friendship is a far more fragile thing.

"Does that sound insipid?" she said, a little defensively. "What else can I say?"

"It's just, I'm afraid I can't return the compliment," I said.

"No. Obviously not."

The darkness, the rain, her silhouette. It all seems romantic when I look back, but it didn't feel that way then. There was none of the energy you'd expect between former lovers alone in a room. None of that crackling of what might happen were the world only to tilt a certain way. Indeed, it could not have been more clear that no matter which way the world tilted, nothing would bring her to my arms. That was difficult to accept.

And yet. Somehow, as I looked at her back, as she took a cigarette, she knew, clearly, what I would have liked to ask.

"*Sometimes* I'm quite sure about him—about Lee," she said.

Jacketed waiters poured coffee in the lobby, but, outside, along Via Ugo Bassi, I passed the remnants of uncountable fires. Chairs and tables interrupted mid-burn; lamps, typewriters, and telephones in varying degrees of smash. By midmorning the bodies—twenty-seven in all, which, sad to say, seemed like very few—had been cleared away, and the business of getting on with it had begun. Shopkeepers picking the teeth of glass from their front windows, vendors sweeping up bruised vegetables, lawyers sorting through documents, drenched and black. Two young boys called for a lost cat. A girl threw her younger brother into a pile of ash and ran away, laughing.

I hoped to find Paul at our hotel on Cartoleria, but in the lobby I found Bianchi instead. His eyes looked as if they'd been boiled. I invited him up to my room, but he told me his schedule wouldn't permit it. He sipped a coffee. He didn't say anything right away.

"Is everything all right?" I asked.

"The hospital is fine. Even the Fascists have very little interest in the insane."

"And you?"

"I am fine." But he didn't look it. "Last night was very instructive, in fact," he said.

"For me too. But you already knew everything I learned."

"What these men are capable of? Yes, I knew. But did you see the police last night? In the cities I thought the police would finally act. Did you see them act?"

"No."

"That makes me afraid." He tried to summon his boyish smile, but what arrived was the brave smile of the terminally ill. "Regardless, that is not the reason I have come. I was awake during the night. I had much time to think. There is another treatment we might attempt with Mr. Fairbanks. There is some risk, but it has proved useful with other negativists."

"I'm not sure I understand," I said.

"Naturally, I cannot promise you that you will find the answers you want, or any answers."

I was tired myself, upset myself, so it took me a moment to see in his red, frightened eyes what he couldn't bring himself to say. And, foolishly, I tried to help. "What would you like me to promise you?"

Bianchi's face always told a good story. Just then the story was this: I had said the wrong thing, or said it in the wrong way. But also I had understood him perfectly.

"We will need to wait several days," he said. "Until Paul is released from the hospital."

Santa Monica, 1950

I went to the window as I heard the car pull into my drive. Paul opened the door for her. Her face was hidden in the shine blasting off the fender. I'd insisted they come for dinner as soon as she returned from New England—Newport, Rhode Island, as it turned out. On the porch she gave me a very un–New England greeting of a kiss on each cheek. And said, "I've been curious to meet you for years, Tom. You're more corporeal than I imagined."

"Should I be insulted?" I asked.

"You're real," she said. "I hope that's no insult."

Her name was Millicent. Her face was as patrician as her name, but her voice and laugh were easy and western. It seemed she had been born in the wrong place, but had been lucky enough to find the right one. California. Certainly the sun suited her skin. And the loose, blue-spotted dress she wore did not suggest temperance.

Dinner was nothing but pleasant. She and Paul could still make each other laugh, and often did, but I never felt excluded. She taught Theater Arts at UCLA, but her way was not especially theatrical. As Paul had promised, she knew quite a lot about the pictures and showed very good taste.

After dinner, just as daylight was leaking away, we went out to the back patio. It was too nice an evening not to, though I'd begun to avoid the patio when I was alone. It was hard not to look into the doctor's yard. I'd seen his daughter once or twice, but, understandably, she ignored the garden. It thickened with weeds, and the flowers wobbled and shrunk. Since no one lived there now, I'd cut the last of the dahlias and put them on my own patio table. They looked rather miserable already, but Millicent complimented them nonetheless.

Of course, she would have paid the compliment to my wife if I'd had one. And it was easy enough to pretend that Faye was sitting right there, to use the small talk of couples on first dates with other couples. How did you meet? I asked. In Italy, wasn't it?

"Don't bore him, Millicent," Paul said, but that was all part of their routine; in fact, Paul seemed to enjoy having mastered banal American small talk.

"I'm still not bored by it," she said. "I'm sorry you are."

They'd met, she said, in 1923, in a town called Sirmione on Lake Garda. She had been staying there with her parents—it was just one stop on the grand tour they'd given their grandly spoiled only daughter. In fact, Paul had met her parents first, during breakfast at the hotel, when she'd been too angry to join them. What was she angry about? She could no longer remember, but it had almost cost her the love of her life. She had promised herself that she would never marry a man her parents introduced her to. Then this Austrian with a drooping eye and impeccable manners joined them for dinner.

"You knew right away?" I asked.

"Hardly. At the time he looked like a foul ball."

I laughed, and looked at Paul, who was smiling politely. He'd heard it all before. "What does that mean?"

"He looked like he'd been hit hard and in the wrong direction. And my father was far more impressed by his stories about the Hussar days than I was." She touched Paul's leg, but she was reassuring me, not him.

"I think I've heard a few of those," I said.

"Have you heard this one? Paul once saw a peasant girl leaning from a train window as it pulled into . . . what was the station again?

"Budapest Kaleti," Paul said, knowing his cues. "It was obviously the first time she'd been to the city, likely the first time she'd been anywhere outside her village. She was elated, terrified. The face we might make upon arriving on Mars."

"That's it. He could see all that just in her expression. And he also saw," here, she began to mock his accent in a way I liked, "a profound beauty, having nothing to do with the paradigms of European culture. A vision of great solace as European culture was crumbling all around him."

We all laughed. "I'm sure he never saw such a beauty again," I said.

"Actually, he did," she said. "In my face, if you can believe it."

"Easily," I said, because it seemed harmless to flirt with her. And I'd drunk a bit too much.

"Believe it or not, I *could* resist." She cut her eyes at Paul. Her voice thickened. The smile slipped, somewhat. "Paul had the most transparently rote charm I had ever seen. He couldn't have cared less if it made any impression."

The practiced part of her story was obviously over. Paul opened his mouth, but in the end didn't object.

"And why was that?" I asked.

"He was in love with someone else. And trying very hard to behave as if he wasn't. That was what made him interesting."

"That *is* interesting," I said. Paul was looking off into the doctor's tangled yard. It was too dark to see much.

"Of course, he denied it at first, but how long can you really deny something like that?"

"You'd be surprised," I said.

"I'm sure I wouldn't. But Paul only managed for an hour or so. We went for a walk around the lake at my parents' urging, and half the time we talked about her."

"What did he say about her?"

Millicent touched Paul's leg again; the gesture clearly meant something different this time. She held her hand there. And while I waited for her to continue I wasn't sure what to do with my own hands. My glass was empty. I'd left the kitchen lamp on, and the window was yellow, full of jack-o'-lantern light. "It doesn't matter now," she said. "Anyway, he never stopped making these old-fashioned romantic overtures, and I think he slowly began to mean them. At least I hope he did. But in the next sentence it was back to someone he'd never have. He really is quite an interesting man. But I never would have known that if not for this other woman. When we met, I actually thanked her."

I would have liked to have been able to test my voice before I spoke again. "Met her where," I asked. "In Bologna?"

"No. It was years later. After we moved to Los Angeles. She lives here."

CHAPTER FOURTEEN

Paul's face had all the colors of a bad beating—blue, red, purple, wax-yellow. His right eye was swollen, his left eye covered in gauze. We used to call the men who had to be taken into the ambulance on stretchers "lying-down cases," and Paul had the look of one.

During the riot they heard him speaking German, Paul explained, and took him for a Marxist.

"Why were you speaking German?" I asked.

"It's embarrassing. I was in a panic. I was telling myself to stay calm."

"It was good advice at least," I said. He didn't smile. "I'm sorry."

"Oh, don't be. It worked quite well, actually. They came at me with truncheons, and soon I became *very* calm."

I helped him light a cigarette. The hospital had discharged him after a day, but only because they didn't have enough beds to go around after the riot and Bianchi had promised to look in on him at home. He lay propped up in bed in his hotel room, the ashtrays full, clothes and bandages draping the chairs, blood visible on the sheets.

"Are you sure you're comfortable here?" I asked. "We could get you a room at a better place."

He shook his head and winced.

"The doctor said I may lose the eye. I'd like to speak to a real doctor before it's too late. I need to go back to Vienna as soon as I can travel. For now, I'd prefer not to move one centimeter."

"I may have good news for you then," I said.

I told him everything Bianchi had said about the new treatment. I told him that he might finally know the truth, that he might finally confront Fairbanks, or Green, or Hagen. Paul listened with what appeared to be indifference. Really, though, it was the face of a badly beaten man who was feeling sorry for *me*.

"Tom," he said eventually. "Do you truly think Mrs. Hagen wants to know who he is? Surely you've realized that she doesn't."

I'm not certain I had realized that.

"Did you hear me?" he asked.

"Perhaps I don't care what she wants."

My agreement with Bianchi was simple enough that we never had to acknowledge it aloud. A lucky thing, as we both would have been too ashamed. In exchange for more aggressive treatment to Fairbanks—call it interrogation, if you want—I offered to help Bianchi and his brother set up a new life in another country.

Truthfully, I never dreamed Bianchi would accept my offer. I never thought he'd believe I could help him. But supply enough desperation, and anything can be believed. It was a lesson I should have learned well enough—after all, I was desperate too.

That evening, I had to plead on the good name and credit of *La Voix* to use the hotel phone. But the minute I heard the crackle of the line and Marcel's voice on the other end I knew I shouldn't have called.

"Tom," he said, "you're not hurt?"

He must have asked the question five times. And when I'd said no in enough ways to convince him, he finally said, "Thank god. It's been eighteen hours. Dictate to me what you have about the Fascists. I'll write it myself. The wires are down, you know, nobody here has any details. As long as you are all right this was extraordinary luck."

I wasn't expecting him to ask for details; I'd forgotten my job completely. And the disappointment in his voice at my vague account was evident, even though he was clearly at pains to hide it. I hung up without asking him about Bianchi.

There was only one other call to make. If it hadn't been for the pictures beginning to form in my mind—the brother's dead face under the iodine, the doctor in tears, the consequences of another lie—I wouldn't have had the courage, if you can call it that.

He picked up on the third ring, perhaps half-expecting chamber music played from Paris. But it was my voice, and I could hear something in it not unlike vibrato. And I could hear the concern in his voice—but when Father Perrin talked to strangers there was always concern in his voice.

I knew just what to say, and much of it was even true. I told him about Bianchi and his brother, about the Fascists. All I left out was what any of it had to do with me. He did not ask a single question or utter a single pleasantry. But he also did not hesitate.

Did they need money? Did they have papers? I explained that they needed work.

"Do they speak French?"

"The doctor can read it."

"He'll have to do more than that. I'll need to inquire, but I believe I can help him, hide him from patients until he becomes fluent. If he's intelligent it shouldn't take long."

"After all, I managed."

"I was just going to say."

"Thank you."

"I can't imagine you'd call if there was anyone else who could help," he said, which was certainly true.

Father Perrin died of a stroke during the Second World War. His bones were placed in the ossuary, just as Father Gaillard's had been a decade before. That afternoon in Bologna was the last time we ever spoke, though I wrote him often in my first years in California. Over time, his replies grew warmer and longer. He may have even forgiven me. Certainly, he kept his word.

Bianchi and his brother left for France not long after I did, and Father Perrin eventually found a place for him with Dr. Fenayrou in Rodez. But for a time he and his brother lived in the Episcopal palace—perhaps even in my old room—where Bianchi studied French. It was hard not to smile at the thought of Bianchi and Father Perrin whiling away evenings in the office, playing cards, arguing politics, spitting out each other's cherished local wines. Sometimes over the years I even imagined myself—why not admit it?—in their company.

It had been a long time—it felt like a long time, anyway—since I'd seen Douglas Fairbanks. Somehow, I no longer expected a mortal man. He'd become so many things at once—Drummond Green and Lee Hagen, ally and enemy, a man I pitied and resented. A man who seemed, as he gazed blankly out, blue circles under his eyes, both alive and dead.

And yet, looking at those heavy-lidded eyes, I could imagine that someone must have kissed them once as my mother had kissed mine. But perhaps Fairbanks hadn't had my good fortune, even then.

He glanced up as we came in, but only the most optimistic reading would suggest he registered much. The single instruction Bianchi had given—especially to Sarah—was not to go to him. The effort was visible on her face.

A week had passed since the riot. Paul's eye was still swollen and bandaged, but he walked and talked now without obvious pain. Sarah was dressed in a black blouse and skirt. All that was missing was the veil.

Bianchi waited until everyone was seated, dabbing at his forehead with a folded handkerchief. The room smelled of layers of Sarah's perfume. The flowers had been replaced by neatly stacked Boston newspapers; on the windowsill sat an oval picture frame holding a girl of eleven or twelve.

Bianchi cleared his throat.

"I have decided to pursue a treatment for Mr. Fairbanks that may help us identify him," he said. We already knew this, so perhaps he only needed to make it real to himself. "The treatment is used by many colleagues. It is very ethical. But it is unethical that you," he nodded toward the three of us, "should be here. I want to say this to all four of you, in case there are objections."

Bianchi blotted his forehead, smoothed the creases of his slacks, blotted.

"There is only a small risk that it will do Mr. Fairbanks permanent harm, but it will be uncomfortable for him. Are there objections?"

My objections, if I had any, were to the way Sarah sat, angled toward Fairbanks, to the way her jaw tremored as if in response to his. I objected to the fact that I no longer knew who I was trying to help or why.

"Aren't you going to tell us what the treatment is?" Sarah asked.

"Yes. If you want, I will inject two ccs of *trementina* into the patient's thigh. His body will respond as if he is ill. He'll develop a fever, maybe for several days. It is possible that in such a condition he will be more receptive to our questions. Negativism has been known to break down under fever."

"What is *trementina*?" Sarah asked.

Bianchi shrugged. "The English word, I don't know."

"Turpentine," I said. "The English word is turpentine."

"Yes, turpentine. Do you object? Does anyone? I include you in the conversation, Mr. Fairbanks."

I did not object. Sarah did not object. Paul did not object.

Fairbanks did not object when Bianchi stuck him with the needle. He did not object when the abscess bubbled up on his pale leg, or when Bianchi lanced it with the same needle and rolled out a white bandage.

"How do you feel, Mr. Fairbanks?" Bianchi asked. Fairbanks did not answer.

"It will take time—hours, I think," Bianchi said, addressing the rest of us, "before the fever develops."

Sarah had said almost nothing since the turpentine, and Paul had said very little the entire afternoon. They both sat in their straight-backed chairs, looking, I have to say, as if they would rather have been almost anywhere else.

"I'd like to begin as soon as possible. Forty degrees may be high enough, I think. It could be in the middle of the night. Perhaps all of you would like to stay here to wait? I've cleared a room for you, Mrs. Hagen."

"Actually, I'd rather not be alone," Sarah said.

"The beds are soft," Sarah said. "But Bianchi must know we won't sleep."

Outside the window there was the blue darkness of late summer. The heat of some animal lying in the weeds. The trickle of the fountain in the courtyard. A bright moon, the light crawling toward Sarah's single bed on its hands and knees. There was nothing to do but wait. I felt surprisingly calm.

"Could you eat something, Mrs. Hagen?" Paul asked.

"Could *you*?"

Paul didn't really look like he could eat. He'd said almost nothing for hours, no one had.

"I intend to try. I managed to go for a walk today and came upon a bakery, baking raisin bread. Amazing, isn't it?"

"I wouldn't say amazing, no."

"The city almost burned down a few nights ago, and they are already back to baking bread, baking *Austrian* bread. I find that amazing."

Paul slid the loaf from its paper.

"I haven't eaten today, actually," Sarah said. She accepted a piece of bread and I tried some too, which seemed to please Paul.

"When I was a boy," he said, as we chewed, "if you went walking after mass on Sunday, the whole city smelled like raisin bread."

"Don't they bake it on Sundays anymore?" Sarah asked.

"Some do. But the smell is different."

Silence again. With the window open you could just hear the last cars of the evening grinding along the boulevard. A ticking from Paul's pocket watch proved that it had survived the beating.

"For us, it was bluefish in mayonnaise," Sarah said after a long pause, "on Sundays."

"What's a bluefish?"

"They have the strength of ten fish, and taste like it. My father used to say that."

"That's the typical meal of Bostonians?"

"Just in my family. It was my mother's favorite food. I suppose part of what I disliked was that she liked it so much. I wonder if I'm still so wicked."

"I'm afraid that doesn't pass for wickedness anymore," Paul said.

Trolley wheels squealed in the hall. Sometime later the thumps of a shoeless runner. The taps of a nurse in pursuit. A metal tray or bowl falling to the floor. Insistent knocks on doors up and down the hall. The hours passed that way.

There was much I could and should have said to Sarah, but I didn't imagine I'd have to. I know that was foolish, I knew it then. But I imagined only feverish Fairbanks saying his true name, any name but Lee Hagen. And afterward: the collecting of the Boston newspapers and the frame with her picture from his room. Or why collect the newspapers? He could keep them, whoever he was, if they brought him any comfort.

"I'll confess something," Paul said. "I had never heard of Douglas Fairbanks."

"I wouldn't call that a damning admission," I said.

"No, but I was thinking the real Fairbanks might be interested in knowing about all of this. I was considering writing him a letter."

"Do you realize how many letters that man receives?" Sarah asked.

Paul did not realize.

"I'm not sure how much you'd like his work," I said.

"I've never understood why anyone likes him," Sarah said.

"You don't watch his films then either, Mrs. Hagen?" Paul asked.

"No, I've seen them all, I think," she said. "But I go to the American movies, no matter what."

In fact, she explained, she'd seen Douglas Fairbanks in *The Mark of Zorro* in Paris, just a few weeks before she came to Bologna. She and Maud had left, disgusted. She began to explain why, but I couldn't follow. All I could think about was the fact that I'd also seen *The Mark of Zorro* in Paris at the theater in Place Clichy. So, she'd been in Paris and made no effort to see me. Sarah didn't seem aware of her admission, and I felt only a little sting.

"Paul," Sarah said, "the girl in Silesia you told us about? Now that I know what you've truly been obsessed with, I have to tell you I think you've chosen wrong. Was she real?"

He laughed. "Real? Yes, but exaggerated. I doubt she'd remember me."

"It doesn't seem like Drummond Green does either," I said.

A man cried out from down the hall. He seemed to be in a great deal of pain, but it was impossible to know what kind. Somehow, I didn't think the voice was Fairbanks's, but it might have been.

"What will you do?" Paul asked. "What will you do if it's not him?" It was nearly dawn. We'd turned the lights out sometime before, agreeing we should at least try to sleep. But no one tried. We just sat in the oily darkness. "I know I shouldn't ask. It seems we have too much time for our own good, don't we?"

She lay with her face turned to the wall, but she wasn't even pretending to sleep.

"I don't mind telling you," Paul continued. "I intend to leave tomorrow no matter what. For Vienna. Can I say something else?

I never should have told you about Drummond Green. I thought it might help. That was a mistake."

Slowly, she sat up in bed.

"Are you saying there is no Drummond Green?"

"Of course not. He's in the next room. But I should not have told you."

"In that case, why would you leave?" Sarah asked.

"Everything is easier with two eyes, you know. I like my chances better in Vienna. And Bologna is not safe now, for you or Tom either."

This was true. The communists had promised another general strike. Mussolini had promised that the Blackshirts would retaliate by storming the city, ten thousand strong this time. Some of the papers were already calling it civil war.

"You're being disingenuous," she said. "Isn't it a little late for that?"

"All right, Mrs. Hagen," Paul said. "Let me not be disingenuous. Once, I intended to kill Drummond Green, but I gave that up a long time ago, truly I did. It was easy to give that up, but I thought that if I ever actually found him I'd feel . . ." He didn't finish. I heard the paper rustling in his hands. A car engine, the first in many hours, turned over somewhere outside the window. "I do not know. Perhaps it is just easier to accept that there is no meaning when one's face and ribs hurt so much."

"Perhaps I should try it," Sarah said.

"I hope you don't," he said. "Anyway, that was disingenuous too. I have a better reason to leave. But *that*, I'd like to keep to myself."

It was not until years later when Paul's wife told me the story of their meeting that I finally realized what he'd meant.

"Tell me at least one thing," he said. "Have you considered it? If it isn't him. Do you know what you will do?"

"Yes, I know."

There were footsteps in the corridor. The door opened, and light from the hall caught Sarah's arm in a slash. A nurse's solemn face filled the door.

"Mi scusi, occupata," Sarah said. The words sounded strangely affectionate. There was just enough light to see the nurse frown and squint.

"I know that," she said in English. "The doctor is waiting for you."

It was just past four A.M.—earlier than I'd thought—when Fairbanks's eyes met mine in the doorway. He lay on his side, breath whistling through his teeth. But the eyes were angry and alert, resulting in a face that looked suddenly intelligent, even clever. It's tempting to say that it looked like there was a person inside him again, though perhaps it only seemed that way because he was so clearly suffering.

Bianchi, for his part, looked like a sleepy boy on his way to school. He'd tried to smooth his hair, but it stuck up in birdy spikes. Even so, he touched Fairbanks's brow with impressive tenderness, asking, "Can you sit up?"

Fairbanks's head lolled back, but then he did sit up, and then he did stand, and point to a chair—my chair, as it happened. He was much taller than I had expected. Bianchi nodded, and pulled another chair in from the hall, and Fairbanks fell into it, pressing his knees together, folding his hands in his lap.

Bianchi wet a pen on his tongue. He sipped coffee. I would have liked some, if only to distract myself from what I now realized would be awful, no matter the result.

"As I have many times before," Bianchi said, "I would like to ask you questions, Mr. Fairbanks. But, this time, because I know you do not feel well, I will not use hypnosis. Naturally, I hope you will do your best to answer these questions. You understand?"

"Yes," Fairbanks said. "No harm in that." The stiff bark was mostly gone from his voice. He refolded his hands.

"I am glad you think so." Bianchi looked back at us, offering one final opportunity to stop him. "What is your name?" he asked.

"I like Fairbanks," the man said slowly. "Can you call me that?"

"If you want," Bianchi said. "Do you recognize anyone here? From before you came to be in this hospital?"

Fairbanks glanced up, then shyly turned his eyes away.

"I don't know. I may."

"Who?"

"Well, it was a long time ago." He didn't look anyone in the eyes. In fact, he appeared to be speaking to his own naked right foot.

"What was your name then?"

He licked his lips several times, as if he might find the answer there. "I'd like a glass of water," he said.

"Why don't I get it?" I said.

"In my office," Bianchi said. "There's a pitcher."

I filled then almost dropped the glass. Perhaps I was thinking of all of the times I'd stood behind Father Perrin with a pitcher just like this one for the families who had crossed the Meuse to speak with him. Perhaps I was thinking of all the other rivers: the Marne, the Somme, the Isonzo. And that even the afterlife was no escape: the Styx, the Lethe. Charon. Well, I think of these things now, but I doubt I did then.

I drank another glass of water, but my throat was still parched, my head light. My heart was beating fast. It was an odd and yet familiar feeling. I was not entirely certain I would survive the next several minutes.

"I don't know," Fairbanks was saying, when I returned to the room and handed him the glass. "Pine trees. Shoveling snow."

He drank the water greedily. Paul whispered, "Nothing yet."

Fairbanks already seemed less lucid than he had before. He was sweating, occasionally clawing at the collar of his shirt. His tongue continued to flicker across his lips.

"Would you rather talk about the war?" Bianchi asked, his voice still smooth as the sky.

"I wasn't really in the war very much," Fairbanks said.

"What do you recall about the war?"

"Lice."

It continued like that, Bianchi calmly asking questions, Fairbanks answering in fragments.

Could he tell us if he'd gone to college? What his parents did for a living? Did he have siblings?

He could not tell us.

"Are you married?"

"I had a girl."

"What was her name?"

"I'm not at all sure," he said to his foot.

I watched Sarah's face as he answered that question. I watched her face the entire time. I saw her beginning to doubt—I feel fairly sure of that even at such distance, even through clearer eyes. It wasn't that he'd said anything that proved he was not Lee Hagen, but something in his manner of speaking, in the faint outlines of lost mannerisms, betrayed him—perhaps the way his tongue just kept flicking and flicking. I saw the desolation on her face, and, yes, I was happy to see it.

Bianchi asked about a trade, skills. Had he been to Paris? Yes, he had. Verdun? He wasn't sure. Had he been in the mountains of Italy? He wasn't sure about that either, but he thought, yes, perhaps.

"How are you feeling, Mr. Fairbanks?" Bianchi asked. "Should we test your temperature?"

"If you want," Fairbanks said. But his voice was growing quieter, his gaze drawing back.

Even so, Bianchi smiled. "If *you* want, I will ask more questions. Describe what you remember of your home."

"I'm afraid it burned down."

"Your house?"

"The entire city. I was afraid it would burn. I checked the newspaper whenever I could."

"What newspaper was that, Mr. Fairbanks?"

"The newspaper was run by cruel people. I remember playing the word search."

"The word search?"

"You know the word search." His voice surged. "You *must*."

"You circle words hidden in a grid of letters, don't you?" I said.

"I knew you'd know it," Fairbanks said, nodding. "All the words they'd chosen were horrible. *Mustard. Flame. Explosion. Lice. Froth. Buried.* I began to scream. And my mother put a blanket around me."

"Your mother?" Bianchi asked. "Where?"

"Not my actual mother."

Soon after, Fairbanks began to tremble; Bianchi draped a blanket around his shoulders. "I hope you are feeling well enough to go on, Mr. Fairbanks."

"I don't. I don't feel well."

Bianchi drew in a breath and turned to us, his face apologetic. "You see that I've done all I can. Mrs. Hagen, would you like to ask him anything?"

Sarah seemed startled by the question. She must have thought nothing would be required of her. She began to say something, and then shook her head. Likely, it was too late, anyway. Fairbanks had curled the blanket tighter around his stooped shoulders. He shifted on the chair, trying to find a better position in which to shiver, receding into his fever.

"Will he be all right?" Paul asked.

"It looks like this when you poison a man," Bianchi answered.

It looked awful. His mouth seemed too weak to work. His lips had gone white, which made the teeth appear all the more broken. Sarah would leave him now. Paul had already said as much. Whoever he was, he would wake from this fever completely alone. Even Bianchi would leave. I would leave too, but now that he no longer posed a threat it was impossible not to feel for him. I told him silently—that is, I told myself—that I'd find some way to help him. At the moment, though, I was too tired even to look at him. I did not want to look at him. As Bianchi finished off his notes, as Sarah and Paul looked on, I only heard the grinding sound he made in the back of his throat. I only heard his heavy breath humming almost musically. And I heard him begin to sing.

I still had a ball, I still had a ball.
I went to the city, but I still had a ball, I still had a ball.

The melody—such as it was—came more from his throat than his mouth, and the words whistled through the gaps in his teeth. Still, there was no mistaking them. And yet I did mistake them. That is to say: though I recognized them at once, I did not fully understand what the words might mean, how Fairbanks might know them, what they might say about who he was.

But, whoever he was, he sang to the white foot, to the ceiling and the window. His eyes flickered open and closed. Bianchi was scribbling in his notebook, completely unaware of what was happening in the rubble of the voice.

I still had a ball, I still had a ball. A ball, ball, ball.
A perfect end, a perfect year.

"What is that, Mr. Fairbanks?" Bianchi finally asked, polite but not quite interested. *A ball, a ball, I still had a ball.* Then Bianchi looked at me and his manner changed. "What *is* it, Tom? Mrs. Hagen? *Tom?*"

I simply could not answer. Every word Fairbanks sang felt like a chisel to what remained of the truth, *a ball, a ball, a ball.*

It was difficult, of course, to look at Sarah in such a moment. But I had to. Thank god, her hands were covering her face, so I couldn't see the expression, though she had already risen from her chair.

"Tom," Sarah said. "Do you hear? You have to tell them. *You* have to tell them."

"What is it, Tom?" Bianchi asked.

Paul had risen from his chair too, though he didn't seem to know what he should do. "What is this?" Paul asked. "Can someone explain?"

What a question. Of all the things I had seen in my life, this was the one I could explain least. And yet I could also explain it perfectly. I could explain that I had met Lee Hagen in Aix-les-Bains, that I had heard him sing this song, that he, in fact, had written it, that he was one of the only people in the world who could possibly know it. And so I did. I explained everything as I recalled saying it to Sarah in the restaurant in Verdun with Michaud the waiter and Michaud the duck. Afterward, I watched her kiss Fairbanks's fingers and help him into bed. And after that I walked out through the ward past the other patients, some awake and shaving their faces in bed, some still turning over mid-dream.

CHAPTER FIFTEEN

Bologna Centrale was mobbed; the trains had only just started running again after another strike. Paul and I waded past families picnicking amid ranges of stacked trunks, past women fanning the sweat from their children with paper tickets, past heads jerking to the snap of flipping numbers as departures and delays were announced on the great black timetable.

Once we boarded the train to Zurich, Paul and I had to *scusa* and push through the crowded corridor. Only his bandaged face secured us seats in a compartment picked clean by strikers. In fact, the train had the look of the trains of 1918, when the upholstery had been bayoneted to patch shoes and coats, ashtrays scavenged for copper, luggage straps stolen for leather, and windows smashed for no reason at all.

We shared the compartment with a family of light-eyed northern Italians with the luggage and look of people leaving a place for good. They were traveling with two children, the younger of whom looked to be about three, a little girl who sat up on her knees and pressed her hands to the window as the train lurched from the station. *Addio, stazione*, she said. *Addio, città. Addio, alberi. Addio, ponti.*

In the countryside it was already fall. The late afternoon sun came in at an ugly angle. The bandage on Paul's eye needed a change. The girl's brother, perhaps nine or ten, clutched a football in his lap. He seemed to want badly to bounce it on his knee but had clearly been warned.

I thought I'd drifted off to sleep, but I must have been speaking, because Paul said, "Don't say that. Take some time before you say that."

There was a young woman crying in the corridor. There seemed something illicit in the way a man was trying to console her. Paul touched his temple where the light hit, and scratched under the bandage. He put his fingers to his nose and winced at the smell.

Goodbye, motorcars. Goodbye, town. The parents were charmed by their little girl, though they kept checking with their eyes to make sure we were charmed too. Goodbye, trees. Goodbye, other trees. Goodbye, church.

The little girl left palm prints on the glass through which low hills fell away one by one.

"Goodbye, hills," I said. The girl turned away from me, afraid. The mother apologized. I didn't like to think of myself as a man who frightened children, though at the time I did rather feel that way.

"It's my fault," Paul said. "Children don't trust a bandaged face. But I have to tell you, Tom, I don't trust the way *you* look right now."

"I'm too tired to talk, Paul, please," I said.

"But wouldn't I be wrong if I didn't tell you that you're destroying yourself for no reason? That there is a more likely explanation to all of that."

I had no doubt what *that* meant. It had been two days since Fairbanks's fever, two days since we'd left San Lorenzo. Neither of us had been back.

"I'm aware *likely* doesn't always matter. But listen to me, if you can. You told her about the song? You sang it to her?"

"Yes."

"She knew it then. Enough to recognize it from a fragment."

"Apparently so."

"And she used to sing to Fairbanks. Bianchi said that, didn't he?"

"You don't think I've thought of all that?" I spat those words. Apologized.

The little girl's brother had joined her in the game. Goodbye, river. Goodbye, sheep. Goodbye, farm. I wondered how I might signal to the parents. Perhaps it was time to put a stop to it.

In Zurich, on the platform, Paul kissed both my cheeks before boarding a train to the east. We did not speak again for almost thirty years. And by the time the conversation finally swung around to San Lorenzo and Fairbanks, we were seated on my back patio in Santa Monica with the dead doctor's dahlias in the center of the table. Dinner was over. Millicent had gone home, saying she was tired, and, to my surprise, Paul did not protest or offer to accompany her. Perhaps they both thought I'd be more comfortable talking about Sarah without her there. Perhaps I was.

"Did Sarah know how you felt about her?" I asked Paul.

"She may have sensed it. I certainly never told her."

"Never told her, why?"

We'd left the plates and glasses. He stretched, and studied his napkin, a red Christmas napkin. They were the only ones I had. "She was in love with three other men already. I didn't suppose there was much room for a fourth."

"Three others?"

"You, and Lee, and Fairbanks."

"Lee and Fairbanks were one and the same, so that only makes two. You see, perhaps you did have a chance."

He offered a pained smile, then another expression, and it became clear he was about to tell me something he wasn't sure I'd want to know.

"It's going to be in a picture," I said quickly. "The song. I wonder what she would think. They're considering Peggy Lee."

"Max said. She'll see it. She goes to all the pictures."

"Then I suppose the question is what will she think."

"You haven't asked anything else about her."

"You can understand how I might not want to."

"Yes. Frankly, Millicent and I have talked about the question quite a lot. In the end I came around to her opinion, as you see. I have wondered, though . . . I do wonder, what it's been like, since we parted? You don't have to tell me."

But, as it happened, I found myself eager to tell him. What had it been like? I explained that by the time I returned to Paris most of my friends had moved on, if not from the city entirely, then certainly from the Chevalier Vert—even Rose, whom I never saw again. I remained in Paris through the rest of the fall and winter, and, by spring, somewhat to my surprise, I found I'd nearly made my peace.

"Your peace?" Paul asked. "What could that mean?"

I tried to explain that, too. For a time, I said, that night in the hospital had full control of my senses: the taste of the raisin bread; the smell of the turpentine; Fairbanks's hoarse, floating voice; Sarah's face buried in her hands. How disappointing, how sad. How was it even possible? But, mostly, how strange.

How strange, I'd think, back in the Chevalier Vert, as a woman sat down at our table and Marcel once again pretended to fall asleep. How strange, I'd think, watching Russian aristocrats in exile tumble from the Eastern Orthodox Church in my *quartier*. How strange, I'd think, as electric lights and church bells announced dusk. How strange, as Marcel cried when I left and tried to give me every centime in his wallet. How strange that the quay at Le Havre was lined with brass bands and fortune-tellers. How strange, the crossing, the ocean. How strange to return to Chicago as one of many men stamping off the slush and unspooling a scarf, and snatching a stool, and smearing mustard to sausage at lunch hour in the Men's Bar at Berghoff's.

How strange to think that Fairbanks could be the man I'd met in Aix-les-Bains, the man who sang the song, who said *I wrote it for my girl.* And if I could think that—as I began to, without reservation, in the Chevalier Vert, in my *quartier*, during the crossing—why not also believe that man was Lee Hagen, found miraculously after years of desperate searching by his faithful wife?

So, how strange, I'd think, shivering my way back up West Adams to the bank where I worked, but how wonderful. It was wonderful that Sarah could demand the return of her husband and have him returned to her. It was wonderful that I had played a part—not the part I would have chosen, but an important part—in such extraordinary fate or fortune. I never felt anything religious in it, I told Paul; rather, I felt as though the oldest stories might actually be true. And that was a comfort, perhaps more so than her hand in mine would have been in the years that followed, as the world burned again. In the years that followed, there were twinges of regret, certainly, moments of painful curiosity, but not as many as I once would have expected. It actually is quite difficult to live in the past, far more so than people make it out to be, I explained.

Paul listened; his face was patient, understanding. He looked at me with heavy eyes and drew on his cigarette. Then he gave the slightest of shrugs, and, in doing so, dismissed everything I'd just said. We both knew it. Just a shrug. That's a true friend, I suppose.

"You haven't asked me anything about her," he said again. "Are you afraid to find out that she's happy or that she isn't?"

"Obviously I'd want her to be happy, Paul," I said. But I stopped there. We didn't speak for a long while.

Eventually he said, "You must be tired. Millicent should still be awake. I'll just call."

"Don't be ridiculous," I said. "I'll drive you."

Once we turned onto Wilshire he asked if I felt like taking some air, driving for a while before delivering him home. I did. We went south on Lincoln Boulevard, the breeze through the windows pleasant after the stillness of the patio. It was all pleasant, the nocturnes of a night drive: the occasional flash of passing headlights, the underwater quiet of gated storefronts.

"I wasn't sure if it was right to ask about her in front of Millicent," I said.

"We don't keep many secrets."

"Then I suppose I wondered what you were doing back in Italy when you met Millicent."

The filling station ahead was closed but still lit up so bright it looked dangerous, atomic.

"I promised Drummond Green's parents I would meet them in Bologna when they arrived."

"Arrived for what reason?"

"To see their son, of course."

"You mean you told them about Fairbanks? After it was clear he wasn't their son?"

"In what way was that clear?" Paul's voice was strained, even offended. "It wasn't clear to me. And I must tell you. It wasn't clear to Sarah. She'd left Bologna, she'd left Italy entirely by then."

The double yellow line curved away from the headlights. I turned on the radio. Nat King Cole was in the middle of a verse. If I heard *her* voice, would I recognize it? Unlikely. I could remember how to describe her but I didn't really remember what she looked like. Nevertheless, this small news of her crushed my windpipe.

"Without Lee?" I asked.

"Without Fairbanks, you mean."

"You're saying that Green's parents recognized him?"

We'd long since drifted from Venice. The headlights caught a sign for Ballona Creek. We must have been passing over it. A few cold lights twinkled on a ridge in the distance. Paul did not answer for what felt like miles.

"No. They said they were terribly sorry for him, but they had never seen Fairbanks before. To be honest, it took some time before I was able to accept they were telling the truth. I was so certain."

"How much time?"

"What has it been now?" He laughed. "Thirty years?"

"Do you know what happened to him?"

"To a point." His voice caught, and he cleared his throat. "The American army tried to intercede. But once Bianchi left he stopped speaking, so there was little to go on. Naturally, the Fascists weren't sympathetic. They moved him to another hospital outside Rome. After that . . . once the war began . . ."

What a fate. But I couldn't fully manage to feel sorry for him. It was too late. I'd pictured Fairbanks—whoever he was, truly—sitting beside some New England hearth, or shading himself on some New England lawn, too many times.

"Now I have to ask you why she left, don't I?"

"You don't *have* to do anything," Paul said.

"I'm afraid I do, yes."

"I believe she left because she came to accept she had been wrong."

"Please explain."

"It's not entirely easy to tell you."

The countryside was ink-black, but I knew the landscape by heart—oil derricks to the west, asparagus farms to the east. And, if we continued straight on, we'd come to the horse ranches on the Palos Verdes Peninsula, the little towns whose drugstores still had hitching posts outside. Paul fumbled to light a cigarette. It was the wind. His hands weren't shaking, at least not in the way that hands used to.

"She and I have never spoken about it. I only know because I spoke with Dr. Boccioni when I returned—you remember him?"

"With the giant eyes?"

"Yes. It's secondhand, but this is what I understand. When they finally arrived, Lee Hagen's AFS and army records showed that he'd always taken his permission in Paris. He was never in Aix-les-Bains. If you truly met Fairbanks there he couldn't have been Lee Hagen. It took Sarah several weeks to admit that was so—to the doctors, probably to herself. Then she did. Then she left. At least that was the reason she gave."

I'd slowed the car without quite realizing it, as if what Paul said might render me unfit to steer. But my hands were steady too.

"She was lying the whole time?"

"Isn't it better to say she knew you were lying the whole time?"

"I suppose it is. Much better."

"There's an ugly stretch of highway coming up. Why don't we turn off here?"

We took a right on Manhattan Beach Boulevard and another on Rose Street; ours was still the only car on the road. I drove slowly, gliding toward the ocean, past silent palms and lawns, while Paul explained that she had returned to America when her mother died in 1924, that she had lived alone for a time in Boston and taken a degree at Boston University.

She'd met a man there, an engineer. She had married him, and moved to California in 1939 when he took a job designing airplane engines for Northrop. She continued her work with charities for the arts. That's how she and Paul met again, at a gala for the Los Angeles

Philharmonic that Millicent had dragged him to. He'd seen her from across the room; she wore her hair very long—halfway down her back—at an age when most women were cutting it. Paul had noticed that about her before he realized who she was.

It was fair to call her a friend, he said. She and Millicent were quite good friends. It wasn't easy to find cold New England manners in Los Angeles, after all. She had a daughter who was their daughter's age and had lost another child at infancy. She'd lost her husband in 1944. He could go on, if I wanted him to. Did I want him to?

"Turn here," he said. "And pull over if you want. This is where she lives."

"What?"

"This is her house."

I did as he said, turning off the engine. There wasn't a great deal to say about the house itself: a ranch with an attached garage; a picture window, curtains drawn; a front door of frosted glass; a doorbell glowing like a fingernail moon. The actual moonlight revealed a sculpture on the lawn. A bronze man with wild hair, sitting at a piano, banging out some difficult sonata. The statue was playful and gaudy and a bit disconcerting, especially in its near-life, but not-quite-life, size. Her neighbors must have hated it.

Paul lit another cigarette. The ocean smell hit us with a wallop through the smoke. Somehow the ocean always seemed to smell the strongest through a car window. Somehow in the middle of the night I always felt the most awake. The engine pinged as it cooled, and my chest tightened in a way I thought I had long since outgrown. I kept expecting the kitchen light to blink on. Or a window to be thrown open. It seemed that something must happen, that such potent feelings must provoke a response. But the house remained silent and dark, and, after some time, perhaps quite a long time, Paul said, "If we sit here like this any longer we may have to explain it to the police."

"We'd better find a filling station before we drive back up," I said.

"I know one in Redondo. But you'll remember the address, won't you? You'll remember the house?"

"I should think so."

"Good. Are you tired? Would you like me to drive?"

"Not at all."

"Don't let me fall asleep, at least."

He did fall asleep. I didn't mind. The entire way back I had a story to tell myself for company. The story of my feet on the porch, the soft chime of the bell, the tremble of footsteps in the front hall, the approaching shadow in the fogged glass. A story too old to be believed—impossible in Europe, impossible in Boston or Chicago—but, as the road coiled through hills of sagebrush and nudged up to the ocean and plunged into the new tunnel under the airport, I did believe it.

And I imagined what it would be like to turn around, to drive all the way back after leaving Paul in Brentwood. It would be nearly light by then, but I still liked to drive when I was bone-tired. It was how I learned, sleepless for days and over terrible roads with the ambulance headlights extinguished so as not to draw fire. Often, it was so dark and I was so tired and the engine shook so madly that I lost all sense of speed or distance, and to arrive anywhere began to seem like a sort of miracle. One night, a sickly and wild-looking horse wandered into the road in front of me, and I stamped the brakes only to realize that without my noticing it the engine had died and that for some time—it was impossible to say for how long—I hadn't been moving at all.

ACKNOWLEDGMENTS

Thank you to the libraries—university and public—and to the bookstores—used and new—in Seattle, Washington; New York, New York; St. Paul, Minnesota; and Corvallis, Oregon. Many books were integral to the writing of this one, some found completely by chance.

I owe a great debt to historical context and detail found in *The Price of Glory* by Alistair Horne; *The Discovery of France* and *Parisians* by Graham Robb; *The Vertigo Years* by Philipp Blom; *Mussolini's Italy* by R. J. B. Bosworth; *City of Nets* by Otto Friedrich; *The Great War and Modern Memory* by Paul Fussell; *Rites of Spring* by Modris Eksteins; *Constellation of Genius* by Kevin Jackson; *The Golden West* by Daniel Fuchs; *The World of Yesterday* by Stefan Zweig; *A Nervous Splendor* by Frederic Morton; *A World Undone* by G. J. Meyer; *No Man's Land* by Eric J. Leed; and *The Beauty and the Sorrow* by Peter Englund.

I am particularly indebted to Pál Kelemen's beautifully written *Hussar's Picture Book*, which inspired the stories that Paul Weyerhauser tells about Ilona and the requisitioned house in Russian Poland. A passage in Mark Thompson's wonderful history of the Italian Front, *The White War*, serves as the basis for Paul's description of the explosion on Mount Tofana. Bianchi's story about Giuseppe Anglani is based on an account found in Vincenzo D'Aquila's strange and fascinating memoir, *Bodyguard Unseen*. The real-life details of Anthelme Mangin can be found in Jean-Yves Le Naour's intensely moving *The Living Unknown Soldier*. Father Gaillard's technique of touching the cold noses is based on the method of a British Chaplain, Cyril Horsley-Smith, a detail found in Emily Mayhew's vivid and incisive *Wounded*. The story Father Perrin tells Tom about the faceless soldier in the hospital at Rouen is based on a French nurse's account I encountered at an exhibition in the Douaumont Ossuary. The letters of Avery Royce Wolfe (compiled and edited by William and Eric Harvey as *Letters from Verdun*) were an invaluable resource for bolstering my understanding of life as an American ambulance driver at Verdun.

Thanks to the College of Liberal Arts and the Center for the Humanities at Oregon State University for crucial support. Thanks to Valerie Steiker, Nan Graham, Sally Howe, Rosie Mahorter, and everyone at Scribner. Thanks to Julie Barer and everyone at the Book Group. Thanks to Peter Bognanni and Brad Liening. Thanks to Tom Dybek. Thanks to my parents. Most of all, thanks to Madeline.